Dancing with Delirium

Dancing with Delirium

The Woodhill Park Experience

JACK BENNETT

Dancing With Delirium

For information: jackbennettauthor.com

Designed by Coverkitchen

ISBN: 979-8-218-40429-1

For all who yearn

PART I

I

I dreamt the night before that I was running through a train. People don't ever really care about your dreams, but I couldn't seem to get this one out of my head. There was death inside me, rotting away the edges of everything that defined me. I sprinted through the train from car to car, opposite in direction yet equal in ferocity. The rolling plains out the window were abstract, an unfinished rendering in a mind focused only on getting back to the origin of the train. Each passenger looked at me with an unfinished face and a distinct ambivalence to my desperate plight. All I knew was that I belonged where the train was coming from and not where it was going. But all the passengers that acquiesced to the train's speed and rode off to its destination sat quietly and patiently, and I could make out a smile forming upon each of them. I envied them, and yet I kept running. Until I woke up.

It was a warm morning. An inviting laziness ushered in the day, differentiating it from the urgent routine of my newfound morning commute. There was no lacing up of a dress shoe a half size too small. Or the other one for that matter. There was no watching minutes melt off the clock as I buttoned up my shirt. Instead, my blinds erroneously let in just enough sunlight, and I awoke naturally in my childhood bedroom that I'd outgrown both decoratively and in size. A glimmer off old little league trophies reminded me that I was back home, that I had a day off. Faces of musicians from bygone obsessions printed onto posters looked down onto me, and I could feel their gaze ever so lightly on my skin.

I wiped the tired from my eyes and sat up on my bed. The main temptress in my room, my pillow, called back for me, but I cursed it, as I had intentions of staying awake. The guitar that hung on the wall across from my bed beckoned me as well, and, in my mind, the picaresque imagery of messing with a guitar in the early California morning juxtaposed sweetly with my harrowing commute to work that it had replaced for the weekend.

I played a few chords, inhaling the fragrance of the transitory notes, and then clamped on my capo to play a riff I wish I'd written. My mother peeked her head through my doorway as I played. I smiled at her. "Reza, when is your train home?" she asked. She looked older than I remembered her, but younger than she was. She'd always had bags under her eyes, a trademark of her face, but they were really starting to pull down.

"Mom, I'm on vacation. Can we worry about that later, please?" I said, with a chuckle.

"Alright, alright," she said with faux exasperation.

"It's Monday night."

"Well, okay, we'll have to find a way to get you to the train station," she said, oblivious to my irritation, which ran lightly, anyway.

"We can deal with that after I get back from the festival," I said with a small laugh. She headed back downstairs to the living room. I kept playing the guitar until my love for the instrument was replaced with the frustration from my inability to play it exceptionally well. Upon setting it aside, I looked around my old room. I caught the smells of my childhood as I studied shirts in my closet that ranged from ones I wished still fit to ones I couldn't believe I ever had the gall to wear. I could taste the dust percolating in a room left behind by time. It reminded me of a simpler time, but it was complexity that I craved.

Still, there was a pleasant feeling to being back home; back where the wonders of childhood once reigned supreme. That my old house is also an hour drive from one of the greatest music festivals in the world is an added bonus, and one I was prepared to fully utilize that weekend.

I headed downstairs and found my parents sitting at the breakfast table. They were both wearing a neutral black, having apparently reached an age where finding self expression through clothing was an ancillary aspect of their morning. Cracks of their once vibrant and expeditious personas seeped through their faces, but the winding down of time gave them a delightfully sedentary look.

My dad read the newspaper while my mom buzzed around the kitchen, focusing on cleaning before even allowing herself to enjoy the breakfast she'd sullied the room making.

"What time is Gordon picking you up this morning?" she asked, half-attentively.

"Probably in about an hour, I guess," I said.

"You know I listened to that new song you all made together," she said while circularly washing a dish. "It's great you guys get to still spend time together."

"Yeah, we gotta get a producer to take a look at it," I said. My eyes darted between each of my parents looking for a reaction. Dad studied the paper, and Mom smiled and said, "mhm."

"Anything riveting in that newspaper, today?" I asked in the direction of my dad.

"Yeah, they're tearing down that old apartment complex on Paxton Mill. That thing's been there forever." I smiled and nodded and secretly prayed that I'd never waste away my mornings reading about suburban construction. But even with the irritations I got from my parents, I was happy to spend time with them and felt grateful to have such a nice family to spend time with. I knew that I should say that more aloud, but I said nothing as I ate my breakfast, and an enigmatic unhappiness grew steadily within me.

"So what genre is this festival again?" asked my dad.

"I mean it's a little of everything," I said. "There's hip hop, EDM, psych rock, indie bands. We get to see it all. There's that psychedelic multi-instrumentalist Warlock's Office I was telling you about headlining tonight. I'm probably most excited for that."

"That's so odd. Back in my day, they didn't mix genres like that. If you went to Bowie, you didn't associate with the people going to Springsteen."

"Yeah, I guess it's really changed."

"So, they're gonna have like Lil's and stuff there too?" asked my dad.

"What, like rappers named Lil' whatever? Yeah," I said, a bit confused at his confusion.

"You know, way back when, the Beatles were bigger than Jesus, and now you got all these Lil' this and Lil' that. Music is really starting to shrink."

"Lil' That actually had to pull out of the festival with legal troubles," I said.

My dad worked in city planning and listened to the same 100 songs he had on CD all the time. He seemed interested in music, but only in a reserved manner. There was a boredom to his life that horrified me. I often wondered how both of my parents seemed so content with pleasant, yet outwardly unremarkable, lives.

At about 10 AM, a van pulled into our driveway blasting music and causing a rowdy scene. The driver honked the horn, and I stepped onto the porch to wave at him. The quiet suburbs provided a dull canvas for their shenanigans. They painted excitement onto the stagnant streets. My parents looked out the window and smiled at my friends as I collected my bags for the weekend. My mom approached me as I went up to the door, and I gave her a hug goodbye. "Alright, be safe Reza," she said. "Don't do anything dangerous." I assured her that I wouldn't. I said goodbye to my dad, and he asked me to make sure I took some pictures at the festival.

I walked out the door and along our front yard walkway towards the car. I felt like a protagonist being called to adventure. Before I got to the car, my father called out, "Reza!" from the front porch. I turned around. "Beware of temptations each step of the way," he said. It sent a shiver down my spine. It was uncharacteristic and oddly prophetic. I nodded back at him. "I'll see you on the other side," he said with a knowing smile. The confidence he had in what he was saying only added to the confusion and slight sense of dread that his words brought me.

The front lawn was perfectly cut, and the scenic house towered over me as I examined my father on the lingering beat of his eccentric statements. His blue eyes caught more of the sun than they had all morning, and he had a comfortable warmth drawn onto his mouth. It was a cozy scene, and I felt a desperation to get in the car not just to head to the festival but also, more bewilderingly, to get away from that serene house.

I mustered up a smile and waved to my parents one last time before hopping in the backseat of my friend Gordon's Subaru.

2

"Ah Mr. Corporate" said Gordon from the driver's seat as he reversed out of my parents' driveway. "How ya been?" He had a perfectly curated bed head, and I could see threads of his brown hair stuck together by the lingering hold of his hair product. He sat casually in the driver's seat, employing a borderline trademarked slouch. His eyes could not contain his excitement, and they didn't even try. In the captain's seat of our ship trudging towards a music festival, he was in his element.

"I'm dunno about corporate, man," I said with a laugh. "I'm still an associate anyway."

"Associate these," said Gordon, clutching his crotch over his shorts, which were made of an elevated bathing suit material.

"With what?"

"With, uh, with a good time," he said. I shook my head in disapproval, but my smile contradicted. I had already found the level of degeneracy that I had desperately missed. I took a seat in the back next to Ashley and craned my neck to see Oli in the shotgun seat in front of me. They were twins, fraternal, and I enjoyed fraternizing with them.

Ashley smirked as if Gordon's antics were both annoying and essential to her car ride experience. She had dirty blonde hair in braided pigtails and a constantly analyzing expression on her face. She greeted me with an inviting smile that welcomed me into a backseat that had once belonged solely to her.

"I'm pumped for this festival!" said Oli, drawing out the last syllable. His sentiment was echoed by Ashley giving out an emphatic yelp. His blonde hair flowed out of his corduroy hat in a purgatory between unwashed and conditioned. I couldn't see his eyes, but I knew that they would have had little to say, acting as a foil to his mouth.

"Dude, I'm so excited," I said. "How have you guys been?" Oli turned to me, and I could see his angular face and printed on smirk.

"Living it up," he said. "But now we got the gang back together." I smiled.

"Well, hey, put on the new song!" I exclaimed. "It's finished now, right?" Oli nodded lifelessly.

"Yeah, I got it mixed by my boy Dickwad. You know Dickwad, right?" said Gordon. As embarrassing as it is to admit, I did in fact know Dickwad. It's a necessity and a drawback of being in the music scene to meet a guy named Dickwad here and there. "It's our first song under the new moniker," continued Gordon as he multitasked by queuing up our new song. Even though my job had moved me an hour or so away from my old friends, I still persisted in getting the band together to cut new tracks.

"Are we sold on the new name?" I asked, hesitantly.

"Yeah man," said Gordon with excitement. "Fury and the Gordon Three goes hard."

"Right but like, why am I 'Fury'?"

"Nah, it's not like that. It's just a band name," said Gordon.

"But the Gordon Three is obviously you three by nature of your name being Gordon and their last names being Gordon, so that pretty heavily implies that I'm Fury."

"Right, yeah, 'cause three of us are named Gordon, so it's cool," said Oli. He gave a little giggle and his tan arm stretched out beyond the confines of his seat.

"I get that part," I said.

"Word. So you like it?"

"Well, I just don't get the 'fury' part," I said.

"I think the part you might be missing that's cool is that Gordon's first name is Gordon and then me and Oli have Gordon as our last name," said Ashley. She smiled towards her brother and bit her tongue. Her five or so bracelets on her right wrist pressed against her exposed thigh just below her jean shorts.

"No, I get that," I said, raising my voice. "But why am I fucking Fury?" There was a quick silence. Then Gordon spoke up to break it.

"Well, I mean that right there is why you're Fury." I couldn't help but shake my head and laugh as I looked out the window.

"Just play the new song," I said.

There's something magical in music, some sort of secret ingredient, that differentiates a real song from some song your friend made. I suppose it's the same thing that differentiates art in a nice establishment or a museum from art you buy at a thrift store just to use the frame. Whatever it was that made a song sound like a real song, we didn't have. I sat quietly as I listened to our newest song, which needed to be our best song, and I felt an overwhelming sense of dread.

It wasn't that Gordon missed too many notes on guitar or that my voice was off key in parts, it was that we just didn't have an 'it' factor. And we didn't have the drive to find that 'it' factor. Also, Gordon missed too many notes on guitar and my voice was off key in parts. We were just having fun making music, but we were supposed to be finding success and making money while having fun making music. That was always the inevitability of the band in my mind, but the band in my mind did not match the band I was hearing in any way.

Every day that I went into the office at my new desk job, I thought about how I only ever took it as a safety net to make money before my music career took off. But every time I listened to my music, I thought more and more about the permanence of my mundane life. I couldn't tell exactly if the three Gordons felt the same. I envied them. Because while they had further to fall, they also had more reasons to keep trying when they failed. They had no stupid cushy job to prevent them from dedicating their lives to their ambition, and that was the most romantic concept in the world. Yet of the band, only I seemed to envision greatness as the necessity that it was.

After our song ended unceremoniously, Oli put on a local indie radio station. I recognized the song that was playing immediately. "Dude, this Light Crab Cake Dinner, I had a class with this singer," I said. I wasn't jealous or anything, but I certainly wasn't happy about it. "Turn this shit off."

Oli then put on the newest Warlock's Office album, which I actually wanted to hear. It contrasted with our music in such an indescribable way. But as I heard the songs, excitement brewed within me. I thought less about my distant future and more about my immediate one. "This song is gonna be so good live," said Ashley, shifting in her seat. Her pigtails moved gently with her movement. I couldn't have agreed more, and believe me, I tried. Ashley might have been happier to spectate greatness than to be that greatness, but at least I shared her sentiment enough to feel the excitement rise within me.

"Oh, by the way," I said. My remembrance had the tone of a light bulb of ideation. "You guys bring the stuff?"

"Yeah," said Gordon. "I got it in my secret compartment in the glove box." Gordon had eight tabs of LSD in his car in a carved out, hidden section of his glove box. Perhaps that contributed to my excitement. Next to him, in the space between the passenger seat and driver seat, was a floral print bucket hat. He kept it off his head while driving to not alert the police that we were headed to a music festival. The closer we got to Woodhill Park, the more police there would be. They were chomping at the bit to scare young festival goers into letting them search their car and score an easy drug charge for their monthly quotas. We'd taken all the precautions necessary to make ourselves and our car look like a group of youth pastors headed for a church retreat who got unfortunately caught up in this heathen traffic.

We were pros by that point. We knew to hide luggage, and not obviously stack cars in a convoy if we had more than just the four of us. We knew to mask our smells and to change into our absurd outfits when we got there. We knew to look like a waste of a cop's time, because every second spent with the four of us meant not pulling over a shaggy, weed-smelling hermit driving barefoot with three grams of ketamine in his lap.

On arrival, we noticed a different atmosphere around the festival than we'd remembered from years past. One that was almost eerie. It all began with the sign out front. It read: *Welcome to the Woodhill Park Festival. Now presented by Vitality Media.* Something creeped me out about the sign. I felt an innate, perhaps evolutionary, need to be afraid of the words "Vitality Media." A need that had been passed down through generations. But as I caught a glimpse of the main stage atop the hill, I traded my paranoia for excitement.

"Didn't this festival used to be owned by Forest Labs?" asked Oli with nothing more than unbiased curiosity in his voice.

"I'm gonna look up Vitality Media," I said, pulling up my phone. On it there was an alert from a Vitality Media app I hadn't downloaded that said, "Nothing seen on the phone can match the joys of the festival." Below was a message from my location services that said "Your location is now being tracked. Enjoy." I opened my phone with hesitation and found that I couldn't google anything. "Are you guys getting any service?" I asked the group.

"No, nothing," said Ashley. I felt a romanticism to my immediate severance to the outside. We had journeyed to this park to be there in that moment, not the infinite segmented moments afforded to us by the internet. And there's a certain level of control you give to a festival when they've booked twenty of your favorite artists. Perhaps Vitality Media was more than aware of this phenomenon, but I was cautiously optimistic towards their judgment.

3

The festival grounds were pre-apocalyptic. In the way that if everything went wrong, one could see events becoming apocalyptic. And then after that, it would be post-apocalyptic.

As we slowly drove through the line, there were screens and speakers everywhere that projected a woman speaking calmly. It wasn't an orientation, but rather a loop of encouragement. "Never give up on your dreams," was one of the things she said. And then "You can be anything you want with perseverance and hard work." Followed by "Everyone has the capacity to be anyone as long as they don't let themselves become nobody." She said these things in such a cheery tone with a warm smile on her face, that I couldn't help but feel inspired. She spoke as if she was speaking directly to me.

"This is weird," said Ashley as her eyes darted around the area, analyzing all the oddities scattered about. When we got further along the line, we noticed that the typical bored volunteers wearing cheap custom T-shirts that say 'staff' had been replaced by paramilitary forces wielding massive guns and leading guard dogs around to sniff out drugs. The dogs were not atypical for music festival entrances, but the weaponry was. Yet there was a distinct lack of smugness from what you'd expect from a young man carrying a big gun and holding a legion of unchecked power. I still felt the whole car tense up at the overbearing amount of security.

To our silent protests, Oli let down his window when a guard passed. "Hey man," he called out. "What's with all the big ass guns?" We all groaned at his brazenness. Especially considering that he was sitting mere feet away from a stash of illegal psychedelics. The guard turned to us and showcased his lifeless eyes.

"We are here to provide a level of safety that you deserve while enjoying the music, art, and social events. Happy Woodhill," he said without the faintest hint of emotion in his voice. He was not bored, because to show boredom there would need to be an eagerness under the eyes for something else. He had an angular face with a pointed chin and a glazed-over look that implied that he was a robotic shell of a man. His weaponry and authority did not scare me, but his blank stare did. Also, as an experienced Woodhillian, I recognized "Happy Woodhill" as a deranged thing to say.

"Okay yeah, this is weird," said Gordon.

"Really weird," said Ashley.

"The only guarantee for failure is to stop trying," said the lady on the screens. I said nothing.

Our nervousness began to dissipate when we got to the front of the line. There were two men by the campground entrance overseeing the cars that passed through, checking for wrist bands and parking stickers. They had a more human aura to them than the armed guards scattered across the area. They brought an energy that was welcome at a music festival unlike the militaristic look of some of their colleagues. While checking cars in two separate lines, they kept a running dialogue for all the festival goers to hear.

"Enjoy it in there, guys," said the one on the left with a Caribbean accent. "It's a beautiful day for a concert. My name's Will and this here's my buddy Testament. We'd like to welcome you into Woodhill Park. If you need anything, holler at us, ain't that right Testament?" Testament nodded. Will loosely checked our vehicle and ushered us along.

The campsite was a giant ring around the main hill that was completely flat and devoid of trees. By the festival's design, we were to sleep on earth before ascending through the forest to experience heaven during the day and into the night. As we rode along the driving path we saw armed guards on horseback, fleets of port-a-potties and a sea of people setting up their living space for the weekend.

Every group we passed had a girl that made me fall in love all over again wearing an outfit that only intensified that feeling. Except for the groups where the girls were too young. If you remember one line from my story, let it be that. Everyone was buzzing with excitement and an exuberant sense of community. The beautiful forest and the equally effervescent sound waves provided a backdrop for us all to melt into one another. All the groups were blasting music from different artists that we were soon to see, and that strong common link made it to where there was not a single stranger among us.

A guard directed our car to a spot about middle distance between the hill and the fence that signaled the end of the campsite. He had a mole on his left cheek, but he didn't seem all that aware of it. We parked the car on the grass next to a spot contained by white spray-painted lines. We began setting up our canopy, making sure not to intrude on our neighbors. I was locking down the back right pole when Ashley spoke up. "Guys, there's something I actually really wanted to talk to you about," she said. Her head was down, and she spoke softly. "I just, I feel like none of you guys," she continued before a pause. I felt a pit of dread in my stomach.

"...Have a beer in your hand right now and it's pissing me off!" she finished loudly with a smile. Our worried expressions all turned to joy as well as she tossed us each a drink from the cooler.

"Woodhill Paaaaaark," I shouted up to the heavens. The warm sunlight kissed us with the promise of a wonderful day. I set up one of the sleeping tents with Gordon, while the twins each set up their own. We all took turns changing into our festival attire with as much privacy as we could get from the small tents. I wore red shades and a bandana around my neck sitting loosely over a green and white downward striped button-down shirt that was a button or two more open than it would be in civilized society.

Once we were dressed, we commenced some very casual day drinking and lounged in our newly forged living room. I grabbed a Fosters out of our small cooler that was not great at keeping cans cool but looked great with its green and yellow painted-on 70's aesthetic. I found Fosters gross, but it was my drink of choice because Warlock's Office, the night's main event, was an Australian band. Oh, the sacrifices we make. Gordon staggered into the middle of the canopy, somehow already drunk yet not close to non-functional, a testimony to his vast experience. He had equipped round wireframe glasses with a slight yellow tint. They were of a prescription that made his vision worse, and I could see the wire digging into the bridge of his nose. Style over comfort was our collective mantra, it seemed.

Ashley poured up solo cups of beer and we played a game called Wig the Woggy. Oli got out the Wig the Woggy rules manual, and the heft of the document snapped one of the lawn chairs we'd brought, so he placed it on the floor. I looked around while Wigging the Woggy or Woggying the Wig, one can never tell, and I felt a sincere euphoria. I looked at how the sun hit Oli's hair. He was equal parts the coolest guy I'd ever met and the biggest idiot, and I'd never have it any other way. I caught a glimpse of Ashley's introspective eyes and sarcastic smirk knowing she had something hilarious trapped behind her pursed lips. I analyzed the moment and felt deeply that it didn't have to constitute escapism.

Once our band started touring worldwide, we'd be doing this every day. I wouldn't party and play music and enjoy my limited time with my friends to justify my boring job. Partying and playing music and enjoying my friends would be my job. It made the moment bittersweet to so clearly recognize what I was missing. I wondered if the Gordons felt the same or if they Wigged the Woggy with blissful ignorance.

As my thoughts had just started turning darker, we noticed a scene down the aisle of our campground. There walked a man, traversing the cars and tents, who stepped with dread in place of the wonder of those around him. If we were at a funeral, only he seemed to know. He was trailed by about fifteen of the Vitality Media army men who walked in step with one another. He had long slicked back black hair and wore aggressive dark green boots. And I shit you not, this is legitimately the truth, he was wearing a cape. He looked like a villain in a sci-fi movie with his hands behind his back as he led his evil forces on a march towards further wrongdoing. He made it known with his presence that he was the human embodiment of Vitality Media, and that alone meant he was villainous. And yet, in his face, there was show-stopping somberness.

His energy, though, had a way of dissipating as soon as he left each area. The warm sun was working overtime to keep our joys afloat. I allowed my gaze to linger on the dark cloud of a man for just a moment before turning back to the comfort of my friends.

"I like my music festivals like I like my coffee," said Gordon. "Run by weird authoritarian dictators wearing capes." I preferred half and half.

We finished setting up our area and began to make plans for our day at the festival. It was hard to fit all the artists we wanted to see across different stages, but we came to a solid consensus. We also had to schedule out when to take the acid to ensure the perfect combination of live music and psychedelia. I often found that talking about the fun things we were going to do was almost as fun as doing them.

As we concluded the conversation, a tall bespectacled man approached us. He lumbered over with an awkward gait and ducked his head to get under our canopy. He looked at us for a second as if he was waiting for us to speak first. We didn't, because that was entirely his initiative. "Y'all need any drugs?" he said with a voice obviously lowered from his natural tone.

"Ah nah we're good, man," said Gordon. We all made it clear with our individual body language that we were not interested in carrying a conversation with the guy. He spoke up again.

"Well, I got all the stuff if you're ever interested. I'll buy from you too," he said.

"Yeah, nope, man," said Oli. "Nothing over here."

"I just really like drugs," he said, every breath adding to an awkward cloud he was filling into our area. "If you have any, I'd love to hear where you got them from. I like to compare quality across drug dealers. An address would be good for my cool drug map. I'm a cool guy."

"Yeah, I bet you are, man," I said, punctuating with a tight, closed mouth smile.

"So, if you see any drugs or drug dealers let me know," he continued. "What are y'all here for, mostly, anyway? Do you like the music?"

"Yeah, there's some good acts," said Oli.

"I like the music because of the sounds," said the gargantuan man at a near screaming volume. We just went silent, and he somehow mustered the self-awareness to take the hint to leave. He presumably went to score the name of a large drug dealer from another group.

"First narc of the fest," said Oli.

"No, I think he just really likes drugs and music because of the sounds," I said, mocking the man. There was a young couple setting up a tent across from us, a guy wearing green aviators and a girl who was wearing green aviators. But the similarities ended there. They do say opposites attract and then put on the same pair of sunglasses.

"Yo, that guy was wack as hell," said the guy. He moved slickly towards us. He had an approachable vibe to them. He was the kind of guy that would describe someone else as having an "approachable vibe." Which meant he was cool.

He had brown hair that flipped out behind his surfer hat in a style that could, on a particularly whimsical day, be referred to as a mullet. He had the face of an actor whose name you can't quite remember, but who you always enjoy when he's on screen.

"Yeah, man, they're desperate out here," I said. "Acting weird as hell."

"Honestly, this whole festival has felt a little strange," said the girl I presumed to be the guy's girlfriend. I was feeling presumptuous.

"Right?" said Ashley. It felt good to meet people who seemed to feel the same way we did.

"I'm Amber, and this is Clayton by the way," said the girl I presumed to be Amber. "I guess we're neighbors for the weekend!"

"Ah sweet," said Oli. "I'm Oli and this is Reza, but he goes by Fury." Oli gestured to me.

"I don't go by Fury," I said in a tone that didn't come off as irritated, because I wasn't irritated. Gordon and Ashley introduced themselves as well. Amber grabbed a thick stack of cards off of a burnt orange yoga mat that sat as an integral piece in the meticulously crafted mess that constituted their belongings. The cards had European Renaissance art on them and seemed to carry a general heft to them.

"Anyone want a reading of sorts?" she asked. "I'm not that experienced with it, but it's fun!"

"Sure," I said, before Oli or Gordon had the chance to jump at the offer. Ashley was the only one in our group who hadn't already lunged forward at the comment. I was feeling particularly introspective about my future that morning so I figured it would be nice to connect my mind to the moment around me.

"Okay, Mr. Fury, sorry, Reza, tell me about yourself," said Amber. She had me sit on the grass across from her as she fiddled with the cards. Clayton, likely a veteran of my predicament, looked on and laughed. In his smile and his eyes, I could tell he was intimately familiar with his girlfriend's silliness and loved her all the more for it.

"Well, I'm a musician," I started. I always did want that to be the start of my explanation of self. "And I'm in this band here, and we're gonna be, you know hopefully, pretty successful. I play songs that I want people to connect with and want to see me perform. I guess I'm in a purgatory waiting to be a star, and that's been a dream of mine since I was a child; to live grand and leave a legacy." Amber smiled.

"A star? Well, let's see what the cards have in store for Reza the star." She pulled out three cards from the deck after pretending to try and feel something from the air. Oli and Gordon each watched intently with a beer in their hands.

Amber's face became a bit disgruntled when she looked at the cards, and then her features fell to that of utmost concern "What is..., I've never even...," she muttered slowly before mustering up a smile and looking me directly in the eyes. "Let's do something else," she said in a cheery tone.

I didn't move at all, but Ashley came over with a bag of red plastic cups we brought and said, "let's play beer pong." We played beer pong.

After a while of drinking with our new friends, I was able to shrug off whatever horrors awaited me in the lines of those bullshit cards, and I found myself back in an amicable mood.

I walked over to the other side of our area while Ashley was showing Amber pictures of her cat and decided to try and meet our neighbors on the other side.

I pulled back the tapestry that represented our living room wall and was met by a trembling man sitting in a chair looking directly at the ground. There was nothing around him but pressed-down grass, and his wiry hair going every which way aided him in looking exceptionally frazzled. His mouth slunk into his neck as if it desired a great revenge for generational trauma brought onto it by the concept of a chin.

"Hey man, looks like we're neighbors," I said with a smile. He slowly turned his head to look up at me. "I'm Reza," I said.

"I'm Jason," said the man who could only be described as shriveled. "But my friends call me…" He paused and then pulled out his phone and poked at it before putting it to his ear. "What do you call me?" he said into the phone. He paused again. "My friends call me Jason." He put the phone back in his pocket.

"Oh shit, are you getting service here?" I asked.

"No," he said. I frowned. "All my friends are in hospice anyway." I didn't really know what to say.

"Oh well, it's good to meet the neighbors," is what I came up with.

"I came here with one, but I'll leave here with two," he said.
"What?"

"I came here with one, but I'll leave here with two."

"Yeah, uh, with what?" I asked.

"Foreskin."

I gently put the tapestry back where it was and turned back to the conversation between the Gordons and Amber and Clayton. Getting to know the neighbors on one side was good enough for me. At about three o'clock, we all began to talk about our plans to go into the venue. Some of the smaller acts had already begun, and we figured it could be a nice way to discover some new music. Plus, we'd exhausted our bags of trail mix and Goldfish and began to crave greasy, over-priced festival food. But first, I needed to use the restroom.

"Imma break in the port-a-potties," I said getting up from my lawn chair.

"If you see anything good in there, bring it back for the group," said Gordon.

"Gross," I said, walking away from our canopy. I walked past rows of tents until I got to the main road. I took in a deep breath of fresh air knowing that I wouldn't have that luxury for much longer. The beautiful buzz of excitement made me feel as though I was levitating. The trees rolled down the hill until they met the cleared-out campground. They posed themselves as an inviting trail that ushered each onlooker to the majestic. I looked away from them, towards the back of the campground, and I saw a thin strain of pitch-black smoke rising from the distance. I squinted to see it more clearly. When I did, an armed guard with swooshing red hair and that familiar hollowed out look stepped in front of me.

"Don't look at that. Happy Woodhill," he said, without any adjective that could be assigned to his tone. I furrowed my brow and turned away. The continued use of 'Happy Woodhill' was beginning to wear me down. I walked on towards the toilets and continued to avert my gaze from the smoke.

Instead, I looked at the sea of people. They went on for rows and rows, each one with a story of their own. Each one with passions and ambitions and grand dramatic experiences. If there was anything that truly haunted me in life, it was the magnitude of it all.

4

I graduated from a college close to my hometown in continuation with what my life had already become. Throughout the experience, I played gigs at local venues with friends I'd known since middle school, and it never really felt like it would end. But I took a job up across the state because it paid well and because I'd been conditioned all my life, that's what people do. Just not the people you see on TV. Or read about. Or the people whose voices play loudly through your speakers. My day job was just a safety net, though. It was a hastily put together backup plan that was to be cast aside once I got that text that a big label wanted to sign my band. Or maybe, once I became a prominent music critic, which was a fantasy I never even bothered to pursue at all.

I took the crowded train to work each day and walked in step with every other suit tasked with business and business-adjacent monotony. But each night, I screamed and thrashed towards the gods that I was different. A job with a title that raised no eyebrows at a dinner party was just a clever way for me to build my promising music career without the fear of financial ruin. But as soon as I dipped my toe in the ocean of routine, a current pulled me in with unfathomable strength. When I got home, I was too tired to put my brain to use on making me into the star I deserved to be. The thrill of making friends or cooking a meal replaced the thrill of stardom that I'd always expected my early twenties to entail. Every week, I lived for the weekend and every weekend wasted away without furthering me along my path once drawn by ancient ambition.

No child wants to be an accountant or a solutions engineer or an auditor. They want to be astronauts and rockstars and athletes and maybe even president if their parents are insufferable. But no one ever really gets that second set of jobs. For every person, somewhere along the way, that dream must die. This was what I thought about as I made my way to the port-a-potties. I had a cynic's bladder.

People were only just arriving and yet the row of port-a-potties already smelled rancid. The odor and the woman's voice shouting encouragement and that sweet taste of musical artistry only a half mile away all grabbed my senses at once. This was what it was all about. Or rather what it could all be about. There was a needless urgency that extended outside my body's pressure to urinate. I was an insect under the thumb of Vitality Media, but if they truly were music personified, then that is where I needed to be. I wanted to look at the dark smoke again, but I thought better of it.

The guy in front of me in line for the bathroom turned around to look at me. "Dude, I'm the number one ranked pisser of all time," he said. He was holding a trophy that confirmed his claim. "You wanna see?"

"Nah," I said.

"Missing out," he said.

"What uh, what metrics do they use to determine that?" He chuckled and crossed his admittedly very impressive arms.

"When you know you know," he said. I admired him. He walked into a port-a-potty when one became available, and another guy immediately approached as if he'd been keeping watch the whole time. The second guy put his ear to the stall from the outside and focus fell upon his face. After a few seconds he shook his head in disbelief and muttered to himself, "Son of a bitch, he really is," as though he had been proven wrong about an opinion he was once steadfast in.

A very big gentleman came out of a different port-a-potty in front of me which meant it was finally my turn.

But when I walked up to replace him in the palace of stank, he looked me in the eyes and said, "I wouldn't. Just got visited by the Ghost of Christmas Blast, man, absolute work of shart. I just wouldn't." I defied him and walked in. What I found was a head-to-toe Jackson Pollock smattering of blood, feces and urine surrounding the cleanest and most pristine toilet bowl I'd ever seen. I darted out of the horrific capsule and took residence in the recently vacated one next to it. There, I found relief.

On the walls, scratched in desperate handwriting, were the words "Mourn with me." Below it said, "Grieve with me." As I urinated, my eyes traced the writing downward as it spiraled into more and more unhinged lettering. Mourn with me. Grieve with me. Mourn with me. Grieve with me. Then at the very bottom of the right wall, it read, "Mourn with me, Reza." For the second time in about a minute, I erupted out of a port-a-potty in horror.

Immediately in front of me was the caped man I'd seen earlier, and he stared at my face. I hastily fastened up my pants as I looked at him. He had a hardened look and his straight black hair against his fair skin created a look less of a sickly man and more of a macabre entity.

"Enjoying the festival?" he asked. I nodded meekly. "Good," he said in return before walking off slowly in the opposite direction of my tent. I felt my breath struggle and my body shiver as I walked back to my group.

I whispered slowly to myself, "And you know something's happening here, but you don't know what it is, do you, Mister Jones?"

5

"Alright, everyone ready to head in?" I asked when I got back. I was met by a resounding "Yes." Ashley quickly grabbed her tote bag that was decorated with the imagery of a 1940s art movie I'd never heard of. She dropped in sour candy and water bottles to join some gems and other trinkets she'd already packed for various reasons such as holding or bartering.

Oli had a white shirt that detailed the pythagorean theorem on it, somehow the coolest streetwear I'd ever seen, and also for the premium price that streetwear requires. And Gordon donned a trippy green and yellow striped poncho. Gordon was the type of guy to don clothes. Maybe there was some mystique to it that I was picking up, but regardless, while others wore or even outfitted, Gordon donned.

We each snuck a tab of LSD wrapped in tinfoil into our wallets and said goodbye to Clayton and Amber who we were sure to see again. Oli and Gordon put on those backpacks filled with water that were designed for consumers who'd always dreamt of sucking from the teat of their own luggage. And just like that, the four of us began our uphill trek towards the promised land.

Gordon and Oli were up front while Ashley and I walked a step behind them. I was glad because I hadn't gotten to catch up much with Ashley, and she was probably my favorite of the bunch what with the whole not being an absolute idiot part.

"How've you been, Ash?"

"I've been good, Reza. Been bartending since graduation and honestly really liking it. It's fun and I meet people that are, like, in the scene and stuff, so I guess that's my way of networking!" She laughed, but there was a small sadness to her voice, as if having nothing permanent to hold onto was becoming draining to her. I wish she'd known how much I envied her connection to a scene, her grasp on her dreams. "And I've been working on my art, of course. But what about you? Raking it in with that fancy data whatever job, huh?"

"I suppose. I'm doing well for myself," I said. I felt bad for ignoring the mention of her art, but I could only respond to so much. "I miss the gang, though. I know we're not that far away, I've just been so busy."

"We'll get some more jam sessions going soon," she said. That meant more to me than I gathered she even knew. It frustrated me that I felt as if I was just living for the sparse moments of seeing my old friends. There was no progression, only a disconnect. Ashley and I caught up with Gordon and Oli as we trekked up the hill.

"It would be so cool to be playing here at this festival," I said. "Even on the undercard." I said it as a goal, a directional suggestion to the rest of the band.

"Yeah that would be cool," said Oli. He said it as a vague dream floating up amongst the clouds as though the sentiment arising from his lips dispersed it from his brain.

"Do you think Warlock's Office is going to play Cosmo Politician?" I asked, trying to grasp the fleeting moment that my ambitions were pulling me from. Gordon's glazed over look hardened and he looked at me with excitement written across his face.

"I've wanted to trip to that song ever since the first time I heard it!" he said. That was all I ever wanted anyone to say about something I had written. The moment simultaneously represented the beauty that music can elicit and the pain from how my desperate plight struggled to reach that beauty. Gordon's brown locs erupted from his tie dye headband like a perfectly shaped bonfire. I admired the intensity in his gaze. He was content in the moment, something I both longed for and restricted myself from attaining through such longing.

"This shit steep," said Oli, struggling up the hill. Feeling the strain on my legs grounded me as I toughed out the journey with my friends. Ashley, being the sibling that she was, started charging ahead of our pace, taunting all of us, but with Oli on the mind.

"How?" yelled an exasperated Oli.

"I'm just a gremlin like that," said Ashley. Gordon and I joined her through gritted teeth and Oli's tan face dropped to a deadpan expression.

"I'm just gonna head back," he said. His blonde hair waved goodbye to us from behind his hat in the stylings of the wind. We all laughed and bid him farewell, and he struggled to finally reach the top of the hill with the rest of us.

As we weaved through the trees towards the entrance, I took note of all the little details that made the festival grounds so magical. There were delicate string lights overhead that would create an enchanting mosaic at nightfall. I stepped over roots and other unchecked disciples of nature's growth, and I couldn't help but feel like I was being beckoned by something greater than us all up ahead. I was only walking to a stage, but there was this heavy sense of going in. Not going into a place of any structure, but into a mental state, into a journey. One with warped time and perceptions.

Walking through the trees to the main gate was like the beginning of a psychedelic episode in of itself. I let it take me. There were a few vendors and art exhibits and yoga areas outside the festival, but most people brushed past them, keeping them in mind for later visits. The crowd began to thicken as we closed in on the front gate. I took in my introspective journey one last time before falling into line with the rest of my group.

At the front of the line was a guard with an angular face and a pointed chin. He held a large machine gun in his hands as he watched the festival attendees scan their wristbands to get in. His eyelids dropped to a spot between bored and downright thoughtless altogether. If this militaristic force was what it took to contain the wonders of the festival, then I was all for it, but I took notice of a nervousness around me. Yet it was not enough to unsteady me. I branched into a second line that was overseen by a guard with a mole on his left cheek. I scanned my wristband and the machinery turned green allowing me into the festival.

Upon my first step into the festival, church bells rang loudly from above. They signified the start or the end. Or both. I turned around and got one last glimpse of the black smoke rising in the valley below me and then continued into the festival, putting it all behind me.

Something wonderful happened to me right when I first got into the festival, and it wouldn't even do it justice to put into flowery words. I bought a big ass corndog. We looked around while we ate and took in all the colorful outfits and people on different wavelengths that all fit together to form an ocean of happiness. There was a merch table with shirts and pashminas from all the different artists and also Vitality Media sponsored shirts that were black with white Times New Roman 12 pt. font lettering that read, "to be as i shall become, i must succumb to the greater plan." I didn't buy any of it. There was a row of tents where artists sold their original art with a big sign above that said, "Woodhill Souk," perhaps a microaggression we let go for its positivity in giving small artists a platform.

We walked through it and enjoyed all the clothing and exotic accessories people had designed. There was also a bit too much framed Jar Jar Binks porn, and I saw our neighbor Jason purchasing a lot of it. I did not greet him. Outside of the marketplace area, there was another tent with a small crowd around it. As we got closer, I heard the same voice from when we were entering the campgrounds. I saw the woman, with the commanding presence of a divine figure, that was on the screen at the entrance. "There are people out there who are trying to tell you what you can and cannot be," she said. "That because they lived this safe and boring life, you must do so as well, because that is just what life is. Being old and retired from an uninspiring job does not make you an expert on what it means to live. Reject those who are adamant that you 'face reality,' as they have as little an idea of what that is as you!" I felt something jump in me as well as she spoke.

"My name is Denny," she continued. "And I will be here all festival, day and night. I will make you the star that you deserve to be. Let me be your gentle reminder that you are more than the world is letting on."

I gazed over Denny's tight blonde ponytail and her stern expression that overwhelmed her warm features. She had the faintest eyeliner that brought out her eyes, and all the wrinkles on her face were perfectly curated to replace the ones that should have been there.

In my mind, I was at the top of a hill, sitting in a red and yellow, plastic Fisher Price car and here came Denny to give me a needed push. I had always thought that everyone, adults especially, looked down on my plight, my yearning. But in Denny, there was a woman that looked like high society, yet spoke directly to how I felt. She was hope incarnate. I hid from the Gordon three my feelings of inspiration and gripped my dreams even closer to my chest as we passed through the crowd surrounding Denny.

"Inspiring stuff," said Gordon with a level of sincerity that I couldn't discern. Ashley and Oli nodded. They too wanted something or other that seemed to be passing them by. But they had it more clearly in their minds that Denny's message was not what we were there for. As we walked closer to the main stage, we could hear the faint sounds of performance.

There were people sitting all around us on the grass as they passively enjoyed the sounds of a band they'd probably never heard of. It was demoralizing that even a band big enough to get booked at Woodhill Park was irrelevant in the grand scheme of things. They were living on the fringes of the dream, and I envied them and pitied them all at the same time. All around us were groups of people with tall signs to mark their presence. The signs represented a landmark for when the group inevitably got split up. We lacked the foresight to bring such an item, but it was probably for the best because it would have had something to do with 'Fury and the Gordon Three.'

As we navigated our way through our peaceful comrades, I noticed a kerfuffle in the distance where armed guards were escorting a man away from the stage. He wore a brown jacket. He was one of those brown jacket guys. His eyes simultaneously displayed disobedience and drug-fueled emptiness. But there was more of a person within him than in any of the guards. And that person wore a brown jacket. In his left hand was a ripped sign, or totem, that read, "Vitality Media sucks butt." Speaking truth to power was evidently against the terms of service.

A girl from his group was yelling hysterically as they took him away and she shouted, "What are you going to do to him?!"

One armed guard said, with a dead expression, "Ma'am, we are going to execute him." She was taken aback and stood there with her mouth agape.

"That's not funny," she finally said. The guards said nothing and showed no emotion as they continued to carry him along. It was all surreal, but the band started playing a pretty cool reggae tune that I was surprisingly familiar with, and everyone's attention turned away from the incident.

Throughout the concert, I couldn't stop thinking about Denny, the talent guru. Part because what she said resonated with me, and part because signs and pictures of her were scattered relentlessly around the festival grounds. I found that her image haunted me, speaking to a core aspect of my own being that either I or my circumstances had stifled. That feeling of desperation for more in life always flowed within me, but never did it take the reins. Denny, in her being and her ideology, was coaxing it out slowly from all around as I tried to enjoy the concert. The concert that I knew in my heart that I should have been performing.

Oli interrupted my thoughts to discuss our schedule. He discussed when we would go to each of the main stages. There were three stages. The main one was called Another Stage and then the secondary stage was called Stage One. And the EDM rave area was the Love Stage. This was because each stage was named for the phrase Love One Another, but it made it all confusing.

"Okay so we'll see Bocce Boys at Another Stage at six," he started.

"Wait, there's another stage?" said Ashley.

"No, the other stage is Stage One?" said Oli.

"The second stage is stage one? Wow, I love that for us," said Ashley.

"No Love Stage is in the back," said Oli.

"Goddammit, I don't wanna do this 'Who's on First' bullshit," said Gordon, but it was too late, What had already gotten to second base. Once we got all of that figured out, Oli continued.

"So, we'll see Bocce Boys at six, then we move stages for Rocco Wealthy who comes on at eight. Then back to the main stage for what it says is To Be Announced at 9:30 and Warlock's Office at eleven."

"Rocco Wealthy playing *Dirt Bike Daydream* live is gonna be so crazy," said Gordon.

"But man, no one puts on a show like Warlock's Office," I said. "I'm so excited." I was telling the truth, too.

"So, we'll drop the tabs right after Rocco Wealthy, so we'll be peaking for Warlock's Office," said Oli. No one had any objections. I was focused purely on the present. I'm under the impression that there is nothing better in the world than being excited for a fun day ahead of you. We walked around the area paying minor attention to the screamo-reggae fusion band that was playing. The songs that were mostly just reggae were a lot better than the rest. Ashley showed me a picture she'd taken that was a candid of me and my big ass corndog. We looked good together.

While we were walking, two very pretty girls walked up to me specifically. They each had one braid in their hair streaming down their face in the front. One had blonde hair and dark eyebrows and the other, the opposite. One could be convinced they performed some sort of swap back at their campground. The one on the left had a green sprout in her hair and wore a two-piece outfit that exposed her midriff and a large flowy pashmina around her shoulders that matched her personality, or so she intended. She bit her lip and said, "Hey, can you settle a bet for us?"

I said, "sure," with a wry smile.

"Game one of the 2010 World Series, Over, under 9.5 total runs?"

"Oh," I said, with a bit of disheartened confusion. Then I remembered that, as a lifelong San Francisco Giants fan, I actually knew the answer. "Over. The Giants scored like eleven runs in that game."

"Shit!" said the girl that had approached me, as both of them pulled out their wallets. Then a fat New Yorker slurping down a cigarette, who I could only be led to believe was their bookie, came and took a wad of cash from them.

"Well, ladies, that settles it. Time to pay the pipah," said the fat man as he thumbed through the cash.

"Screw you," said the girl to me as she walked away. It didn't really seem fair. I felt like that bet should have been settled long before that moment, anyway, but I brushed it off and went along with my evening, forever more skeptical of what is and isn't a pickup line. I spent an amount of money that would literally sadden me to type out on a beer at a vendor, and my group chatted about nonsense in between waves of raucous laughter.

Finally, Bocce Boys played their set. It was quite nice. In the words of that massive undercover police officer, I liked the music because of the sounds. With every melodic stroke, I felt a deep appreciation mixed with a deep envy. It must have felt so fulfilling to be up there performing to a crowd of that size, knowing that the notes flowing from the instrument were both perfectly placed and uniquely yours, your tangible mark on the world. That I could only hypothesize the feeling was perhaps my greatest sadness.

The fans around me sang along. With each familiar song came a memory or a feeling that was deeply personal to them. An artist's set isn't just a celebration of their songs, it is a celebration of music itself. When it ended, the crowd dispersed back into the flow of their unique schedules and out of a once strong, attentive collectivism.

It felt like we were ants scurrying along atop the hill. It was just another silly little day in our silly little lives despite how grand it all felt. The eyes on the ever-prevalent signs and advertisements for Denny pierced into my skin as if to try and burn off my growing feeling of frivolity. We made the quick journey between stages as the sun worked its way to its final resting place of the day.

I noticed that my mind had been moving in waves all afternoon. The lulls between sets were broken by intense peaks of focus. Thoughts about the past and the present built and dissipated rhythmically as I entered, mentally, into each song. The musicians had a profound control over their audiences that I craved. The way time flowed through the day, effected gently by my own flows of focus, felt like a whimsical hint at the perhaps underestimated fluidity of its structure.

We settled in the crowd about a half football field from the stage, or about 0.6 field hockey fields, or 0.089 nautical miles from the stage and decided that it was a comfortable place to be. The crowd was simmering at a low murmur waiting for Rocco Wealthy to get on stage. I saw, to my left, a young girl have something whispered into her ear, and she turned to me after hearing it. She was as short as the day is long, or something like that, and had an extremely round face that was covered in glitter. Her right ear, facing me, had three piercings, a green, turquoise and blue gem, from top to bottom. She stood on her tippy toes to reach my ear.

"Only in Vitality Media can we find purpose, pass it on," she said. I immediately turned to Gordon next to me.

"Only in Vitality Media can we find purpose, pass it on," I said. He nodded and turned to Ashley. I looked down at my twiddling thumbs and wondered silently why I'd complied so easily.

The game of telephone, one that did not elicit even a single smile across the audience, made its way through the crowd. I would consider the stark joylessness a failure as far as a childrens' game goes. After a while, the lights on the stage began to lower, and I could feel a breeze as the crowd's split attention collectively flew towards the front in unison. There was a large cheer, and Rocco Wealthy ran out onto the stage to perform his disgusting yet catchy song "Drip off the Old Cock," a pun-filled tune about fatherhood. At its conclusion, he began some banter with the crowd.

"I never thought I'd be where I am today," he said. This was met by scattered shouts from fans. "I remember when I was sleeping on the floor, no idea if I was finna even eat the next day. Now I'm a multi-millionaire off this rap shit." There was a loud roar from the crowd for his inspirational tale. It was the perfect segue into a hit song, but he kept talking. "My mama told me I wasn't never gonna amount to anything," he said. I felt like that was just bad parenting. "My teacher said I was gonna be in one of two places by the time I hit twenty: the jail cell or the coffin," he continued. It seemed like there should have been some education reform somewhere along the line to prevent that. The crowd was still hanging on his every word. "And when I tried to make something of my life, every day I was held down by the crooked, greedy Jews," he said. The crowd began with an uneasy murmur. Rocco, though, was unaware that he'd lost his audience. "The Zionist overlords control everything we do with their filthy ways, and still here I am!" He finished, hoping to be met with some raucous cheer, but many in the crowd just looked around in shock.

Then he began the song "She Like It How I Lick Like That" and all was forgotten. The crowd was wild throughout his set. That the same crowd that passed a blunt around and hacky sacked for Bocce Boys could mosh like they did for Rocco

Wealthy was, to me, the great beauty of music festivals. And drugs that make you happy. As soon as the final loop of 808s faded away on his last song, we all collectively booked it back over to the main stage for the final two headliners.

"I wonder what To Be Announced means," said Ashley, glancing at the schedule as we quickly walked across the festival grounds. Her fingers curled around the three rings on her left hand, and she wondered aloud. "Like is it a special guest or something?"

"I bet it's going to be Drake," said her twin brother. His beady eyes darted around between the three of us under the shade of his hat.

"Drake is a concluded social experiment conducted by a team of grad students at the University of Toronto. The project ended, he doesn't exist anymore," I said back.

"Oh right," said Oli. We theorized who TBA might be but didn't come to much of a consensus. We were at the whims of Vitality Media and, as wonderful or horrifying as that might be, we were all excited.

When we got to the main stage, we sat down in a spot of our liking. The act that was playing simultaneously to Rocco Wealthy had just finished, and the new crowd we'd immersed ourselves in, which was largely the same crowd we'd been flowing through all day, waited impatiently for the surprise guest.

Once we sat down, we all pulled a little piece of paper from our respective hiding places and held them out for a toast. "Down the hatch, Bon Appetit," said Gordon as we all placed the acid on our tongues. The uncomfortable feeling of paper in my mouth was a small price to pay for ten hours of absurd introspective bliss. The sun was almost all the way down, and the festival grounds had been lit up with neon lights spread across the sky. The area looked like a giant's playground. Massive glow sticks illuminated the small areas they inhabited, and the limited sight brought on by the darkness created a true sense of disconnect from the world that only strengthened our connection to those around us who were right there with us in that moment.

"You think Batman or Elmo would win in a boxing match?" asked Oli. He put that question into the world and looked at it with satisfaction as it rode the haze of marijuana smoke that passed over us.

"Tie," said Gordon, curtly. Ashley nodded.

Before any further elaboration on the topic, the crowd's potential energy turned kinetic. The lights dimmed, and everyone around us leapt to their feet. I looked up to the stage and tried to make sense of the wild flashing lasers that had just begun. Then I felt and heard one strikingly loud note from a guitar.

6

My life flashed before my eyes as the sound slammed into my head. It was brief and unexciting and redundant. It was completely disorienting to be jolted with everything you've ever known and to feel so little. The person I saw was not who I was supposed to be. I felt that it was now or never to do something to shrink that dissonance, but for that moment I was trapped in the audience and hypnotized by a guitar.

As a melody began to form, I regained my balance and composure and immersed myself back into the performance. As soon as the first note played, the crowd crunched together and pushed towards the stage with murderous intentions. Every person had the attitude that if they were to accidentally kill the person in front of them for a better view, then so be it. Tomorrow's problems did not affect today's wants and needs. My feet left the ground as I was ushered closer to the stage. Oli, Gordon and Ashley floated along with me. The wild band raged on, clashing with the natural laws in place that limited the maximum volume an instrument could make. I finally found my feet again as the crowd around me began to sway to the music. I looked up and saw the lights on stage swirling and making patterns they were not supposed to make.

On the screen there were words that read Dreadful Art By Dying Artists in a wavy font. They were a five-piece band, but I was too far away to make out anything besides the fact that they seemed to have two women and three men. The chaos of the music caressed the chaos in the crowd and created a wonderful explosion of passion. I had not heard of Dreadful Art By Dying Artists, but I heard them then loud and clear. The trance-like guitar and desperate pleading vocals shot through me as my dilated pupils pulsated with intense focus towards the stage. The lights around the band bounced with the music either from meticulous set-up by the stage director or only within my own mind. It was enthralling regardless. When the first song ended, the singer leaned against the mic and said, "It begins again as it always has and always will."

The second song they played had a chorus that went like "I killed the man who wrote my autobiography." It was catchy and intense. Each member of the five piece, who I could only see as silhouettes, moved themselves to their own unique beat, but it all tied together in a knot to make a cohesive song. While they played with infectious enthusiasm, I couldn't help but feel that they were everything and that I was nothing. I wasn't even me. I was just a small part of the mob, a small part of the moment.

I wanted more. Whether through art, through charisma, through performance, I wanted to create the moment, not just be a part of it. I was witnessing that, for a brief moment, a person could be God, and I desperately craved just a taste.

I noticed that the wall of the stage was lined with armed guards who stared indifferently into the rowdy crowd. I could not pick out their impact on the moment at all.

Every new song the band performed captured me all over again after releasing me with the previous fade out or ringing conclusion. It was both exhausting and invigorating. Then they released me for the final time. "There will be no encore," said the lead singer. "You know when it's over. Once it begins, it cannot begin again. It can only end." The band walked off the stage in opposite directions. I stood paralyzed with shock. My soul had been spoken to, and it had been told only harsh truths. I looked behind me, but I did not see any truths at all. All I saw was a sea of people who I recognized even less than I would a stranger. Then three faces rendered in my view that I deeply recognized.

Gordon's face was more pale and gaunt than I remembered it being and he had a nosebleed beginning out of his left nostril. "That was…" I said to him, but I didn't have any more words. Oli looked at me with a soft, meaningless smile and I noticed that the design on his shirt had faded significantly. And Ashley jittered ever so slightly, even down to the excess brown hairs that frizzed out of her pigtails. This amalgam of uncertain and undriven people was my vehicle to create and experience what Dreadful Art By Dying Artists just had. Without succeeding in whatever it was I was so passionate to achieve, I knew that I would die.

"Oh man, they were phenomenal. I'd never heard of them," said Gordon finally, his strong voice unaware how strung out he looked.

"Me neither. It felt like they were speaking directly to me." I looked into Gordon's green eyes. "Yo, you tripping, bro?"

"A bit," he said with a laugh. I was starting to feel it too, with the aid of that raucous band.

"Yeah, me too," I said. We both laughed. I didn't even really know why I was laughing, but it was hilarious. Ashley sat down as the crowd fell back to a low murmur waiting for Warlock's Office. We joined her.

"Not to be too sentimental," started Ashley. "But don't you wish we could do this for the rest of our lives? Just holding onto the idea of being musicians, holding onto the idea of being artists. Just going to festivals and being around like-minded creatives. It just feels so fleeting and final and scary. But maybe that's the beauty in it all." I grasped at Ashley's sentiment and came up empty. That big break, that grip on a life well lived still remained just beyond my fingertips.

"Yeah, but it almost feels like all the old people here are even sadder than the old people who aren't here," I said. There was a smelly old man in front of me, but he didn't hear my ageist comment. "And sometimes it's not enough to just love Warlock's Office, I want to *be* Warlock's Office."

"You still can," said an auditory hallucination in the bowels of my mind. I blinked and the sound and the thought dissipated.

"Yeah, but then Warlock's Office's music would sound like shit," said Ashley. I pushed her playfully.

As we waited for the headliner to start, I examined Gordon and Oli and Ashley's faces. I wondered if they were experiencing an inner turmoil quite like I was. My mind was swirling from the Dreadful Art By Dying Artists set, and the world around me had an ambiguously different look about it. I again felt as though I'd gone in but still couldn't place where to or where from.

The anticipation built in and around us. I knew the Gordons so well through my time spent with them, but at that moment, I could only focus on the present versions of them. Only the them right then and there truly knew the me that existed in that one individual moment. And then a giant wall of lasers appeared above us. The crowd hushed their individual conversations and melted into a sea of onlookers.

A man's face distorted with swirls appeared over the large screens on either side of the stage. He spoke with an aggressive echo. "A journey. Journey. Journey. Into. Into. Into. Your Future. Future. Future." Then washed-out C, Cmaj7/B, and Em chords floated into the crowd. I could make out Kendall Paulson and his backing band on stage playing the music. The crowd erupted. Kendall began to sing with his unique high psychedelic singing voice.

"As a kid I saw myself / A starlight man in weaving threads of wealth/ As a man I see myself / A worried man in dire need of help / I wanna go backwards in time / To when it never weighed so heavily on my mind / Oh how it'd be so heavenly to rewind." It was a deeper cut off his second album, but we knew all the words. So did most of the rest of the crowd. We were at home.

Next to the stage stood a tall, intimidating building. It was presumably an air-conditioned space for the artists and VIP members to comfortably experience the festival. It seemed to be one of the only permanent parts, one that didn't need to be reassembled every year, but in my prior trips to Woodhill Park, I never remembered its architecture being so Draconian. It had a balcony at the very top of it, about four stories high. On it stood who I'd assumed was the Vitality Media leader with his cape and jet-black hair. Which means that his hair was as black as a B-52 Stratofortress aircraft, but don't look that up because no one likes a know-it-all anyway. In front of me, the old man I'd noticed earlier was standing perfectly still with terrible posture.

I focused on the music. Warlock's Office had full control over me. The intricate walls of sound they created filled me with crushing inspiration. The first song ended, and a chill ran down my spine. Every little sound had been curated for me, and even more so for my brain on psychedelics. In creating these songs, Kendall Paulson knew me.

He grabbed the mic and spoke into it with the pedals beneath him still caressing his voice with angelic intentions. "California," he said. "We are Warlock's Office, and we come all the way from Northern Beaches, Australia. Tonight, we get to go on a journey together." A woman in an upper-class Antebellum dress put her hand to her forehead and fainted into her boyfriend's arms. She was all of us. A girl in front of me pulled out her phone to film, but there was no way the video could capture even an iota of the moment's true beauty. And if that makes me sound like a pretentious douchebag, then my intentions were clear. There was a purity in the air, an essence of exceptionalism that made me unapologetically pretentious. Everyone truly experiencing the concert was better than everyone who wasn't.

The laser show picked up its pace at about the eighty-minute mark. It waged war on the night sky in a truly climactic nature as Kendall Paulson played "My Night in Cairo," perhaps his biggest song. I felt a bittersweet release as he played the final note. I was sad that it was over, but ecstatic to have it now in my memory forever. "Thank you," he said leaning into the mic. "May the rivers run with your love." The band hadn't even finished walking off yet by the time the crowd began strategizing a way to get an encore.

As the crowd chanted for their return, the old man in front of us turned to face Gordon, the twins, and me. He had a wild white beard that fit his curly white hair, and he wore suspenders. His stature was large, but his hunch brought him back to our eye level. "You'll never be that," he said, with an oddly adversarial tone. He tilted his head at us. His left eye, the one closer to us squinted and twitched, while the right remained wide open. "He has thousands of people under his thumb. He comes up with a melody in his spare time and you, like the rest of the world, spend your time memorizing it. He goes city to city and people trip over themselves just to see him. Now that we can see a life led like that, how can we settle for our own dull lives? Look at you all, obsessing over another person's actions. Don't you want it to be you? Don't you deserve a taste? Every day, the world goes by, and the life you do live slips further from the life you could live. I pity all four of you. A half decade of nothing remains and then an eternity of forgotten. Think about the day that started, the day it all ended, for that day is just as much today as any other."

We just looked at him as he walked off and disappeared into the crowd. Perhaps I was just in a vulnerable state, but his words resonated with me in the worst way. I looked over at Gordon and saw him staring at the ground. "Damn," he muttered to himself. Oli stared up at the clouds in a malaise.

Warlock's Office came back and played one of my favorite songs, but I barely even heard it. I wanted to be up there instead of down on the dirty ground. I didn't want it all to be over. When the song ended, Warlock's Office left, and the lights turned on.

"I want to be up there," I said.

We walked aimlessly in silence.

"Wait, follow me," I said to the group. I took the lead of the pack. The Gordons said nothing and followed.

"That old man's wrong," said Ashley. "There's more to life than fame and success."

"Like what?" I asked. Ashley said nothing and looked at the ground. Perhaps we were truly privileged to get to care so deeply about what the old man said, but we cared nonetheless.

"Like getting twisted," said Gordon. He knew I didn't agree with him, and I wasn't sure he even agreed with himself. The parties and drugs and alcohol were a wonderful symptom of a wild successful life, but alone, they stood hollow in my mind.

There was an emptiness within us that we tried desperately to never think about, but at that moment, it was all we thought about. We came to a crowd near the front gate of the festival. People were gathered around a tent that had a light post next to it creating dramatic shadows. Facing the crowd was Denny, the talent guru and inspirational speaker whose face filled the screens around the festival grounds. I looked into her eyes from afar, desperately seeking answers.

7

"We are told from a young age that we can be anything," said Denny to the crowd. Every fixating eye locked onto her as she spoke, and she knew well enough to harness that energy through her presence and tone. She'd created a forcefield around her, somehow curating the only spot in the festival without a tinge of feces and sweat wafting through the air.

"And then we're told at a slightly older age, by the world, by mentors, by parents, that we can be anything within a range of these sensible options. And so, we have imagination instilled in us and reinforced every time we consume media involving and created by the select few that live their dream only for it to be pulled from us." The crowd around her murmured indistinguishably yet positively. We were like budding revolutionaries listening to the novel ideas of a great orator.

"But we live in a unique time, where enough people fall victim to the trend of settling for less, and those who just keep trying end up facing a small enough level of competition that they actually can succeed. It takes talent, perseverance, and connections. If you can bring me even the smallest amount of the first two, I can provide the third. And we can get you to your dreams together."

"I have talent," said a lady in the front.

"Do you have the work ethic to keep trying?" asked Denny warmly.

"No, absolutely not."

"Hmm," said Denny, scanning the crowd.

"Well, I have perseverance," said a guy next to her.

"Awesome," said Denny. "And talent?"

"That I do not have."

Denny made a face as if it were weird that these people spoke up despite knowing these truths about themselves that directly contradicted what she was looking for. Then she looked to the back of the crowd and stared right at me. "You four," she said, gesturing towards us. "Come here." We looked around for a bit and then finally approached her. I could now place her at around forty. Her blonde hair was still in her tight ponytail. Her clothes were plain, but you could tell they were fancy through their fit and material. She wore modest jewelry that only dazzled as you got close. She looked like a woman from an '80s exercise video had been dropped into modern high society. The griminess of a multi-day music festival over a hot weekend in the woods had yet to touch her.

"You look different from all of them," she said quietly once we'd approached her. Then she turned to the crowd and spoke to them. "Give me a moment; enjoy this quick video." She put a video of herself on the screen using a remote in her hand. On the screen she said, "Vitality Media loves you and your dreams..." but she pulled us aside before I could watch any further.

"You four are talented, aren't you?" she asked. I was happily perplexed by her singling us out.

"I like to think so," I said. Oli giggled, but I ignored him. All I could think about was being a musician. That was a life well lived, a life Denny saw for us. I ignored the concept of trying to be a musician. I could not glorify the struggle. It was the struggle that had led me astray, sedated me from true passion. In Denny, I found the strength to shout, "to hell with the struggle, now is the time for results!"

"I love that. My job is to find talent, and I'm very good at it. What are your names?"

"Reza Donegal," I said, proudly. It was a name that would soon be known to the masses for its excellence. Gordon and Oli and Ashley also said their names, but they don't get quotations. Denny said that there was a place that she wanted to take us where we could talk to some Vitality Media execs about how we begin our journey towards making it in the world. The convincing way she spoke made me feel like the future I could not help but envision for myself of wasting away at my desk job and giving up on the dream of playing large shows or dropping hit albums was not inevitable.

She saw the potential in me that I had once seen, but that had also been fading from my vision. It was validating and magical. As we walked through the much emptier festival, we saw that the guards with their soldier gear were still walking around with glazed over faces and a determination in their step that didn't seem to belong to their mind. Denny touched two of them gently on the arm as they passed.

"Jim! Andre!" she said. Jim had a mole on his left cheek and Andre had swooshing red hair. They said nothing, and Denny turned to us behind her. "Oh, I love those boys," she said. She led us along the festival grounds as we walked over trash reflecting buzzing blue lights. There was a calmness reminiscent of the aftermath of something chaotic. Massive fluorescent light posts stood high above us to illuminate the main path.

We went around the back of the main stage and saw the other side of the centerpiece building that felt like an eerie castle.

"What is this?" asked Ashley.

"Woah," said Oli. Their interest in Denny's direct message seemed to ebb and flow, and I began to slightly resent them for it. We had a chance to actually become someone. The castle was unimportant to me.

"This is the cathedral of success," said Denny with a cheery tone that implied that her statement was less mysterious than it was. The castle became important to me.

"Woah," I said, with the same tone as Oli. I looked through a stained-glass window to see inside one of the rooms. There were hundreds of girls in sundresses, and they swung their arms about and shuffled their feet in some sort of trance-like dance. Their faces had the same indifference as the armed guards all around the park. Their movements were unnatural and unkempt, but they never bumped into one another. It was all a cacophony of calculated randomness. Peering through the window, I could make out a second floor that looked down on the girls, and it was lined with silhouettes of onlookers.

I let the Gordons and Denny go past me as I tried to make sense of the weird room, and when Denny realized I was behind, she snapped at me with a stern voice, saying, "Don't look in there." She then warmed up considerably as she gently pulled me away. "Those girls sure do love their dancing."

Denny brought us to a little forest within the forest on the hill that was roped off from the rest. There was only one entrance and exit, and it was guarded by a whole troop of soldiers. They let us in upon seeing us with Denny. The tall trees created a bit of a ceiling, and warm yellow light lit the whole area from the ground. There was ethereal music playing, but I couldn't spot any speakers. Scattered about were people on yoga mats with massive headphones on. They all seemed enormously at peace. It was a serene little spot, and Denny sat us at a picnic table. "Tell me," she said in a whisper. "What are your ambitions?"

"I want to be fulfilled," I said immediately. It was as if the forest was drawing these words out of me. "And fulfillment to me is success. And success to me is to create an identity through music. Every day, I wake up and I get to be a renowned musician. And I captivate people with my music. And in that, I actually exist in this world."

That goal, as vague as it seemed, became clear to me. All I ever did was wait for it to fall in my lap, but in Denny, there was a chance to actually go for it. To love music was not enough, I needed to embody music. I needed to make it my life and be remembered for it. It was a future that I desperately craved. Denny turned to Ashley.

"I want people to truly connect with my art," she said. Her face was so envious of something she had created in her mind. "I want people to feel something, anything when they look at what I've created." Denny smiled.

We all turned and looked at Gordon. He said nothing for a little while and then jerked his head up to face us.

"You know what? I want the rockstar lifestyle. The drugs, the girls, the parties. I'm not ashamed to want these things!" He looked down at the table in shock. His breath was heavy, coming out through the light brown scruff above his upper lip and on his chin. "I've never articulated it like that," he said.

"I wanna just vibe," said Oli. His statement was, amongst the four of us, the most directly aligned with his character.

Denny scanned us slowly with deliberating eyes.

"I like you four," she said. "You have presence, talent, chemistry with one another. You have what it takes to be a creative collective. The industry is looking for unapologetic desires, for a band that wants to deliver at a high level." She turned to me. "This success you mention. It's right there for the taking. It's easier than you think." I fell in love with her message as she laid it onto me. The world only existed in that singular moment. My dreams were not dead.

For the first time in my life, I looked into the future and saw a concrete path to really reaching my dreams. Sometimes people make it in the most random of ways. I'd, just moments prior, felt that my ambitions had firmly cemented themselves as delusions, but with Denny, I felt as though I could reject that feeling. And so I did, fully and blindly.

8

Denny talked at length about how she could feel the dedication we had within us. She spoke in exciting and vague phrases throughout, as though to be very careful yet casual with every word. She said that the details were for the morning and gave us each a massive pair of headphones.

"Find a spot in this enchanted forest that calls to you and put these on. Then we will advance to phase two. Under no circumstances should you take them off. You'll be instructed when to do so."

Her eyes switched rhythmically between bright and dark as she spoke, likely a symptom of my own mind fluttering through the night.

Gordon, Ashley, and I walked together with Oli a step behind. We branched out to find our own little nook. Gordon, actually in a complete antithetical, found a cranny. I laid back against a tree and looked up at the Edison bulbs above me as I placed the headphones over my ears. I sat comfortably against the bark, and a night breeze flowed slowly through my chosen area. I felt like the main figure in a ten-hour lo-fi beats YouTube video.

"Sit as perfectly still as possible," said a voice in the headphones. It was Denny's. All other sounds in the world around me were blocked out. "You are in the Zen forest. Breathe in, relax. You're here because we see something in you, in your ambitions. The very same ambitions that the rest of the world is telling you to abandon. They are wrong. Take a deep breath. Do you smell that? Can you taste that? It's pleasant, isn't it? That's the sweet feeling of all the beautiful lives you thought you'd never get to live coming back into reach. Now close your eyes. Do not open them under any circumstances." I closed my eyes. There were circumstances, so I did not open them, as instructed. It was dark in there, in my own head with Denny's voice replacing my inner monologue. It was as dark as how dark it is when your eyes are closed. "Reach out and grasp at the air. Grasp at your dreams." I followed her instructions. "Don't think about your silly data analysis job up north. Think about your God-ordained life. The one you deserve. It's not gone. It's right there in your mind, as potent as ever. You're receiving an award at a fancy banquet. All eyes are on you. It's so vivid. What's the alternative? Sitting with your family watching other lives succeed. It's blurry. It's what they want you to think is inevitable, but they're wrong. You can barely see it. Do not open your eyes."

I didn't think any thoughts that weren't Denny's as I meditated in the Zen forest. The Gordons were presumably still around me, but they faded away in my mind. I was floating through space with Denny's rejuvenating words caressing my fall towards nothing. She led me to feel the future. It was bliss.

At one point, a fly flew on my face as I enjoyed the moment. I tried to shake it off, but it wouldn't let go. It was uncomfortable and began to pull my focus from the voice in the headphones. I brought my hand to my face to no avail and finally, briefly, opened my eyes. I saw Ashley and Oli sitting perfectly still listening to the headphones, and I saw Denny directing some guards to push around some trembling teenagers that were so skinny I could trace their rib cages with my eyes. The eyebrows Denny had presented to me earlier were replaced with much angrier, pointed ones. She swiftly gave directions with short finite movements, and the guards followed their conductor's orders with well rehearsed, symphonic actions.

My eyes met hers, and she gave me a horrifically scathing look. My eyes had never closed quicker. Except for that time when I got poked in the eye by Jimmy Fontaine on the elementary school playground, and he didn't even apologize. And then the teacher still gave him a smiley face for the week, but I got a so-so face because I was talking too much during independent reading time. But besides that time, this was the quickest I'd ever closed my eyes.

I kept my eyes closed tight and waited for some sort of repercussion that never arrived. Denny's voice in the headphones trudged on about the rejection of a boring, quiet life. "Create a man in your mind," she said. I pictured a man in a suit who was a bit scared and very confused. He had a strong chin and stood about six foot two. "Give him a family and a home. Perhaps something picaresque. Use as many cliches as you can." I envisioned the renderings of the world around him, but as I turned back to my protagonist, I winced at the sight of him. He looked horrifically similar to my father. I shifted his facial features and edited his family as best I could, but every time, his nose and brow would morph into the realm of familiarity.

"On TV is an episode of *Alf* for some reason. The kids enjoy it for the relic of the past that it is. The man falls in and out of sleep with a pleasant smile on his face. Time goes on and on and on. Days repeat. *Alf* stays on. When season four ends, they just pop season one back on. I'm dead serious. There's a knock on the door. It's you. You stand in their doorway. The man is confused, but the rest of the family nods knowingly. Now kill the man."

I imagined myself unsheathing a small, ornate dagger. It was silver and its handle was patterned in an ancient design. The fear ran down the man's face and sewed a quiver into his frame. What did this man have to fear? What real loss would he find in death? I poked his chest through his sweater vest with the knife before he could get away and pushed in slowly. It was so easy. There was no blood until I pulled the knife from the wound. By the time it was gushing out I had made a new hole. I was like a kid splashing in a shallow pool above this man. I was entirely apathetic.

"Good," said Denny. "You may now open your eyes and remove the headphones."

I opened my eyes, and the sound of the wind brushing through the trees returned to my ears. I could see Oli and Ashley do the same in congruence. "Oh wowee pour spaghetti on me!" said Oli.

"Huh?" said Ashley with almost angry confusion.

"Oh, that's a new catchphrase I've been working on for when crazy stuff happens," said Oli.

"Ew, why?"

"Just a little something I been cheffin' up," said Oli. Gordon emerged from his cranny. I gave him but a glance.

"That's terrible, Oli," I said, through obvious distraction. I was looking over at Denny who had gathered another group around her. Their eyes were locked onto her, and she was locked onto her own message. The group contained three girls and a guy. One girl had nearly the same hat as Oli. The guy had Ashley's thin eyebrows. I felt a dark jealousy towards their time with Denny.

Denny caught a glimpse of us in her peripheral vision and handed the group each a pair of headphones before taking off towards us with a warm smile.

"Ah, good to see you back awake," she said. I didn't dare bring up anything I'd seen beyond the confines of my own head. Denny told us to cut down the tree I'd just been leaning against. It was a nice tree. I felt that a stump would create an eyesore in the serene forest, but the warmth in Denny's eyes told me that she wanted us to do this for a reason. She had such passion for our personal ambitions that I was willing to reciprocate the effort.

She gave each of us an axe, and we got to work. "When you're done, we can move to the next phase," she said as she sat down to watch. The four of us picked up our axes and immediately got to work.

"Why are we doing this?" whispered Gordon. No one really answered, and we kept working. I wanted to scold his unwillingness, but I held my tongue. Every time an axe hit the tree, Denny exclaimed "Good!" or "Nice!" or "That's it" or "Oh yeah." Some of the exclamations seemed reminiscent of sexual gratification, but I'm not going to speculate.

"Shouldn't we be wearing goggles?" whispered Oli. He spoke with a little giggle to convey that he found ridiculousness where I found a need for total compliance. The bright lights above us gave just enough visibility to finally get the tree to fall. It narrowly missed Ashley as it fell, and she leapt out of the way. With the tree out of the way, I could see pitch black smoke clear in the distance, cutting through the moonlight. It arose from somewhere near the campgrounds. I felt a shudder down my spine, for lack of literally any less trite description of the feeling.

"I don't like this," said Gordon quietly to the group.

"You don't wanna be a star?" said Denny loudly. I hadn't realized that she was right behind us. "Come on," she said. "Let's advance to the next phase. You all are doing great."

Denny led us out of the Zen forest, and we felt the peacefulness we'd once been ensconced in dissipate. Instead, there was a lingering tension mixed with excitement. I grabbed onto the excitement, but I worried about the varying levels at which my friends were taking hold.

We wandered to an area behind the stage where the hill began to slope back down on the other side. It was a part of the park that was strategically cut off by the way the stage and vendors were set up on the festival grounds. It was covered in soldiers who walked in optimized routes with little thought.

"It seems quite heavy security for a music festival, no?" said Oli. I felt a strange tension, as though he'd crossed a line with Denny that he wasn't supposed to. I analyzed his statement to be wrought with more carelessness and curiosity than brazenness, but I feared Denny's interpretation.

"Oh these young men have so much more to give than protection," said Denny. She gave Ashley a shovel. We were in a large meadow surrounded by trees that petered out in the distance into the Vitality Media workers' campsite. I could only make out outlines through the darkness that surrounded it. "Sweetheart, will you dig me a small hole? And make sure you pile up the soil next to it?"

"Sure," said Ashley. There was a faint smoky smell like a great fire had just gone down. The area around us was filled with ruts and bumps in the grass. Every blade of grass around me had been stomped on five times over. It was a particularly busy and decimated section of the park.

Industrial grade light fixtures illuminated the entire field, but I focused only on Denny and Ashley as people walked all around me onto the next chapter of their own story. Ashley's shovel dug into the soft ground, and she started to create a small hole. Gordon and I stared down at the movements silently. Denny stood above the hole and seemed to be analyzing its quality intently. She finally directed Ashley to stop when there was a sufficiently sized hole in the ground and a nice mound of dirt next to it.

"It is like art, isn't it, Ashley? What a creation. When you carve your mark into the ground, look at the mess you leave behind," said Denny. "It needs to become your mission to only ever focus on the depth of the hole, not the size of the mound of dirt." I gave a knowing nod, as though I had some clue as to what the hell she was getting at. I was beholden to this feeling that she knew so much more than me. She held my attention and deepest desires in her clutches, but I believed in her because of her steadfast proclamations to reject those who'd have me end my dreams of a grander life. She spoke the words that I barely ever dared to let myself think. I focused entirely on the hole in front of me.

"Brandon!" Denny called out to a group of soldiers walking by. A young man with a blemished face and bright red hair walked over to her. His expression was aggressively neutral, and each of his facial features looked like gravity was working overtime on them. His glossy eyes conveyed many units of absolutely nothing. "Eat the mound of dirt," said Denny. Brandon looked at me, and his expression changed immediately to an extremely whimsical smile.

"Help us," he said towards me in a cheery tone. Then his face dropped back, and he got to his knees and put a handful of dirt in his mouth.

"Woah," said Ashley softly.

Denny chuckled nervously.

"Sometimes they say outrageous things. Never mind him," she said. She led us away from him, but each of us craned our necks to watch the young man scarf down the dirt. Every action he took was so methodical, from scooping the dirt to bringing it to his lips, to forcing a swallow. There was no enjoyment or even purpose, but any pain from the ordeal was in the observer's imagination. His movements acted only in service of Denny's command.

She led us to a spot across the field that wasn't nearly as well lit. When we got there, I could make out a circle of young people standing perfectly still. A young Asian man with a bowl cut was staring darts into us from the side of the circle closest to us. I gave him an awkward smile.

The circle had a small opening in it, and Denny led us towards it. As we got close, she turned around to face us.

"This is where it all begins. This is the humble beginning where your success story starts," she said. She walked into the center of the circle and gestured us to the open area. I noticed, in the moonlight, that each person in the circle had a mound of dirt in front of them. In the opening of the circle, there were four unattended mounds of dirt. Everyone in the circle had emotion weighing heavily on their faces, and the emotion that pushed its way to the front was desperation.

I saw Ashley and Oli hesitate, but I stood in front of my mound proudly. Each of the Gordons then followed. I knew that out of everyone there, I was the one that Denny truly saw. I had the talent and the want. I was no longer sitting back waiting for a big break. I was there to take it, by any means necessary. I stood right next to the Asian fellow I'd noticed before. He continued to stare at me. Did he hold disdain for me, for competition? Was there a mutual respect for our willingness that got us to this point? I wondered if this man was more my compatriot than the Gordon's whose ambitions I was beginning to doubt.

The moon lit Denny like a spotlight, and she spoke loudly through the warm night air, as if she was channeling divine words to her chosen subjects.

"Very few have what it truly takes to make their mark on this world. It's easy to dream, but it's so much more difficult to take. You've all been on a journey with me today because I saw something in you that you have seen many times in yourself. And you've given me your time in proof of your dedication," she said. She seemed to feed off the undivided attention she was receiving. She spoke as if she'd just completed a triumphant conquest. The other people in the circle were either looking intently at her or their respective mounds of dirt.

"In the twisted winter of a life let drift away, a man can only focus on regrets. What could he have amounted to? How far could his reach have spread? It's easy to let the day go by, the easiest thing to do in the world. But as he shivers his last shiver, he wonders where he lost it. He wonders what the moment was where he did not go 'No! No, I shall not let the world beat me down. It is not dead, and I reject those who say that it is.' Just as much as you must reject the naysayers, you must also accept those who see the path forward. Anyone can be powerful and famous, but only if they fight for what they want." Denny took a deep breath through her nose, as if to inhale the moment. Then she continued her speech at a low whisper that worked its way slowly towards a shout.

"In this world I've come across two people: Those who understand that small difficulties today lead to great rewards tomorrow, and those who lack the foresight to work towards anything but a quiet, sedentary, forgotten life. You have, today, an opportunity to join me. You have, today, an opportunity to be the person you see on the news, in the media, on stage, winning the big game or doing any incredible feat life has to offer. Which person will you be? What life will you live?!"

"Now, to prove your loyalty in defiance of anyone who might tell you that your dreams are dead, you must complete a task. You must do as I say for the betterment of your own career. This is how all your idols began, and now you shall as well. Ladies and Gentlemen, eat the dirt."

Across the circle, I saw each member drop to their knees and scoop their hand into the dirt. But they did not want it more than me. They did not hold onto or deserve Denny's message and her promise more than me. So I dropped to my own knees. Only Oli, Ashley, Gordon and the man staring darts into me remained hesitant in the face of opportunity. I put the soil to my lips. "It's not dead," I muttered to myself in reference to something vague, perhaps a dream, and ambition, a youth.

I slipped the dirt into my mouth in a medium sized bite. The granular texture was more immediately unappealing than the taste. I tried to swallow unsuccessfully and coughed, turning my face to the ground, dripping a concoction of tears and muddy saliva. Gordon put his hand on my shoulder.

Gordon and Oli and Ashley were my only vehicle to success. They were my band. We had chemistry and presence. But all along, they had sabotaged my push for more. I noticed Denny walk over to her only dissenters, and the embarrassment my friends brought washed over me. I took another mound of dirt in my hand, as I still worked on the one in my mouth, and I shoved it into Gordon's lips.

"Eat it!" I shouted. "You want to be something don't you?" Gordon and Oli threw me to the ground as Gordon spit to the side. The dirt fell loosely from my palm back to whence it came.

"This isn't you Reza," said Gordon, quietly, perhaps patronizingly. "Where did this come from? If you wanted it this bad, so bad that you'd eat dirt, then where was that before? Back when you showed up late to practice or goofed around while playing shows at bars? You went and got a job, and that's great, but where did this desperation come from?"

"I thought it was gonna happen!" I yelled. "It was just going to happen eventually. And now I realize this is my last chance. And you're- and you're giving up on me."

"Reza, your last chance was a long, long time ago," said Oli. Denny approached us with an expression that had lost all its warmth.

"You don't believe in yourselves?" she asked with a biting coldness.

"We do!" I shouted. I reached for another mound of dirt, having spit out most of the first one.

"Reza, this isn't you!" cried Ashley. I didn't want to believe her. I wanted to be tenacious and persistent in my reach for my goals. All of my idols were. Denny brought over a couple of guards, and they closed in on the Gordons.

"So you too hesitate in the face of this idiocy, chief?" said the Asian man next to us towards Gordon, awakening from his post as a silent observer. I felt a dreadful panic wash over me as Denny approached, and the moon lit up the worm-infested mound in front of me.

"Yes!" said Gordon. "Sure I want to be a rock star. I think everyone does, in their own way. But I no longer see how cutting down a tree and eating dirt contributes to that." The young man nodded, his bowl cut accompanying his movements.

Denny took a gun from one of the guards and gave it to a kid who had finished his entire pile of dirt. His eyes, once filled with the similar desperation as my own, were now devoid of any emotion at all. "Restrain them," she said to him softly. He methodically stood up and looked at us. Gordon and Oli pulled me to my feet and away from Denny. The young man who had allied himself with the Gordons stood in front of us, providing a buffer between Denny and my group.

"Well then, bossmen, if there's no takers on the dirt eating thing," he said, before a long pause. He reached down and grabbed a handful of dirt. He held it for a second and then threw it in Denny's face. "Then run!"

PART 2

I

All my life, I wanted to do something amazing. I would write songs and envision myself performing in front of thousands of people. I would watch documentaries of musicians on the tour bus goofing off and I craved that excitement and notoriety. I would try to understand how they could create art that truly connected with people. I wanted there to be a massive headline in the news when I died. I idolized celebrities, but I was also deeply jealous of them. I didn't understand what they had that I didn't, but I knew it was something big. Denny had promised to bring me that big intangible thing.

But, instead, I ran from her. My legs cycled in panic like Scooby-Doo, but I actually moved forward like real life. It was a bit of a blur running for our lives across the festival grounds.

Denny sent more and more armed guards after us, and we followed the young man who had thrown the dirt in her face. I heard a gunshot that only further pumped the adrenaline inside me and sent me running faster into the distance. We ran through the Zen forest and passed an ugly stump lying next to a fallen tree. The people spread around the forest with their eyes closed and headphones on didn't even notice us. We used the shadows to our advantage hoping to cut through the night and avoid the guards under Denny's control. Our leader forced open a door to the cathedral of success, and we all weaved through the expressionless girls as they danced in chaotic unison. We popped out the other side of the castle and felt the tension of the pursuit begin to die down. On the other side, I peered upwards to see if the horrifying Vitality Media leader was still perched on his balcony. He was not.

"Hey man, so, like, who are you?" asked Oli between breaths to the man who threw dirt in Denny's face. I was running out of ways to refer to him in my mind, so the question was an urgent matter.

"Never mind that, broski," he said as we ducked through the trees back towards the main part of the festival. "I'm Angus." I figured that we didn't have to mind it anymore because he literally just told us. He held a stern expression that was unrelenting. He wore a white button down shirt that was buttoned to the top button, but one of the middle buttons was unbuttoned, likely erroneously. He wore those gloves with the fingers exposed. I was under the impression that those gloves always looked stupid, and Angus's appearance was an excellent exercise in confirmation bias.

Once we felt safe from the pursuit, Angus stopped and took a breath. We were under a tree on the far side of the main stage which was once the edge of a raucous crowd. As soon as my heart rate calmed, I pushed Gordon aggressively. "You stopped me," I said.

"From what?" he said back, angrily. "From falling victim to your delusion?"

"Oh I'm the only one here with a delusion," I said, sarcastically. "Because I want to be a success, to make something of our band, and I'm willing to try anything." I looked over the other members of Fury and the Gordon Three. It was an apt name. "Cocaine skinny doesn't look so good when you're pushing 25, does it Gordon? Partying every night feels a little worse and it's hard to be a local legend when everyone in a college town doesn't know who this sad drunk old guy is. So your delusion that you can party like that forever and live like that forever is totally fine, but my delusion that I can make something special of myself is too far, yeah?"

"But you only seem to want to make something of yourself if it's easy," said Ashley. Angus analyzed each of us as we stood under that far reaching tree. I felt a deep animosity for Ashley wash over me.

"Oh well Ashley, sorry my goal can't be as pure as your's. Making art that really connects with people is so noble. That on-commission furry art you make is really just deeply digging into my soul. You must be so proud. Or are you just selling it because you don't make enough money bartending? Because it would sure be a welcome surprise to see literally one original idea in your art, but I guess you're just waiting for that dream to come to you like the rest of us." Ashley's bottom lip quivered, and she turned away from me.

Oli looked at me and winced, knowing he was next. "And Oli," I said, because why not? "Not having any ambition at all doesn't make you cool, it makes you pathetic. Everyone thinks so."

"Yes," said Angus, after watching the whole explosion with a twisted smile. "This is what Vitality media does." He turned to me. "You're not angry with them, you're angry with the whole system, brother."

"Well we're angry with him," said Ashley.

"I'm going to bed," said Gordon, he turned slowly from the rest of us.

"Good!" I yelled at him. "And when you wake up, you can keep holding onto a reality that doesn't exist." Ashley gave me one last disappointed look and joined Gordon in a slow walk away. It was like they were exiting stage left from a play that was about me and me only. I would not miss them, and neither would the audience. Oli hesitated for a moment and followed them.

"Bye, Reza," he said, too stupid to realize he was supposed to shun me. And in an instant, a moment of emotional vigor, I now stood alone on the precipice of all these tiring emotions with only Angus there to keep me company.

"So why didn't you eat the dirt?" I asked in mumble.

"Ah, sports fan," he said, continuing to use nicknames without even a hint of irony. His eyes were a dark brown and he had a large protruding mouth. "I was never going to eat it. I've been watching Vitality Media for a long time now. I've seen a million different Dennys, and they all use the same tricks. I'm studying. Trying to find ways to break it."

I didn't want to believe that Denny could be leading me astray, but away from her charismatic aura, it was difficult to deny. The tree and the dirt and the guards all seemed more like symptoms of control than perseverance, a trait I had begun to over-romanticize. Still, I did not regret my words towards my friends. I knew then that they had always held me back, always pulled me away from pursuing my goals.

We walked slowly through the festival trying to blend in. It was dark and the crowd had thinned out, but there were still unrelenting hippies all around trying to tease enjoyment out of a night that had long since peaked. I passed a girl in a floral print bra and jean shorts with energetic glitter on her face that juxtaposed comically with her drooping eyelids and slow, struggling gait.

In the distance there was house music playing. The late-night rave paused for nothing.

"So, you've been tracking Vitality Media for a while?" I asked.

"I have. Have you not seen how many human rights violations there are here?"

"I guess, but I mean they got Bocce Boys and Rocco Wealthy and Warlock's Office all in one day? This lineup slaps," I said.

"That's what I mean," said Angus. "No one does anything. They have the elites in their pockets and the little man brainwashed. It makes me furious."

"So, Denny is an agent of that brainwash?" I asked. I'd rolled my ankle as we walked, but I didn't tell anyone because it was embarrassing. This will be the last you'll hear of this.

Just know that the rest of the story, I'm in a bit of pain. Also, my tummy hurts. I'm a real trooper.

"The best, homeslice," said Angus. "Every guard you see around here, dead-eyed and following orders, went through the same routine you did. Some Vitality Media 'guru' told them they were going to be a star if they followed orders. So, they started small. Follow them, do little tasks, cut down a tree, then eat some dirt, then grab a gun and eventually they lose everything they ever were. It's the biggest incentive in the world, being someone remarkable. And those in power use it to manipulate those that aren't."

"That's wild," I said. I felt a bit of shame for following Denny, but I knew the blame was on her.

"Sure is, buddy boy. All the guys become soldiers for some kind of army, and all the girls do a creepy dance for all the people Vitality brings here to entertain. It happens every festival, and it's only getting worse. They're creating something awful by using people's desire to be more. A desire they are also a major part of manufacturing."

"How do you mean?" I asked.

"They have their hand in the culture of worshiping celebrity just as much as the grass roots brainwashing that goes on here. You can enjoy music without coming to a show and crying and falling to your knees and acting as if you are looking in the eyes of God. It's goddamn unhealthy." I thought about it for a second. I thought about the part of me that wanted to be more, my drive. It was pure and innocent and a core aspect of the human condition. And Denny exploited it for her own gain. Through Angus's eyes, I saw the festival grounds for what they were, a war zone of control and manipulation. But I did not accept that his eyes were the lens to reality.

"But some of the artists are truly groundbreaking. They're geniuses. They worked hard and made it, and it's impressive," I said. I wanted to push back at the absoluteness of his stance.

"Oh yeah? They worked hard?" said Angus. He lowered his voice for a second as we passed a group of guards. We stuck to the shadows and walked past them.

Just like you're gonna work hard, and then boom you'll be just like them right, champ? No. You think with millions of people in the world that the son of a president would just happen to be the best man for the job? Every time you apply for a job in the arts you go up against someone whose parents paid for them to go to Juilliard or some other prestigious art school. And you lose. You lose to them, boss. It's a tight-knit club that gets its power from telling everyone else they can get in if they just do this or that, but no one ever gets in."

"You're a cynic," I said.

"Vitality Media would have you believe that so that they can run the world as they please. Do you know the book *The Time Spouse*?" asked Angus.

"I think I've heard of it," I said.

"Yeah, it's a popular book. Probably pretty good too," Angus continued. "It was written by Amy Neggeniffer."

"Woah!" I said. "I don't think you're allowed to say that."

"Well, I was reading Ms. Neggeniffer book's Wikipedia recently, bucko," said Angus. I winced. "It was a quality book with a small publisher. A fun little story. But then it says, 'The book became a bestseller after an endorsement from author and family friend Tom Scuttle on NBC's *Today*.' And that is how the world works. Everyone who's family friends aren't on NBC can eat dirt and grab a gun and go to war protecting Vitality Media in pursuit of a life led by those whose friends are."

Angus's words cut me. What did he know about the world? That Vitality Media would exploit my ambitions did not make my ambitious nature inherently exploitable. I looked into his dumb face. His brow was permanently furrowed both literally and metaphorically. Regardless of whether I respected him, I wanted to use him to learn more about the detestable nature of Vitality Media.

We made our way towards the music that was playing on the other side of the festival at the Love Stage. It was more of a struggle for me, because my ankle hurt. Wait, I mean it was the same for both of us. It seemed as though the guards were no longer looking for us. They were onto bigger and better things, whatever that was for them. Denny was getting her dirt eaten without us, which was one of the most vile innuendos I had ever thought.

We walked past a row of closed vendors and stepped over a smattering of couples making out and tweakers shaking in a blanket in a ketamine hole or people laughing maniacally as they played with bugs. Midnight at a music festival employs a cast of characters for sure, and the casting director is one twisted sadist.

"Wait. I want you to see something before we finish blending all the way back in with the crowd over here," said Angus. We were at the tail end of the row of closed vendors. The area was strikingly clean, as the Vitality Media workers had picked up trash in unison at the exact conclusion of the main stage's headline set. It seemed like there were some areas where having a brainwashed task force at your disposal made for an efficient event.

Angus brought me to an unoccupied tent that still contained the remnants of what was once a bustling kitchen. It was the very one I'd purchased my corn dog from earlier. It was a big ass corn dog.

Angus stepped over the side and got in the tent. It was surprising how easy it was. He opened up the cooler and pulled out a brown sack. He looked back at me with a smug expression and put the bag into my line of vision. On it was a title with rustic lettering that said Buffalo Gooch. "This is what they serve us," he said.

"Ugh," I said. "Is that even a cheaper alternative?"

"No, it's more expensive," said Angus. "Someone along the way thought it was funny, and here we are." My stomach rumbled.

"Maybe that's what I need to eat to become a star," I said. Something in me felt, despite the mounting evidence, that if I complied with Vitality Media enough, I could one day grace their stage.

"What? No. They're toying with us. 'Look at all the silly little people who will never amount to anything. Look at them eat their buffalo gooch and do whatever it takes in desperation to be someone.' The thought of it all sickens me more than buffalo gooch ever could."

"I don't know," I said as I clutched my stomach.

"It's all an illusion," said Angus. "There's always someone to envy and someone to look down on, and the powers that be manipulate you using both. It's either 'do this because you don't wanna be like him' or 'do that because you want to be like her.' And it always gets done." I nodded along emphatically.

We made our way into the rave by the Love Stage, and it was no longer possible to have a conversation. The beat rang in my ears as the crowd all swayed to their own sound. By this point in the night, everyone was either asleep in their tent or awake deep within their own minds. There was no longer any collectivism. Still, I could not help but notice the way the crowd worshipped the DJ. The lights on stage cast his massive shadow onto the backing behind him. He did not seem human. He seemed to levitate a couple of inches off the ground and his pupils took in more than just light. They took in adoration. He raised his fist to the beat of the music. He was both the marionette and the puppet master. Actually, that's kind of how everyone moves, but still. He existed in a form that was strictly unattainable standing above us all forcing our minds to move to the beat of his drum. I hated him.

I've always looked at two main aspects of my idols. I studied their craft, and I studied how they got big. The craft here seemed attainable. The looping beats did not seem all that complex. He was but a middleman between the sound and our ears. And as for his journey, he was just a DJ that got chosen. He did not eat the dirt. He was a one in a million, a lottery winner. He was the randomly chosen one that could be used to convince the millions that weren't chosen to keep wasting away in pursuit. He, statistically, did not exist.

We watched the DJ set a while longer. I could see Angus looking around still focused on the guards. He was the picture of paranoia. He made very little effort to enjoy the music, although the DJ was making it equally difficult. I turned to him and said, "It's quite loud, should we get out of the crowd." I had nowhere to be, but somewhere else was a good start.

"What?" said Angus.

"It's quite loud, should we get out of the crowd."

"What?" said Angus.

"It's quite loud, should we get out of the crowd."

"What?"

"It's quite loud, should we get out of the crowd."

"What?"

"It's quite loud, should we get out of the crowd."

"What?" said Angus.

I finally snapped my head back and awakened from the loop, out of breath. We were eventually able to work together to realize that we both wanted to leave, and we made good on that want.

"Wasn't there three of us?" I asked.

"There were your three friends, but they left," said Angus. "They seemed more interested in their misplaced anger with you than with the festival."

"No, I mean after that," I said.

"No, just the two of us." I was a bit disoriented.

Angus immediately got back to musing about fame and fortune once we could hear each other again. He wasn't so much trying to convince me of anything as he was merely venting. He had no plan of action and no hope of being an agent of any sort of change, so he just shouted into the abyss. But there was a sick comfort to that for him.

"It's always been bad," he said to me, giving me no choice but to listen. "And in many ways, it was worse back in the day. But at least there was an emphasis on intellect and quality in the past. Kids who wanted to make it in television or movies saw sharp writing and well-developed theatrics. In most realms, being smart was considered being better. The lives dangled as bait for manipulation were at least, commonly, lives of culture. Obviously beyond the horrid social climate of our predecessors. But today we have so many celebrities to look up to and envy who place such little value on intelligence. To make fame on social media or YouTube is not a scholarly aim. I sound an old curmudgeon, I know. But my fury points at the tactics of companies like Vitality Media. Never has it been harder to make something real of yourself, and yet, in parallel, never has it seemed easier. Therein lies our true yield to those in power. Therein lies the manipulation that leads to this." He pushed his hand to gesture out to the whole festival. It looked more like a nightmare to me than it ever had before.

I could see little dotted lines outlining the stages and the VIP areas and the artist's clubhouses. There was an in group and an out group. Angus despised that format, but I felt more resentment that I could not wrestle myself into the in group. Vitality Media had created glory and told me specifically that it was not for me. I realized while looking around that much of my desperation to achieve something had been uprooted and replaced with rage. The festival, without the luster of my favorite artists performing, looked nothing more than a slaughterhouse for delusional commoners.

We walked up to the water station that was devoid of its daytime lines. I leaned against it. "You know that lake near the campgrounds down at the bottom of the hill?" said Angus.

"Sure, the little pond down there by where we sleep?" I said.

"Yep."

"That little reservoir down by where everyone gets their rest?"

"That's the one, old sport."

"Oh, that itsy bitsy loch down by where we all get our forty winks?"

"No!" said Angus. "Not that one." I went silent.

"But anyway," he continued. "I saw a young man down there this afternoon. He couldn't have been older than forty-five on account of him being a teenager. He was having trouble with the sun. It was hot, and he probably hadn't had much water, and he was on God knows what drugs." This statement implied Angus's belief in an all-knowing God. "And he passed out. I saw it with my eyes, musta been heat stroke or the like. And a couple of guards came by, tied some cement blocks to him and just tossed him in. He was their burden, and they found the quickest resolution. It sickened me, but there's nothing to do here. Our phones don't work, and by the time we get out it's too late. Because the police officer I report to, well, he wants to be sheriff. And the sheriff above him, well, he wants to be mayor. And Vitality Media is the only path to their individual salvation. So why would they go after them based on the word of some loony kid."

This terrified me. I didn't know how much of what Angus said held truth, but his disillusionment seemed valid regardless. He asked me if I had a water bottle, and I did. Three cheers for me. I offered it to him, and he chugged it quickly. Then he refilled it at the festival water station where we had made a temporary base. "Taste it," he said, passing it back to me.

"Why?" I asked.

"Just do it."

I imagined a cartoon guy in my head named Ribbity Rabbit cheerfully saying "I'll do it Angus!" and I got jealous of him being more open to new experiences than me.

"Okay fine," I said. Angus handed me the water, forever unaware of the absurd reason I acquiesced. I took a big sip. I was intimately familiar with the taste of water, yet there was an unwanted and unrecognized added aspect to this one.

"It's odd isn't it," said Angus. I made a small cough and nodded my head.

"It's like…musty," I said.

It tasted as if it had just recently gone bad, but that wasn't really a quality that should ever be applied to water. It was confusing. Angus told me that this was a trend of the Vitality Media festivals he'd been to and kept tabs on. We inspected the water tank for a bit, but then Angus told me to follow him. I did dutifully. The house music that raged on through the night grew fainter as we walked to the outskirts of the festival grounds.

2

I followed Angus to an old steel building that had been kept primarily out of sight. The fact that it was tucked away didn't seem as sinister as some of Vitality Media's other endeavors because it was quite an eyesore borne only out of practicality. Attached to it were two spigots that could be used for showering. Everyone at the festival had their own lazy methods of staying just clean enough to avoid retching at their own filth. Some did less than that. There was no one around us, and the area was barely lit from light overflowing over from where people were actually supposed to be at night.

"This is the main water source for the festival," said Angus. He said it with such dread, but I felt that providing water was actually one of the few pluses for the festival. "And what you'll see is a horrific commonality among all the festivals they run." Angus reached into his pocket and pulled out a key. It opened the maintenance entrance to the small building. Inside, we saw a long spiral staircase leading down into the abyss.

"How do you have a key to this building?" I asked.

"Don't worry about that, chap," said Angus. I looked at him inquisitively but said nothing.

"How did they manage to put this building so deep into the ground in just the few weeks they spent setting the festival up?" I asked, hoping to get an answer to at least something. "I've been to this park several times, and this was never here."

"Having thousands of brain dead workers at your disposal will do that," said Angus.

We walked down the stairs towards the bottom, and our footsteps echoed through the tight confines. Only a sliver of light from above illuminated us until I had the genius idea to use my phone flashlight. Angus told me he didn't have a phone, so I had to produce enough light for the both of us.

The air cooled off considerably as we went underground. It felt like the safety we had from being around crowds, and the safety we got from the ignorance of atrocities, was slowly being sucked away with every step down. I feared whatever Angus wanted to show me.

"So these people who are under Vitality Media's thumb," I started as we walked. "What are they like outside? How do their families and friends not say something?"

"What is there to say? Have you never excused behavior in the name of ambition?" said Angus. "On the outside, they just talk of opportunities and 'grinding' and 'hustling,' and everyone leaves them be." I started to wonder just how many people I knew had been affected by Vitality Media and the takeover they were enacting. While I was blindly following Denny, I felt justified in my actions. It was a noble pursuit to try and make something of myself. And yet, I was being used the whole time, manipulated by the one thing I held dearest, my ambition. It was not fair, and it certainly was not right.

We got to the bottom of the staircase, and Angus told me to round the corner. I could hear the sound of gushing water and could see only where my flashlight pointed. I looked back at Angus with a quick glance before I turned to whatever it was he wanted me to see. He just shook his head knowingly.

At last, I laid eyes on what floated in the water tank, and that I ever did at all remains a headlining regret.

Bodies floated lifelessly in the large vat of water encased in fiberglass. My flashlight reflected off their pupils, and I felt a sickness come over my whole body. It was a menagerie of the dead tucked away in the water supply. It was an aquarium of nightmares.

"Casualties of a world gone by," said Angus. His tone unmasked an even further depth of anger than before, but his focused eyes and tightly wound brow showed nothing in the way of surprise towards the ghoulish scenery in front of us.

"No," I said. "These are casualties of a company. Of the people who murdered them." I thought of the raven-haired bastard who pranced around the festival without even hiding his evil. I thought of Denny who did his bidding and ruined lives along the way. I felt the rage.

"Same thing," said Angus. The foul beat in my head pointed its gaze on even Angus. This was his reality, but it did not have to be mine. I was a dumb fool for giving myself to this machine, but Angus was wicked to instill his turmoil into me. I longed to be in bed back at camp, where Oli and Ashley and Gordon were allowed to both not eat the dirt and not have the world's cruelty unveiled to them. They were free to wake up tomorrow and continue to float aimlessly through the void.

"Where are the police, the news, the parents and families of these people who come here and die? Surely someone should be at least, like, canceled for this," I said. I was still trying to make sense of a worldview thrust upon me.

"For every Hannah Montana, ten die along the way," said Angus. I couldn't tell if it was a metaphor, but I just let it go.

I was pretty sure Angus didn't even know that Hannah Montana was fictional.

I glanced back at the bodies and felt lost. They were all martyrs. I felt as though I was face to face with true evil, and perhaps that gave me some semblance of purpose.

"So what exactly would you have me do about all this you're showing me?" I asked. I felt a sickness that was beyond eating buffalo gooch and drinking corpse water. And the sickness was coupled with passion. "Have you just given up?"

"I have not, my comrade," said Angus. "There are things in motion. Recruiting you is a step towards exposing them. We need a coalition, and we need action. I have a plan. I only require your patience." He picked at the left cufflink on his dress shirt as he outlined this process.

"So you shall have it, Angus," I said. Just as I began to feel the excitement of revolution brew within me, I heard the echo of footsteps coming down the stairs towards us.

"If only we'd had more time," said Angus. He looked down at the ground, and his face went white. We were sitting ducks down by the water tank where we shouldn't have been. The whole festival, I'd endured oddities with only the goal of making it in this world, only the dream of gracing that stage. Maybe it was the drugs, but I never really felt the severity of the situation. But standing there as the guards descended on me, I was as fearful as I was disillusioned.

The world had offered so much in life, but it never had any intention of actually giving anything. And here it was to take away once more. I cursed any God that anyone might believe in for the unfairness of it all. The reasons to live, to slave away towards the brightness at the end of the tunnel were fake, and so a small piece of me welcomed the oncoming danger. But I only welcomed it with hatred in my heart.

I turned off my flashlight and stood perfectly still in perfect darkness. Yet I was so far from perfection. I slowed my breathing and hid my thoughts just as I did my physical form from the searching party. A flashlight found my face regardless.

"Freeze!" said a guard to the two of us. We stared back at him in both horror and apathy. They forced us to our knees and shoved their guns in our faces. There were two of them. They wore black vests over camo jumpsuits, and their faces said little that had not already been said before. I thought of my mother and my father. I thought of their gentle love and the comfort I felt around them. I wished they were there with me. I felt anger towards myself.

The left guard turned on a walkie talkie. He had a mole on his left cheek and an angular face with a pointed chin.

"We got two people here by the water tank," he said. "One of them decent looking; one really, really ugly." Angus and I glanced at each other. "Looks like they've seen everything. What's the call?" There was little inflection to his voice, yet the most emotion I'd seen a guard show all festival.

"Eliminate them," said a voice with a disappointed sigh over the handheld transceiver. They unclicked the safety on their machine guns in unison and pointed them at us.

"Woah there, daddy-o," said Angus. He was looking right at the right guard. "You have a model's face."

"M-me?" said the guard.

"I mean, who am I telling? You know you've got the goods. You know you're a star, right?"

"Yeah, of course."

"You know, I run a modeling agency. You've got that perfect look. That stern, killer instinct. They got you shooting people underground. Think about how high I could take you out there."

"You run a modeling agency, for real?" asked the guard.

Angus stood up and approached him. The guard did not stop him.

"Yeah, it's called Eat Shit talent agency."

"Woah, vulgar yet cool," said the guard. Then Angus grabbed the guard's gun and hit him in the face with the blunt end. He fell to the ground, and a pistol fell out of his pocket.

I took the opportunity to attack the guard closest to me who was too distracted thinking about how he, too, could become a star. In the struggle, a few errant gunshots hit the water tank behind us, and water gushed out, flooding the bottom floor.

We pummeled the guards with their flashlights and sprinted up the stairs as water chased after us. In the faint light from the flashlights we carried up, I saw Angus pick up the dropped pistol. We had been unable to secure any of the heavy duty artillery, but I felt a small rush of power as Angus tucked the pistol away. We booked it up to the top step and dashed out of the water building.

We ran until we were as far away from the horrific scene as possible. When we stopped, Angus stared forward. I simply muttered, "We have to do something, we have to do something," over and over again bordering on hysterics. Angus did not seem to disagree with me. He began to walk slowly towards the campsite, and I followed him. His anger was ever-present, but in the pounding of his perfectly pointed footsteps, he now also had direction.

3

Angus walked me through the campsite towards his area. It was on the other side of the grounds from where I'd set up my tent with Gordon. That felt like eons ago, whatever an eon is. Angus's setup was predictably more apocalyptic than ours — than any festival attendee, for that matter. He had industrial string lights lining his canopy. There was a generator and a hot plate, where he was cooking some beans. He seemed like the kind of guy who only ever ate beans.

There were a few lawn chairs scattered about next to his beat up '80s looking red car. He gestured for me to sit in one of them. "I just gotta empty my shoes," he said.

"Of what?" I asked.

"Of me." I didn't like that very much. He took his shoes off and sat down in the chair closest to the old beans. The tension left his body, but the fire didn't. He seemed to take almost dying in stride. Interestingly enough, though, so did I.

It was as if the events of the night existed in a vacuum. I could not see future consequences as clearly as usual, and I was not tired. There was so much more to go.

"So, what's your deal?" said Angus. I pondered his intentions with the question and decided to answer earnestly.

"Well, I just came here with my band," I said. "And I had this horrible realization that the chance for all the success I'd always envisioned for us was kinda going away. And I guess

I hadn't realized how unfair it all was. But I saw Warlock's Office and felt more envy than appreciation."

"You are exactly who Vitality Media looks for and attracts," said Angus, the pessimism oozing out of his every word. "But you aren't wrong or broken to feel that way. That's what's so unfair about what they do. They turn valid human emotion into a means for control."

"So what of you, Angus? What's- what's your deal?"

"I'm Vitality Media's greatest enemy," he said. "Don't remember much before I became that." He was messing around with some item on the floor of his campsite as he spoke. He was fidgeting with it and inspecting it, but it didn't really look familiar to me. It looked like an AI generated item. It was all one color. A nondescript gray or maybe a neon pink. Trying to conceptualize it gave me a headache, so I looked away.

"I've got a coalition going. A rebellion of sorts," said Angus. I perked up and looked around his empty campground trying to understand exactly what he meant. "I hate Vitality Media and the celebrities who back them to ruin the lives of the masses, so we plan to overrun them. Then our lives shall have purpose, yet. To see you not eat the dirt was a revelation, even with the aid of your less ambitious friends. You have shown an understanding of how dire the problem is. We are starting to put together a group. We can combat hopelessness with violence if we must. We can send a message."

"What do you have in mind?" I asked.

"First, there's things you must know," he said. Then he turned to the tents next to his car. "Worm Man, get out here!" A very tall, very tired man emerged from the tent. "Good morning, boss!"

"Is it?" said Worm Man. He spoke with a slow, low voice, then sighed. He was like an elongated regular person. He had thick, drooping jowls and gangly arms that seemed to pull his shoulders down with them.

He walked slowly over to us and scanned me with his eyes. He looked at me with pure frustration. "Twenty-four, five eleven, one seventy-five." he said.

"Yep," said Angus. "Worm Man here is quite sexually accomplished."

"Okay," I said.

"I screw, I kill, and I feast," said Worm Man. I decided that I didn't really care about any of that, but I figured I'd indulge.

"Is that in respect to one person or separate people?" I asked.

"No respect given at all," said Worm Man. It was hard to understand how Worm Man was related to anything else that was going on. It seemed like he was Angus's surreal travel companion. I began to tune him out as he spoke nonsense to us.

The warm night was peaceful when I looked away from the hill or the constant black smoke in the distance. But even as the comforting air hit my skin, I felt despondent. Vitality Media and the people who willfully enabled them infuriated me. My whole life had been manipulated by ideas propagated by Vitality Media and adjacent power grabbers, and what was I left with? Eternal unfulfilled ambition and irritation. I took an aggressive spit into the ground.

"We should make a statement," I said. "Take a stand. Here tonight." I had cut off Worm Man talking about his idea for a cryptocurrency only strip club where the women are NFTs.

Only Worm Man was bothered by my interruption, and I didn't care about that at all.

"Aye, brotherman," said Angus for some reason.

"Who is that unsettling black-haired man who roams the grounds like he owns the world?" I asked. Worm Man chuckled.

"You want to know of him? I know him well," said Angus.

"Aye, brotherman," I responded, emphasizing each syllable, mocking the idioctic way he spoke.

"Tell him then," said Worm Man to Angus. Angus nodded. "Tell him the story of Ross Kluber."

4

As Angus told it, Ross Kluber's past is largely erased. Without much digging, all you'll ever find is that he was born in NYC to a coffee shop owner and a medium- tier talent agent. He was conceived by them as well. He saw from a young age that there were two very powerful weapons that his parents wielded: manipulation and desperation. Young people would slave away for long hours making iced lattes because their boss's wife was a talent agent. "Hey, you gotta start somewhere," they'd remark, but Ross never saw anyone get past that start. He saw it in politics too. The power of a promise with no intention of delivery. The promise of a better life while using the people's support to strip them of access to anything they'd actually want.

He worked with the church for a bit. Angus had found old documents of his time there. Ross found it a haven for the same tools used in Hollywood while keeping his image squeaky clean. His career as an evangelical lobbyist was lucrative and powerful. He stayed in the shadows and fed off of people's desire to be one with God. He offered politicians the support of the church and the money that came with it, and in exchange, he had a hand in lawmaking. But as he turned his attention to the arts, he realized that a religious past was actually looked down on.

At his core, according to Angus, he was a chameleon. He needed to be cool and authentic to get artists to respect his brand. He found that the desperation of a struggling artist to make it in the world was the strongest he'd encountered. He was power hungry and well connected, so he founded Vitality Media, a creative conglomerate that made promises of an idealistic life if only you do as they say in the budding beginnings. Those beginnings, however, turned into eternity, and an upstart media company turned into a militarized empire.

All of that is easy enough to uncover and even to digest. It's the rise of a power-hungry man who knew the secrets to profiting off of the separation between the elites and the masses. What's hidden is the events of the first ever music festival he ran. One that Angus attended many years back as a naïve teenager. Before then, Ross was not a murderer or a cultist, at least in a literal sense. One could argue that his political influence could characterize him as both. But he was simply a powerful man who bent the masses to his will. He painted the picture of an ideal life and used it as bait to get people to do his bidding. An outsider listening to Angus's story might even say he was a genius.

But those years ago, on the first night of his inaugural music festival, his beloved daughter died. She'd caught the all-consuming bug of depression and succumbed to its might. Angus saw him the next morning, parading his nightmare around the festival with a newfound ghostliness. The vigor had been drained from him. The vitality had been drained from him.

Evil is far more dangerous when the propagator thinks they are doing good. Ross Kluber began to believe that his daughter had died because she'd lived a life devoid of purpose. He was building an empire where he gave young people purpose. No one would be lost if they were living directly under his thumb being given definitive direction. And so each line he crossed became justified. Each body left in the water tanks was a means to an end. Angus was but a lost young concertgoer when he first saw Ross's apathy lead to death.

He was with his girlfriend, who he kept emphasizing was really hot. He made an hourglass shape with his hands and described her "big ol' tits" with more detail and descriptive language than any other part of his story. It was kind of weird how badly he wanted us to be impressed by the fact that he was with this attractive girl, of whom all pictures with proof of her beauty mysteriously went missing. But anyway, Angus and his girlfriend, who probably had a great personality, were at a music festival when they saw Ross Kluber walking around after the conclusion the second night. His face was blank, and his keel was even. Angus was very observant towards others' keels. Ross told Angus and his girlfriend, Margery, that the popstar Dana Rae was looking to try out potential backup dancers after hers had, as she put it, "boofed it" that night.

Whether it was providence or meticulous care on Ross's part, Margery was a skilled and ambitious dancer. Ross spoke with the sadness of a man in the wake of tragedy, but his mind and his goals were ever true. Margery was thrilled at the opportunity, and Angus tagged along through the late night, as a doting boyfriend should. Ross led them along through the festival grounds, not unlike the way Denny had led us, and he brought them to a beautiful backstage banquet. It had an ornate fountain depicting a leaping dolphin in the middle of it surrounded by massive, clothed tables holding tiny, unclothed food. Angus soaked in the classiness. It was a different tier of living than he was accustomed to.

There, they saw Dana Rae. She was glowing. She looked larger than life, and Angus remembers thinking that, although he loved his girlfriend, Margery didn't have the intangible divinity that seemed to bless Dana Rae. No layman did. He noticed then and there whatever it was that people referred to when they said the "it factor," and it disheartened him. Next to Dana Rae was Liana Lexington of the famous Lexington family, who had nothing to do with Kentucky. Together, they frolicked as the famous do, and they lived a lifestyle that was cherished yet impossible. Angus noted the flowing dresses, the enchanting yet exclusive giggles. Time, the untamed beast that ruled the common folk, seemed to bow down to them.

Ross introduced Margery to Dana, and Angus looked on. There were a few other girls there too, and Angus watched the display, in awe of these famous figures. Dana thanked Ross and mentioned that her backup dancers had "totally boofed it" and then she had them all do a little twirl. It was a game of Simon Says, and Dana knew exactly how high the stakes were.

These girls were that evening's playthings, and Liana Lexington laughed at everything Dana did. Back then, Angus wasn't filled with rage; he was too starstruck. Dana pranced them around and got them to dance and then she convinced them to build a massive Lego Star Wars ship. None of the girls questioned it. It was actually pretty cool, as Angus told it.

After it was apparent that the girls would do anything Dana asked of them, Dana invited them to come to the next music festival to play an "important role." They had been completely indoctrinated, just like that, and Angus felt nothing but pride for his girlfriend.

After getting everyone's contact info, Margery asked Ross Kluber where the bathroom was, and he lazily pointed down the hallway. "'Second door on the left,' said Ross," said Angus, as he told the story. Margery walked down the hall as Angus waited, and the first door was a maintenance door and then there was a second door, but Margery figured that the first door didn't count for some reason, so she opened the third door. I assumed that something bad was going to happen in that room considering the way Angus was telling the story, but I felt like it was kind of her fault because he obviously said the second door on the left, giving no reason to not count the maintenance door as a door. I found myself rooting against Margery, but then I remembered my hatred towards Ross Kluber, and I reconsidered my allegiances.

Margery walked back from the room quickly and immediately went up to Angus in a fit of panic. She had the crushing look of realization, of letdown. She had a pain in her eyes that could only ever come from truth. She had grown flush in her curvaceous bosom. Yuck, perhaps I should transcribe Angus's story more loosely.

Margery told Angus that she had walked into the wrong room, which I found to be obvious because she'd blatantly disregarded the directions. She said she saw some executive types and some famous people she vaguely recognized sitting around a white board. They were looking at a flow chart. "'"We weaponize the desperation to 'make it' in the world to militarize the men and turn the women into playthings," said the main executive,' said Margery recounting his words to me," said Angus as he told us his story. If Angus had nested just one more layer of speakers into his storytelling, we would have had an altercation.

Margery didn't watch for much longer but came away with enough to understand that she was being fed control under the guise of opportunity. She pushed Angus to leave, but Angus wanted to know more. He looked around the room, which they'd been left in unattended, and saw all the women being herded to their dreadful destiny like cattle or like sheep or like goats. Llamas also get herded.

Then Liana Lexington shouted out, "Hey, I think this girl heard too much!" with a big, silly smile on her face. Ross Kluber walked over. "Yeah, she went in the wrong room over there," continued Liana with a casual laugh. Margery looked around in trepidation. Ross came over and grabbed Margery by the arm.

"If you wouldn't mind coming with me, darling," he said. "We'll just have to handle some debriefing. It's funny actually, not knowing what 'second door on the left' means." His expression implied that he didn't actually find it all that funny. He looked Angus directly in the eyes as he pulled Margery away and into a separate room. Angus waited nervously. Then he heard a muffled scream. He lunged towards it, but he stopped at the sound of Liana Lexington's jovial voice.

"I wouldn't, love," she said. Angus froze. A single tear ran down his face. "You should head out. She'll be out soon." Angus walked outside and waited all night, but he didn't see Margery again. Ever. He got to his car on the last day to find a $10 Amazon gift card with a note that read "No one will believe you. So don't bother."

Angus did bother for a bit. He went to the police and was subsequently shut down. He tried to contact members of the government but ran into friends of Ross Kluber's at every step. He even contacted the board of the ATP, but they said that while the situation sounds messed up, it doesn't really have anything to do with tennis so it's out of their jurisdiction.

His only method of justice was to follow Vitality Media from festival to festival gathering both information and anger. And somewhere along the way he met Worm Man. That was how he finished his story.

"Damn, that's crazy," I said. "I don't really get why the maintenance door wouldn't count as a door, though. I mean I'm not saying she deserved to die, but, you know, second door on the left is second door on the left."

"That's not the point!" said Angus.

"I know, I know, I know," I said.

"There's a space between what we want and what we have," said Angus. "Therein lies suffering. Ross Kluber and his lackeys have spent their lives widening that gap and using it to their advantage."

"And what retaliation do we have? What recourse can be done to dampen the wounds they've opened by painting a picture that we never can attain?" I asked. I was becoming less hung up on Margery choosing the wrong door.

"We have our anger. We have our right to be furious," said Angus. "Ross wants us to be desperate, but he does not count on us to be mad. That is where we win."

"To live our lives angry is no different than the suffering of living our lives in constant pursuit of a facade, no? It's all just unhappiness in different forms," I said. But no one answered my question. And that made me angry. And I embraced it.

"Where does Worm Man fit in all this?" asked Worm Man. I was also wondering about that. But Angus just told him to go back to sleep. He obliged and moved his massive body back into the small tent. As he unzipped it, a thick smog emerged from it, and Worm Man disappeared into it. Perhaps he was just there to be like a zany guy that Angus brings around with him.

"I have more to show you," said Angus. "Our lives can have purpose yet. Tonight." He pointed out into the distance, where the daunting smoke did battle with the moonlight. "There is the epicenter of evil," he said. "We must go there." I licked my lips and brought my eyebrows down near my eyelids. I felt my call to action more clearly than ever before. And it was fueled by the sweet nectar of hatred.

5

At the dark smoke's source
you finally feel remorse
you feel regret for those you've met
all the lives that you've made worse

But at the dark smoke's source
from your pain you are divorced
A purpose for your life
A path to stay the course

Oh, it's the source of the smoke where
your answers lie
It's the source of the smoke where your answers lie
Why alive one day and then we die
It's the source of the smoke where your answers lie

I remembered these lines suddenly. It was like I'd been injected with a memory by an ambivalent and experimental doctor. They were the lyrics to a song by Dreadful Art By Dying Artists. I'd heard them at the concert as I bobbed my head to their sweet yet uncontained melodies. And I remembered, just as suddenly, that I'd also heard them once before. In the earlier memory, my head was also bobbing, but not to the sound of the music. I could vividly remember the wheels of a hearse bumping on uneven pavement. I rocked in my seat in the back. I was looking out the window watching unfamiliar plains roll by me. It was an aggressively unremarkable landscape. The song had a pace to it that seemed out of place. We were the second car in my grandmother's funeral procession, following closely behind the car holding her casket. The driver, who worked ambiguously with the funeral home, turned on the song, which cut through the dour mood but did not break it. I remember now that he stared at me through the rear view mirror and did not break his gaze through the entire drive. The song played multiple times, and I remembered thinking that I would have quite liked it if the circumstances were different.

Remembering it in concert was better. I remembered enjoying it without recognizing it, but I couldn't help but begin to hate it. I was filled with jealousy that I could not and would not make a song like that. I did not have world renowned talent or impossible timing and luck. And for that, I did not matter. I cursed the unfairness.

Angus poured beans just loose into his fanny pack, and after I realized that I simply had to accept that he did, in fact, do that, I followed him on a journey to the source of the smoke.

It was either a few minutes, a few hours, or a few days since we'd last run from the dead-eyed guards, but I knew for sure that it was still nighttime of the same night as it had basically always been. I walked a step behind Angus, who led me with his hands clasped behind his back.

We tiptoed through the rows of tents until we got to the main road that once led to the festival entrance, but now simply housed a smattering of drugged-out zombies and the guards who kept their eyes glued to them. The guards did not recognize us as the troublemakers we were and likely wouldn't have done anything anyway without direction to do so. We walked past a row of port-a-potties that smelled of anger in their own right. I recounted how much joy these festival grounds had once brought me, but all they became was a bitter reminder of my own unimportance.

I'd always felt that the need to be special, which caused my everlasting anguish, was an innate feeling that came packaged in with life itself. But as the night went on, I realized that it was a manufactured premise designed to belittle me. And I was too far gone. I wondered if I had it in me to become a martyr.

I started to notice the smoke get slightly closer, but I realized that it was just because I was walking towards it. As we got closer, we noticed fewer and fewer people milling about. I began to hear a faint clang that sounded like hundreds of people sharpening their own respective knives over and over again. It grew louder as we approached, which led me to believe that the sound was probably coming from the bottom of the smoke. I'm a pretty clever guy, being able to deduce stuff like that.

Angus stopped me as we got dangerously close to the area. It was tucked away on the outskirts of the festival grounds at the bottom of the main hill. There was a tension derived from how much the smoke called to me clashing with how secretive it seemed to be kept. I could see the top of the rising smoke dissipate into the night sky, being swallowed up by the vastness of the atmosphere it entered.

Even such a dramatic thing that captured our full attention was powerless against the enormity of our universe. We stood behind a row of trees, and Angus peeked through, towards the smoke. He gasped as though he'd known what he was going to see and yet still was overwhelmed by the image. He turned to me, taking up the entirety of the sliver between the leaves that we could peek through.

"Did you ever date, Reza?" he asked. I nodded in the affirmative, but I was put off a bit by the timing of his question. "Did you ever love?"

"Perhaps for a few fleeting moments," I said.

"It's the only thing that comes close to the fulfillment of reaching our dreams," said Angus. I nodded. "There once was a man whose only dream was to love. And he died alone surrounded by no one."

"That's a sad story," I said, dryly. Angus moved away from the opening and gestured for me to look through it. I pushed a low-hanging branch aside and moved towards it.

"There's love in there," said Angus, and I peered through the leaves to see what he'd seen. "Perhaps the love I once felt for Margery bottled up and set aside. And then there's so much evil in there. And there's a twist." I listened half-attentively to Angus as I made sense of what was in front of me. There was a large cave that rose from the ground, spewing a blinding light from the inside, which illuminated the whole area. The opening of the cave had a door attached to it, and it was open, allowing the light to flood out. The cave was almost archaic. And around it stood hundreds of guards ready to protect it at all costs. They looked more sinister and together than the guards that waltzed around the festival. These were the higher quality guards tasked with the most important job. They stood fully upright and watched the area around the cave. Above the cave, from a small hole in the top, there was smoke rising out.

I had never been more horrified, intrigued, or curious from anything in my life. I felt as though there was something being kept from me, and it took every fiber of my being to not sprint into the cave and into almost certain death by bullet. Then I thought about what Angus said.

"A twist?" I asked.

"Yes," said Angus. "There's a lot of loose ends, and the twist that brings it all together is in there."

"I've been to this park many times before," I said. "There's never been a cave here."

"No," said Angus. "Vitality Media brings it to every festival they run. It is their centerpiece, their climax, the final piece to the puzzle, and they dangle it in front of us just as they do everything else." I became filled with white hot rage. I also felt pity for Angus that he'd spent so long knowing that all the answers he was looking for were there but never being able to see them. "The biggest question in any story is motivation. Tales live and die by it," said Angus. "And my question has always been: What is Vitality Media's end goal in gathering this ever-growing brainwashed army? All I know for certain is that the answer is in there. And now you have to share my frustration in knowing that the truth is unattainable." I did feel frustration.

I pried Angus on whether he'd ever attempted to sneak in, but he assured me that it was impossible. It was the most heavily guarded and controlled area on the festival grounds, and this was the case for every festival. Even the artists and VIP celebrities knew not to so much as even look at it. So we sat and stared, and it felt good to defy the wishes of our authorities even if it was pointless and from afar.

"When we get enough numbers, will we storm it?" I asked. I wondered where those numbers were.

"Perhaps one day, in the distant future," said Angus. He had no intention of doing anything but following Vitality Media from festival to festival gathering information and troops and anger. I understood that desire. It was a noble pursuit. At least it was a life of some purpose. Fighting trumps acquiescence any day. And each day in the future was just as much a day as any other.

I studied the smoke as it rose from the top of the cave. Smoke in general can be such a vessel of mystery. It's a beacon for something eventful happening, and yet it also conceals the details of all it surrounds. I wanted to know so badly what was in that cave, and Vitality Media knew that feeling and exploited it. I hated how well the company knew people, and I prayed that if nothing else, at least my anger could be my revenge. I was one of the few they could not swindle.

Angus sat down in our little enclave of nature that hid us from the surrounding danger. I studied him, and I started to understand him, and then I started to idolize him. He knew the virtue of patience in the face of unjust evil. How could he feel such hatred towards what the world had become and still have the control to bide his time and wait for the right moment? I envied his skillset, and I was determined to learn from him.

I felt as though I was learning from a revolutionary. I used to think that this was his fight that I was merely getting a glimpse into, but I knew then it was my fight too. There I was being led by a generational prophet.

"Damn, my dick itch," he said, scratching his groin while I looked at him. He then looked at me.

"I want to take them down," I said sternly. I needed to take them down. But I didn't want to sound too eager out loud. Angus nodded.

He then told me that Worm Man was on meth. He told us about a wicked K hole Worm Man once went into and how he's now 100% convinced that he went back in time and was Gabriel Princip when he pulled the trigger killing Archduke Franz Ferdinand. I didn't care about any of that, though, as Worm Man was uninteresting and unrelated to me.

"If you keep bringing up Worm Man, I'm gonna have to kick your ass, man," I said.

Angus conceded that my threat was reasonable and promised not to. It gave me the first glimmer of happiness in a long while, but it quickly dissipated when a guard locked eyes with me through a gauntlet of shrubbery.

"Oh rats!" I exclaimed because I was too panicked to remember all the curse words. "We've been spotted. Let b-b-b-book it, gang!" I'm not really sure why I was talking like that, but it is my eternal burden to relay these events as truthfully as I can.

We sprinted out of the woods and back into the campgrounds, where we easily assimilated into the crowd of late-night wanderers. The guards seemed like video game characters with their short memories, reduced areas of movement, and limited communication with each other. We were able to navigate through a minefield of danger with relative ease.

We were getting close to Angus's camp again when we walked past a trio of girls smoking a blunt on the roof of their car. They embodied every cliche a festival girl could. They all wore floral head wreaths and had a free-flowing energy about them. They wore bikini tops and trippy shorts and were decorated with glitter and henna tattoos from head to toe.

"Hi," said the one on the left. Angus kept walking as I slowed. "Up late?"

"Suppose so," I said.

"I'm Hannah," said the one on the left who I'll call the one on the left because she was on the left.

"Me too," I said. "Wait, I mean, I'm Reza."

"That's a cute name," said the middle one.

"Thanks, I brought it from home," I said. I literally had no idea what I was saying. All three giggled. It was one of those giggles where I was imagining our wedding reception.

"This festival really brings you closer," said the one on the right, who was the one on the right. "Closer to yourself, closer to the world, closer to the truth, closer to…" She approached me and brought her voice to a whisper, "each other." The one on the left threw her head back and cackled while the other two simply giggled again. They had completely surrounded me.

The middle one touched my hair playfully and the one on the left walked closer to me.

"There's something about the hot night air and the good music," she started. "That can make people just melt together." She got very close to me. The moon illuminated her face.

"The moon's making a spotlight on you," I said. She giggled. I saw Angus storming towards us out of the corner of my eye, but I didn't pay it any attention.

"On us," said Hannah or the one on the left or whatever. I looked into her eyes. "It's a funny thing, guy like you up this late."

"Yeah?" I said. She smiled. Then Angus began to spray all three with a spray bottle filled with some sort of liquid.

"Begone! Begone!" he shouted.

"Ahh, what the hell, okay!" yelled one of them as they all ran away from the water.

"This is how they get you," said Angus. "The sirens of the festival luring you away from your true calling."

"Yeah, I don't know if that was what that was," I said, adjusting my waistband. "Those were just sexy festival girls," But Angus didn't want to hear it.

"Come with me," he said. "There's work to be done yet. Come morning, all the girls and guys will still be around, but you will only be dug deeper into the control of evil." I hated it, but I felt that Angus was right. I followed him back to his campsite where he prepared to lead me to my next revelation; our next move.

6

It makes my blood boil that a desire for creative expression could be so callously turned into the oil that runs an apathetic machine. It should be that we create art for the sake of art, and if that art is good enough or powerful enough, then people will take notice. But instead, we'd been coerced into making art for profit and fame. And it goes for scientific discovery, political philosophy, mathematical academia as well. Every one of our passions has been warped in our minds into being something that only holds value if it is appreciated by others. We don't just idealize geniuses for their genius, but also for their lifestyles. The same lifestyles that Vitality Media tells us will soon be ours.

"Gimme the gun," I said when we were back at camp.

"What gun?" asked Angus.

"I saw you pick it up in the water tank."

"Oh we got Mr. Eyeballs over here, Mr. Vision," said Angus. I scowled and he gave it to me. It was heavier than I expected. And equally as cold as I expected, but I had expected it to be pretty cold, so that's to say it was pretty cold. I twirled it in my hand.

I had never held a gun before, but only because I never felt a reason to. My head was lowered to look at the gun, but my irises hit the top of my eye sockets to pierce into Angus.

"There's power in disobedience," I said. I handed the gun back to Angus. "If I cannot live my life to flourish, I'll damn well live it to fight."

"It's useless to fight without a plan," said Angus calmly.

"Everything's useless anyway!" I shouted as I stood up. This complacent fool in front of me began to piss me right off.

"I'm just saying, it's a good thing I have a plan, old sport," he said. I had forgotten that he did the weird nickname thing, and I think he did too. I guess he was trying to be more conversational and friendly, but it was actually quite off-putting. I sat back down. "Every night of these festivals, they throw a big celebrity gala at the top of that castle by the stage. I don't know what goes on there, but I suspect that there's a sinister gathering of elites who discuss plans to further control our lives. I've studied the badges they use to get into these VIP events, and I've made perfect counterfeits. Would you like to join me in getting a glimpse into the other side?" He looked at me with a sparkle of determination that he had often let get trampled by his defeatist nature. It was inspirational to see.

"Perfect counterfeits? Perfect, perfect? That still sounds a little dangerous, and what exactly would we even do?" I asked. I could feel my skepticism linger in the air, but I quickly shooed it away.

"And also, they have free champagne," said Angus.

"I'm in," I said. I again stood back up as Angus gave me the fake pass.

"Tonight, we seek truths and actions," said Angus. "Tonight, we begin to take back our lives!"

"Yeah, I'm already in," I said, sweetly patting Angus's shoulder, making sure he didn't launch into a whole impromptu inspirational speech. We both placed the badges around our necks and took our first steps towards the main stage. I was excited to check my step counter once my phone started working again.

"I feel like it's been a wild night, but then again, I've kinda just been walking back and forth the whole time," I said to Angus.

"There has been much to see, chief," said Angus.

"You know what time it is?" I asked.

"I actually don't," he said.

"It's feet hurty." Angus and I both became even more mad than before.

"Is it actually 3:30?" he asked.

"I have no idea," I said. "Yeah, I guess I didn't even realize feet hurty sounded like 3:30."

"Then what's the joke?" asked Angus.

"It's just like if I replaced the famous tooth hurty joke with a nonsensical phrase. It's an anti-joke."

"An anti-joke?!" said Angus. He paused. "I've killed for less." We continued on towards the slope of the hill in silence.

It was a relatively still night, and time navigated it differently than usual. We walked through the areas that were once occupied by crowds of people and saw the beauty that lay in the emptiness. Only a few stragglers shared this view with us, and each one of them was on a similar journey of some sort of self-discovery. It's a journey we're always on, but particularly in the wee hours of the morning. The area by the main stage had been cleaned by the fleet of workers and its pristine, refreshed look reminded me of a sleeping lover. The final piece of the puzzle was sunlight, and I knew that its arrival would bring on another gorgeous day of music. But it was my burden that I must see the sinister truth behind the gilded front.

We neared the castle for the one billionth time, hyperbolically, and I was yet again in awe of its gravitas. Angus opened the front door, and we were hit with a blast of cold air that felt like an eternal relief compared to the hot outside air where we were to sleep and eat and pee and poop. But the seemingly infinite feeling of pleasure dissipated quickly, as it always does, and I began to even feel a bit cold. When we walked in, a whole squadron of guards stared us down. Angus approached them with a confidence that I had not yet acquired. He'd been antagonizing the guards for so long that it no longer made him nervous. It felt nice to be led by him. He showed them his badge, and I followed his lead. The guard in front gestured over to the elevator.

"Which fl—" I started, but I was cut off by Angus. "Thanks!" he said loudly to the guards. He pressed the up button on the elevator. "We should know which floor," he whispered to me.

The elevator arrived, and it opened to a ghoulish man standing directly in the middle facing the wrong way. He turned around and studied us with his eyes. He split the two of us as he exited the elevator and said, "Enjoy the ascent," with a laugh. We got in the elevator, and I looked at the buttons. They were 'Ground', '2', '3', '4', and 'Glory.' Angus pressed 'Glory'. The elevator closed and slowly made its way to the top before stopping at '3.' A short man entered the elevator as it opened. He had a joyous face, and he looked at us and then at the buttons. He saw that 'Glory' was clicked and he turned to us.

"We're gonna make it," he said. He had a huge grin, and his eyes were tearing up. He was wearing a shirt I used to own in high school. I wanted to point him towards reality, to tell him what the 'Glory' really was, but I didn't even know myself. So I said nothing.

The elevator finally reached 'Glory,' and the three of us got off. The doors opened to reveal a vast room with no furniture that was scattered with bones. They looked like human remains. The short man chortled, and even though that word sounds like he shit his pants, it doesn't mean he shit his pants. In the corner there was an old man in a slick white robe who stood by a door that appeared to lead to a staircase. Angus led us to him, and the short man trailed a beat or two behind.

"VIP passes?" said the robed man. We presented ours with the nervousness of a college freshman trying to get into a bar. He let us through with only a glance. The short man tried to follow us in, but the robed man stopped him. He did not have a pass. I looked to the back of the room and noticed that the elevator was no longer there; it was just a blank white wall. Then I shook the image from my mind and finished my ascent to the top floor.

At the top of the staircase, I was met with more beauty than I'd ever seen concentrated in one room. If the Beauty Density Index was a real thing that I didn't just make up, this area would top the charts.

There were celebrities filling up every corner of the large room with their own massive presence. The air was suffocating with personality. We had traveled deep into the night, but you wouldn't have known it from the golden banquet around us. It was an enchanting hideaway where those that were better got a needed and deserved break from those who were worse.

A woman in a fancy suit approached us as we concluded our wide-eyed gaze on the glamor in front of us.

"Champagne?" she asked. "For the monsieur and the other monsieur. She had a wide smile and distraught eyes. We accepted. I took a sip and turned to Angus.

"Woah, this champagne is really good," I said, knowing nothing about champagne or whether or not this one was particularly good. I thought to myself in a jokey fake pretentious voice, "You know it actually has to be from the Champagne region of France to be called champagne. If not, it's just sparkling wine." The Gordons would have appreciated that one.

Angus didn't hear me, as he had wandered off a bit and looked around the venue half in paranoia, half in search, and half pretending he belonged. He was somehow a person and a half in that moment. He walked back over to me, looking a bit stressed.

"How do you like your champagne?" I asked.

"You know it actually has to be from the Champagne region of France to be called champagne. If not, it's just sparkling wine," he said with a straight face. "You see that woman, there?" he asked, gesturing towards a gorgeous woman in the middle of the room. I nodded. "That's Lacey Lexington of the famed Lexington family and the younger sister of Liana Lexington."

"Oh, true," I said. Lacey Lexington was one of the most famous people in the world for something or other. I studied her jovial face as she laughed at something said to her, and then I swung my head around to see Angus's furious, hardened face juxtaposed with the rest of the room.

"They tell you can be anything you put your mind to. That success is created from hard work and effort and that you are awarded on merit," said Angus. "And then you see one of the most famous people in the world born into wealth with no discernible talents. What did she set her mind to? What was her hard work? It's all made up." I thought about what he said. Lacey Lexington wasn't really an actress or a musician. She modeled, but not in the sense of any real fashion artistry. Her biggest success was her endorsement deals which she promoted on her vastly followed social media, but she only secured those for being famous. She was, quite literally, famous for being famous. It worked in the same way as me being unknown for being unknown. Fame is just as much a trap as obscurity.

For actors, they can't get big roles because no one knows them, and no one knows them because they're not in anything. It works the same for trying to work your way up in any industry. The famous get more famous and the obscure, more obscure. I felt great resentment towards that, especially looking at someone who was famous for no reason. "She's an 'influencer,'" I said. "Influencing what? Her whole job is to live a lifestyle that people want but cannot attain. This evil that infects our way of life and tears down our inherent right to happiness is not some secret plot. It's right out in the open. It's right beneath our nose."

"Feel the anger, Reza," said Angus, looking past me towards the gossiping celebrities. "She only exists because we put her on that pedestal, and in return she exploits us for everything we have. Oh, it's a fickle world."

I felt a rage that I had never felt before. I thought about my own silly attempted music career. We wrote songs in my garage and desperately tried to get people to listen. I couldn't even squeeze out a drop of happiness from the memories. It was a pathetic waste of time. I thought of all the time I'd spent on the guitar, and I hated myself for it. The world had taken my love for the instrument and replaced it with my lust for attention. And all I was left with was emptiness.

I looked around the gold room that was so quick to point out how much of an intruder I was. I took a sip of champagne and felt the helplessness slide down my throat, but then I saw, in the corner of the room, a man who snapped my focus back to the present. "Hey!" I said to Angus. "It's Kendall Paulson, it's Warlock's Office!"

I was still starstruck even after all the epiphanies I'd had. Angus was unimpressed.

"There's a reason we came here," he said. "There's more to be done, more to be actualized."

"It'll only be a moment," I said. I left Angus behind in the spot we'd chosen by the wall and approached Kendall Paulson who sat at a small table in the corner underneath multiple chandeliers. He was sipping on a big, wide can of Fosters and talking to one of the guys that he tours with. He saw me approach and gave a faint smile. He had stringy brown hair under a bucket hat, and he wore a plain T-shirt with the words 'Not Present' written in plain text. The slacker, minimalist outfit was a carefully selected choice to be paired with the massive walls of psychedelic sound his act produced.

"Hey," I said, without any plan or goal. His bandmate glanced at me and turned to a girl next to him.

"How ahh ya?" he said in his patented Australian accent.

"Your set was amazing," I said. Every sort of odd revelation I'd made in the hours prior was undone by my admiration for his musicianship.

"Alright, thanks heaps, brudda," he said. "Thought it was shithouse, frankly though." His accent was much thicker than the one he sang with.

"Suppose if I know every note and every li'l way it should sound, I pick up when there's a miss here and there." I sat down with him to pick his brain about his musicianship. He was so unbelievably talented that I found it hard to hate him for his own fame. It was refreshing to meet someone who did, in fact, earn his place in success. It was a lens into the positive aspects of aspiring to be the best you can. One that I was having a harder and harder time seeing the world through.

"This festival's weird, huh?" I said. I wanted him to be like me and not like Vitality Media.

"Yeah with the army men and that," he said. "Beautiful town though, mate. It's a marvel all the places I've gotten to play at. And this place, oh man, the parties this company throws after every night are mental. Look at all these people. What are you VIP for anyway?"

"I'm friends with Ross Kluber's daughter," I said quickly. I was hoping it would be an airtight lie. Kendall looked at me suspiciously, and then his gaze lifted and was replaced with a soft smile.

"How noice," he said.

"How does a melody come to you, and how do you know what sound to put it in when you're first coming up with a song?"

"It's all just messing around," he said earnestly. "You gotta fall in love with just dicking around. I'll just noodle for days and file away all the small teased out parts I find interesting. And then I experiment with any and all combinations of pedals and effects I can and file my favorites of those away. And then finally, I just mess around combining the two. It's the greatest joy. And for me personally, let me tell you, the most time comes with fiddling with the drums. It may not be so obvious, but they're the backbone of my songs." It was an absolute thrill to get insight into the creative process of a Warlock's Office sound.

I let out a soft, "Wow." It was one of the coolest conversations I'd ever had, but I needed to know the answer to the question that haunted me every day.

"How did you make it?" I asked. "How did you go from, you know, just a guy to a global superstar?" He got a bit more sheepish than before.

"Ah you know," he said. "If you keep working at it, you'll shine through." He got closer to me and spoke with more of a whisper. "And sometimes you have to think about just how much you're willing to give up to get where you want to go." He looked at me a bit more suspicious than before. He seemed to figure me out with his eyes and his face hardened. "Forget all that, though, there's actually a lady here named Denny Dawson that can get you where you need to go." He reached into his pocket. "Here, I've got her card."

He gave me Denny's business card. My face dropped. It was as though he finally saw me for who I was. He knew a nobody when he saw one. I could see, for the first time, how disingenuous he was in his eyes. He could see that I was one of the little people who needed to be reined in and brought to

Denny. He talked to me like a peer until he realized he needed to lead me to the slaughter. The betrayal enraged me.

"Now I gotta see about this girl here. They tell me she's 18, and who am I to mistrust a friend. Thanks for chatting though, have a good one." He gestured for a wandering young girl to sit next to him.

I stood and looked at him and trembled with rage. He was my hero, and yet he was just another agent, doing the bidding for those who've made it to suppress those who never will. All of his music and his personality and his wonder was just another instrument to control us. I wanted so badly to do something brash. I walked back over to Angus.

"Did your beloved star tell you how you can be just like him if you keep pushing?" asked Angus.

"Shut it," I said. I looked around the room. All the celebrities laughed with one another while leaning against golden furniture and sipping on fancy sparkling wine. But it was so much deeper, what they had and I didn't. I wanted to be able to create a song and release it and have millions of people feel what I felt. But I never would.

I could not relate with the people who create art for consumption, and the most beautiful thing about art is relating to it. The entire purpose of art had been ruined by manufactured feelings of jealousy. The only outcomes I could see were delusion and anger. Those were the two destinies of man brought on by the latest version of society. I finally felt what Angus did. Truly and entirely this time. The world had taken my ambitions from me, and it had no right to do so.

"It's weird being all mad in a party full of celebrities, huh?" said Angus with a chuckle. "But when you take the mask off a world with unlimited possibilities to find that your choices are to chase an impossible dream or work an unremarkable job until you die, it's difficult to enjoy yourself."

"Yep," I said. "I feel like I'm talking to my younger self and telling him all the cool things that he'll never be. He would be disappointed in me," I said.

"No," said Angus. "He would be disappointed in this." He gestured to the air around us. It was a pathetic thing to blame the world for our own shortcomings, but we were right to do so. Perhaps blaming ourselves is just what our antagonists want. I thought, only briefly, about God. I hated him.

I felt the room spin as all the people laughed and yelled out in joy towards the creator of their wondrous fate. I had never felt as though I did not belong somewhere more. I was not one of them, and I feared that I would soon be found out.

As this fear set over me, a guard poked me in the back with his rifle. I spun around with pure paranoia in my eyes. "Hey," said the guard, but not in much of a greeting sort of way. I grew pale in the face. Apathetic guards lined the walls around us, but none had moved from their stations except for this one who had joined our excluded conversation. This guard has a mole on his left cheek, and he'd left his spot next to one with red swooshing hair. The one next to that one had an angular face with a pointed chin and the one next to him had a mole on his left cheek. They were infinite. The guard that approached me was lanky in nature. His face remained expressionless, but his eyes began to crack like there was a real person imprisoned inside his body.

"Can you see me?" he said.

"Yes," I said, with the full range of confusion. He let out a sad yet relieved chuckle, and then he caught himself and his face resumed its emotionless state. He straightened his posture back up. Tears began to fall from his eyes.

"There's more to it."

"What?"

"There's more to it, man. It's a cautionary tale. I don't exist."

"You do exist," I said. I began to feel his sadness. "You can break free." I grabbed his arm to ground him. He began to break down.

"The cave. The cave. The cave…" he said over and over. I began to console him. Angus looked on, unimpressed. The guard caught just a bit of composure and looked me directly in my eyes. "Don't get stuck here." He glanced at Angus and then back at me. "If you get stuck you lose. You have to fight through."

"You can break it too. You can break through," I said. His eyes were those of a real person.

"It's not about me," he said. He glanced quickly at Angus and then back at me. "It's about you." He looked past me and the life in his eyes left. His face became stone once again, and his posture became horrifically upright. Take this as a cautionary tale. If your posture is good, you are brainwashed by an evil corporation. He was looking at something behind me as he transformed back into the rest of the guards.

Then I felt the coldest hand I'd ever felt grab me by the back of the neck. I spun around again to see Ross Kluber staring directly at me.

"Never mind him," he said, casually. "The festival volunteers sometimes forget themselves." I could feel Angus staring daggers through me at his personal antagonist. I could tell that I was just a side character in his revenge story. But Ross was talking to me. I was too frozen to speak. Half in fear and half from his cold ass hand. "Didn't realize you were VIP," he continued warmly.

"Yeah," I said meekly.

"I saw you outside of the portable bathroom zone. I didn't take you for a VIP. It's nice to see you." He had weathered skin on his cheeks that was somehow sun damaged and extremely pale. His eyelids drooped and his eyes seemed to produce a natural eyeliner around them. His arms, underneath his cape, were long and skinny. In his stature and position of power, he lorded over me.

Ross completely ignored Angus as he looked at me. "Have you enjoyed the festival so far? I see you're staying up late into the night."

"It's been, uh, great," I said. I could feel myself tense up.

"I hope nothing we've done has caused any ill will towards Vitality Media," he said, calmly. "I'd hate for that."

"No, not at all." Ross looked at me while I spoke.

"Good," he said as the smile left his face. "I'll be watching you to ensure that doesn't happen." I didn't say anything. He smiled again. "To mitigate any problems you run into, of course." I hated myself for being so scared of him. He already held power over me, and he knew it. "I've gotta go talk to Sir Paul McCartney about how long strawberry fields last but let me know if you need anything." He walked away slowly, and I turned to Angus.

"We have to do something," I said. "I don't know what, but I'm too angry at him, at the world, at my own personal fate to stand here and do nothing." I expected Angus's usually calm fury to bring me back to reality, but he just began to hyperventilate.

"I don't know," he said. Then he said it again. "People are closing in; they're talking to us. They're noticing us." As Angus's worry grew, so did mine. Something was boiling over. We were the focal point of the room, and I had trusted Angus this far. He had pulled me from Denny's grasp and showed me the true horror of the lives we lived. He unveiled my captors and pointed me in the direction of my enemies.

Perhaps the prospects of a life of glory had died in my arms, but he pointed me in the direction of a life of revenge. I shall kill those who killed my ambitions, and it is Angus who's mentorship brought me on that path. So, I looked at him with admiration and trust.

"What is the next move?" I asked.

He said nothing.

"Angus?"

"I don't know!" he screamed. His voice rattled around the room, and hush fell over it. All the celebrities who floated above turned to look at us. I looked around as all those eyes fixated themselves onto me. We stuck out. I was where I was never meant to be. I thought about all the times where I'd found a beautiful melody or performed a solid set at a college bar, and I dreamt of where I'd be one day. I'd study genius musicians who received accolades and kind words and I dreamt of being their peer. I always had doubts, but at the same time, there were flashes where I didn't. I always knew that maybe I had a place amongst the famous for my creativity and my wit and my talents. But standing there, in that room, with all those eyes on me, I knew that I did not belong. Why did I not belong? My face grew bright red as the silence thickened.

Then there was a soft D chord played from a piano. No one's gaze drifted from us, but the silence had been filled. I glanced over and saw Kendall Paulson, my hero, on the piano. He began to play a beautiful melody. And he sang. His voice projected as golden as the furniture it bounced off of. I felt the hair on my arms stand up. The words flowed smoothly through the crowd of famous superstars.

A child dreaming asleep in her bed
Desire creeping up into her head
Her life is her future, the lies she's been fed
And when she awakes, she finds she is dead

Welcome to the slaughter, the slaughter, the slaughter
The one that she was and the one that she is
Could never be further, be further, be further

You find a box of old clothes slipped under your bed
Painful memories of the things left unsaid
And each garment you find is stained with red
Blotches of hurt, the blood that you'd bled

Welcome to the slaughter, the slaughter, the slaughter
The one that you were and the one that you are
Could never be further, be further, be further
Apart

Look at your prophets and ask how they profit
On the death of a child or a fictitious adult
It is not your fault, no, it is not your fault
In death there is peace, and in peace there is hope

He played a final haunting note on the piano. and then he looked over at Angus, who still captured the attention of the room from his outburst. I felt Lacey Lexington's gaze on me. She was larger than life. I was smaller than life. I suppose life is medium sized. I tried to conceptualize what was important. The panicking Angus behind me whimpered and began to turn red. The eyes of all the celebrities othered me further with every passing second. I could feel uneasiness suffocate my space.

There was a profound transitional moment going on in my head. I couldn't seem to maintain the amount of importance I'd placed on my hatred and anger. I turned to Angus and saw a small, confused man.

"What now? What is the plan?" I whispered to him. The last note of the piano lingered vaguely in the air, but it stood alone in its fight against silence. Angus did not look at me. Instead, he turned his vision skyward, and was blocked by the ornate ceiling.

"Dear God," he said aloud for the room to hear. "It is now that I must act. Show me the strength to wage war on the world. Point in the path to start anew. It is your fault that I am here, and so it shall be by your grace that I escape. I curse the circumstances that took what I've lost from me. I curse the divine ambivalence and the negligence and the carelessness that brings us to this predicament. I speak with the tongues of my ancestors and the tongues of descendants who share my hatred for those who took what was mine!" Then he looked back at the room. He pulled the small pistol he'd stolen from the guard at the water tank out of his waistband. He handed it to me. "Kill something," he said. "Actualize your anger."

I stuttered and loosely gripped the gun as Angus yelled commands in my ear. The guards around me, with all their weaponry, did nothing. The celebrities held their breath. They were in a club designed to keep others out. They lived a life that made all normal lives pathetic and insignificant by comparison. They were the true cause for my unhappiness. But the gun felt cold and uncomfortable in my hand. The people it loosely pointed at were just that, people. As my journey unfolded, I'd found that my life had less meaning than I ever thought it did, but it still had more meaning than this. I held the gun, and my hand shook and everything in the world was still—except for Worm Man, who writhed in his sleeping bag a half mile away. My contempt gave way to lonely sadness.

The anger in me knew I needed to pull the trigger. But the me in me hoped desperately that the gun would jam. And because there was no certainty that the gun would jam, I simply did not pull the trigger.

Angus yelled, "Coward, coward, coward!" Then finally, he ripped the gun from my hand and cocked it. He took two steps towards the center of the room and placed a small sphere of lead right into the center of Lacey Lexington's head. It was one quick knock on the door of unhappiness, and I was the stranger in the room. This was the destination of one long journey of unhappiness. The crowd screamed as she fell to the floor and the guards seized Angus. He looked at me as he fell to his knees with five guards throwing him to the ground.

"Now my life has purpose," he said. One of the guards pointed to me.

"That guy was with him!" he shouted. "Get him!"

"Oh wowee pour spaghetti on me," I thought silently.

PART 3

I

My dad used to drive me to school when I was little. We'd talk about the sports teams I'd inherited from him and music we listened to and general happenings in our hometown. He never really talked about anything grand. He'd tell me about small dramas at his work and what was going on at my mom's office. I'd listen and form my opinions on the world along the way. We'd talk about politics and the horrors on the local news. Each car ride was a new, forgettable, pleasant memory.

I used to think I was special. Every time I was good at something, I got the idea that I was the best at it until I met the harshness of reality. There are just too many people in the world to be good at anything. But my dad lived in a small world, and he raised me in a small world. I was promised happiness so long as I didn't peek my head out. But as my dad showed me the world, piece by piece, I built a vision of who I would be. I built that vision in those car rides and at family dinners and in elementary school classrooms.

And one day, that vision began to fade. My dad no longer drove me to school, but he continued to show me his world. A world I began to reject because I was special. But the vision of myself got blurrier and blurrier. I grew up and did all the things I was supposed to do. Nothing less, but nothing more. And that vision faded further. Until one day, the first day of the festival, I looked at the vision and could not see it at all. It was gone. All I could see was all the things I was supposed to do, just like my dad. Nothing less, but nothing more.

And as the festival raged on, I saw gunfire zipping past my head. I'd busted out of a window on the top floor of the central castle and leapt to a tree that was conveniently placed to aid my escape route. It was like it had been put there, with express written consent, for the sole purpose of my journey. And the bullets had been placed similarly, in a way that would not spell an end to that journey. Again, I felt in some way chosen by this twisted story, so I did not fear for my life as the guards chased me, guns ablaze. The protagonist does not die like this.

I'd weaved past Angus getting pinned to the ground, Lacey Lexington's blood spilling around me and a calm, ambivalent Ross Kluber all the way to the window to make my great leap. Once I got to the ground, I sprinted down the hill as every guard in the festival was alerted to chase me.

I watched a bullet fly past my leg, and it jump started me into the next gear. I looked back to see how many guards there were behind me. There were many, but before I could count them, I tripped on a root and tumbled ferociously down the hill.

I pulled myself up, aching and alone and saw a fence that encompassed the entire festival. I could hear the clammer of guards closing in all around, but a clear path emerged in front of me. The moon lit the straight line to the fence, as if to give me a shining invitation to freedom. I sprinted towards it as a warzone erupted around me. It was the climax of an action movie, but I did not feel the adrenaline that was meant to accompany it. Never once did my mind fear death at the hands of a climactic explosion. It was life in the hands of anticlimactic boredom that haunted me and seemed my devilish fate. The prophecy that I must survive rang true as I climbed the fence and escaped into a thick forest. I looked back and could not see a trace of the music festival grounds, except for a thin line of black smoke reaching out into the sky. I knew where the answers lay, and I turned and walked the other way.

I wondered briefly about Angus's fate, but before I could think with any momentum, the trees began to dance rhythmically in front of me.

2

So much had happened that part of me, perhaps even my mind, had forgotten that I was on those psychedelics. But the psychedelics had not forgotten about me. When the calm of my escape finally came over me, they rushed in to fill the void. I was surrounded by outlines of trees that got traces of light from the festival behind them, the moon above them, and some spec of civilization in front of them. They received nothing from below. I navigated through them, and as I got deeper into the forest, they moved with more wiggle and bounce. It was as though they were rubber, and when I touched one, it failed to persuade me otherwise.

I began to see patterns form in their leaves. At first there were kaleidoscopes of nature swirling in front of me. Everything that moved was mirrored ad infinitum. I became unsure of my footing on the ground and even further of my place in the world. As I intensified my stare, and softened my focus, the patterns seemed to transform into lettering. There were words in front of me in an alphabet that did not exist. The tone of the writing was adamant, but I could not make out what it said.

I was moving through the forest, but the lettering never left my vision. The trees bent down and back up as if an inflatable tube man at a car dealership moved more responsibly. I began to translate the words from one language I didn't speak to another I didn't speak. It was a bit counterproductive. As I was making a breakthrough of no real substance, I began to have auditory hallucinations. It wasn't as if there were clear voices in my head but rather a murmuring of a crowd just behind me, out of eyesight. I came to a fork in the forest and watched as the roots of the trees ran through both ways. They danced on the forest floor and weaved with an elegance I hadn't seen in a long time. I chose the path to the left, but the murmurs in my ears rose in disapproval. I stopped and laughed at the absurdity. Then I went right. I pushed through the forest, figuring out which of the growth was real and which wasn't as I went along. All of the patterns enthralled me but did not requisite meaning. I simply thought they were cool and liked looking at them. Perhaps there's more profundity in that than anything.

I kept moving past the trees, following the directions of the murmurs in my ears. Each time my path led to an uproar, I changed direction until I found the right way. Eventually, I saw a small clearing that led to a massive tree; the biggest I'd seen yet. *Go to it,* said one of the voices, sharply. It was clearer than any before it. *Go,* said another. I walked slowly up to it. *Touch it,* said a voice. I placed both palms upon its bark and felt its essence flow through me. I flung my head back and let out a soft moan. *Not like that, damn, just touch it normal,* said another voice. I touched it with only the fingertips of my right hand. A great fog emerged around me and filled the clearing. I could barely make out my surroundings. I felt a loud, booming voice suffocate me. It wasn't like the others. It was clear and present. Like danger, but pleasant.

The voice came from the tree and from something ancient. Something celestial and originating. *You're not satisfied?* it said in a loud, low tone.

"No," I said, so softly that I struggled to hear it over my own bizarre thoughts.

You want more? asked the voice. All I could see was fog surrounding total darkness.

"Yes," I said, again with a meek disposition.

The voice was silent, but I could hear its judgment. "I just want one more chance. Give me to the end of the year. Give me a lucky break, just a small one. Let me make a small album that I'm proud of and that I can reflect back on with happiness when I'm on my deathbed." My voice began to quiver. "That's all I ask." I could feel a response brewing like a loud bass hitting my chest but not my ears.

And what do I get in return? asked the voice.

"If I get that, I'll, I'll never play an instrument again," I said.

Why would I want that? The fog jumped to the rhythm of its voice.

"Because it is your plan," I said. There was such desperation in my voice. I did not want to believe that my dreams were mere delusions, and I was furious that they were. But those feelings faded as I scrambled to find something to hold onto, even if it meant giving away the rest. "You want me to live a quiet, sedentary, unremarkable life, and I will. If you just give me this chance."

No, said the voice. *I want you to live* your *life.* It then mumbled something softly that I could not make out.

"I beg your pardon?" I said. The fog grew perfectly still.

Then beg! said the voice. It was so loud that the fog dissipated all at once.

I fell to my knees.

"Please," I said. "Please, please." I pawed at the ground and let the desperation take me, the voice was very faint as though it was leaving the area.

Perhaps we can strike a deal, yet, it said. I continued to dig into the ground. I felt overwhelmed by the emotions and self-discovery running through me. I did not want it to continue, but I did not want it to end.

"Excuse me," said another voice. I couldn't tell where it was coming from nor what it meant.

I muttered to myself, "No more voices." But it did not listen. It repeated itself. It was a woman's voice. I opened my eyes and found that I could see a bit of light. Then I felt a hand on my shoulder that brought me all the way back into the world around me. There was a middle-aged woman with brown hair and kind eyes in front of me. She had a warm yet concerned look on her face. She had just come from her picturesque suburban home, which had a porch light on and an open door. Below me there was torn up grass where I'd dug into her lawn. I looked all around and found that I'd wandered into a beautiful, secluded neighborhood just on the other side of the forest from Woodhill Park.

"Oh, oh my God," I said to the lady. "I'm so sorry. I just—"

"It's okay," she said with a smile. "You seem to be having quite the night. We've all been there. I'm glad you're okay."

"Yeah, I-I just got lost," I said. "I'm sorry about your lawn."

"Oh, please," she said. "The way this lawn won't seem to stay cut, it'll be regrown by sunrise." I laughed, and she helped me up. "I know it's late, but would you like to come in? You can have a glass of water and get your bearings. I don't want you just wandering around."

"Sure," I said. "Thank you so much." She was so kind that I felt safe around her. I needed a break from the dangers of my hallucinations and the searching guards.

"I'm Elise," she said.

"Reza."

She led me inside to a living room straight out of Ikea. There was a magazine with Lacey Lexington on the cover sitting on the coffee table. I began to fill with panic at the association but found the strength to calm myself. Lacey Lexington's face is everywhere.

Elise brought me into the kitchen and turned on the light as she poured me a glass of water. As the light came on, I saw a completely bald child sitting in one of the dining room chairs staring at me menacingly. I jumped and gave a frightened gasp.

"Who's this bastard?" said the kid. He couldn't have been more than nine. I figured that I could have said the same right back to him, but I held my tongue.

"This is Reza," said Elise to the kid. "He was outside and just needed a glass of water." She then turned to me. "This is my son, Maxwell."

"I'm dying, Reza," said the kid. "I'm going to be dead soon." His mother gave a sad smile, and she turned back to me as I sipped my water.

"Yes, Maxwell has an inoperable brain condition and unfortunately doesn't have much time left." I could feel the pain in her eyes. She was in a strange limbo, where the shock of the prognosis had begun to wear off, but the sadness of the death had not yet happened.

"Oh my God, I'm so sorry," I said. It wasn't really my fault, but you know how people talk.

"Only got to live nine years," said the kid with a completely deadpan expression and tone. "Still long enough to bang your mom, though." He made a thrusting motion from the highchair he sat in, and I watched his feet dangle in the air.

"Aren't you a little old to be in a highchair?" I said. Two can play a game of disrespect.

"I don't know," he said. "What I know is that if I lived, I would have done a lot more with my life than you."

"Is that so?" I asked confrontationally.

"Yes, Maxwell is quite talented in a lot of ways," said Elise, sweetly. It took me aback how earnest she sounded. It didn't seem like a compliment born of pity or motherhood. For whatever reason, I truly believed her.

"I liked to draw," said Maxwell. "I made a new color."

"That he did," said Elise with a soft chuckle. "That he did."

"What do you mean, he made a new color?" I asked.

"See for yourself," said Elise, gesturing to the kitchen. "It's over there on the fridge."

I walked from the dining room to the kitchen, which were barely separated in the open floorplan that characterized the back half of their house. Sure enough, on the fridge door was a white piece of paper with a scribbled mass of a color I'd never seen before. It was astonishing. It was as if the color red had grown sentience and learned of all the suffering that's ever existed in the universe. Or if blue was mixed with a child's love for his teddy bear and then exposed to the sun of a planet that did not know pain. But neither of those descriptions come close to doing it justice. I returned to the kitchen with my mouth agape.

"It's quite nice, isn't it?" said Elise. Her brown hair sat loosely in a bun atop her head. It was sweetly disheartening that she was up in the wee hours of the morning just sitting there marvaling about her dying child. "He's also developed countless machine learning algorithms that have done wonders to help out around the house. Especially since his father passed away." The scumbag in me felt a tinge of excitement upon hearing that a husband was no longer in the picture with Elise, but I quickly suppressed it.

"I'm also an historian," he said with his high-pitched little kid voice. "Do you know Indira Gandhi?" The expertise in his tone contradicted the youth small jeans he wore that traded out belt loops for a scrunched elastic waistband.

"Sure," I said.

"Well, I wrote a biography of her brother Cho Gandhi, who is relatively unknown, but quite remarkable. Are you familiar with him?"

"No," I said. I was a bit distracted, looking around the room. There was a framed picture of Elise and her husband holding Maxwell as a baby. It was a constant reminder of a happier time. I wondered if Elise ever felt the urge to take that painful reminder down. And then the self-hatred at even the mere thought.

"You're not familiar with Cho Gandhi?" asked Maxwell again in a goading manner.

"No, I don't think so."

"Well how 'bout you Cho Gandhi's nuts then," said the kid while grabbing his crotch. Elise chuckled while I stood silently. There was a long pause.

"It's like 'choke on these nuts,'" said Elise.

"Yeah, I got it." I thought about Maxwell's impressive, prodigy-like life, and it made me sad. Here was a remarkable life cut down by the cruelty of nature. I felt a harsh tension between him and me. I had begun to see my life in front of me that would only ever quietly fade away in the nightmare of suburbia. And in Maxwell, there was the possibility for a remarkable existence. The thoughts of our antithetical futures lingered in my ever-growing existentialism.

"I wish I could give my life for his," I muttered.

"You can!" Elise perked up, but I wasn't listening.

"But the world is so cruel deciding who lives what lives and for how long…"

"You can though," said Elise again. This time I heard her.

"What?"

"Yeah, we have that," she said.

"Have what?"

"Have a way for you to give your life for his," she said. "I can go get the equipment from the basement." Her voice was so clear and adamant that it snapped me further back into reality. And with an understanding of reality comes an understanding of consequences. She turned to Maxwell. "Oh Max, what a blessing this was today! What a blessing!" Maxwell just smiled. Elise made her way towards the basement door.

"I don't know," I said, weakly and flustered. "I don't wanna, like…"

"Huh?" said Elise. "You don't wanna do it?"

"I mean, why don't you do it?" I asked.

"And make an orphan of my son?" There was a long pause. "So, you actually don't wanna do it?" I shook my head. "You tear up my lawn, come into my house and lie about wanting to save my dying son?"

"I didn't know you actually had, like, a way…" I said.

"So, you just lied, because it was an easy thing to say?"

"I-I-I," I said. I had no real response.

"Get the fuck out of my house," said Elise. Maxwell started to cheer.

"Get the shotgun, Mommy," he said while clapping his hands. "Get the shotgun." Elise reached into a cabinet next to him and picked out a double barrel shotgun that she began to load.

I sprinted towards the front door and busted back out into the night air. It must have been about 3 AM. I ran faster than I had all night through the quaint neighborhood. Each house looked the same as the one next to it, and each porch light turned on as I passed it. It was as if the world was rendering around me. I heard a loud boom of a gun, but I felt nothing, and then the night went silent. My harrowing, aimless journey had spilled me out into what looked like the main street of a small town.

I passed a few closed stores and restaurants. There's a dreadful darkness to a closed establishment. It's a wicked reminder of how still the world can be without life. Nothing really exists without someone living their life's journey through it. In the distance, though, I saw what looked like a hotel with lights on. It never seemed to get any closer as I approached it, but then it started to after a little while. It wasn't another surreal hallucination; I was just kind of a simpleton who couldn't judge distance that well.

Each step took a noticeable toll on me as I approached the hotel. My mind was just as energetic as it had been at the festival, but my body was starting to wilt under the strain of all the running. My body told me to stop and rest and my mind rejected it, and they argued on for a while as I waited patiently until I was finally at the hotel and my body realized it had lost but also, in a way, won.

The lobby was lit up, but the light almost made it seem even more empty from my vantage point through the windows from the outside. But I could hear and vaguely see what seemed like a festive rooftop bar on the second or third floor. The party raged on into the night. I reckoned that I could use a drink, and I don't reckon often. I entered the lobby and saw a concierge whose head barely peaked above the front desk.

"More people have died here than have lived here," he said in a child's voice. He was speaking at me, but not to me. I got the impression that he still would have said it at that exact time even if no one else was in the room. I smiled and nodded at him.

"Most people don't stay here long," he said. I could taste a faint sulfur in the air. The concierge moved around behind the desk with extraordinary fluidity, as though his legs were wheels. The ground floor of the building felt like a brand new design installed into an archaic structure. It felt like someone was trying to mask ancient secrets with new smells and decor.

"I see you have a bar up top," I said.

"Go to the elevator and hit the roof button," he said. "But you won't be here long. You're waiting for someone."

"Not particularly," I said.

"I wasn't asking," he said.

I walked to the left and found a hallway that led to a waiting area surrounded by ten elevators. There was an incredibly old woman waiting by the buttons. It appeared as though she'd clicked the up arrow button on account of the up arrow having been clicked. She looked even more decrepit than my paternal grandmother looked at that moment, and she had been dead for almost two years. That would be an outrageous insult had it not been true.

I stood next to her, awkwardly waiting for any of the ten elevators to open. About a minute went by as we stood in silence. I began to wonder if the elevators were even up and running.

"Have you been waiting long?" I asked the elderly woman.

"Since I was a child," she said.

"No, I mean for the elevator," I said, trying to avoid whatever philosophical reminiscence she had in store for me.

But all she said was, "No, I know." I looked around to see if there were stairs until finally an elevator arrived. "I'll take the next one," said the old lady, and I didn't fight her on that choice. I got on the elevator and saw the buttons for one through twenty and then a button with an 'R' on it. I clicked that one. The elevator took its merry time hitting each of the many numbers before letting me off at the top. This confused me, and that confusion was affirmed when I got off to see that I was at a rooftop bar only a couple of stories off the ground. All I knew for certain was that I definitely needed a drink.

3

"You guys sure are open late," I said to the bartender after ordering a Moscow Mule.

"We cater to all kinds of folks," he said. "Some folks are up late." He then gestured to a man sitting at a table by the edge of the roof. "See. All kinds of folks." The gentleman he was pointing at seemed pretty normal. He wore a suit with a tie that had been loosened through the night. He was joking around with a girl he was trying to flirt with. I watched him take a sip from his drink and then put it down. He looked up at the night sky and smiled and then turned back to his conversation. He was completely and totally ordinary. I wanted to ask the bartender what he meant by his comment, but then I saw something on the other side of the roof that distracted me fully.

There was a side profile across the bar equipped with yellow tinted wireframe glasses and brown locs escaping a tie dye headband. A connected hand brought a cigarette to the lips as the eyes stared out over the town from the edge of the balcony. I was among the top ten people in the world with the most expertise in knowing this fact: That face belonged to Gordon. Before me was a piece of the Gordon Three, and although I no longer felt like it, Fury had just found him once more.

I wondered if Gordon resented me at that moment. I wondered if I would have been sitting at the bar in my own internal predicament if I'd parted from him much earlier. If I had pursued my dreams on my own, would I have not been held back by ineptitude or a lack of passion or simply the weight of depending on others? I wondered if cutting the Gordons from my life would have been a worthy price to pay for real success. I let these thoughts sit in my brain longer than I ever would have before, and they only cleared when Gordon made eye contact with me.

I felt the slightest trimmer in my head as if I could still jerk away and pretend I didn't see him, but I knew that was impossible. Instead, I approached him.

"You see that building over there?" said Gordon. If he was surprised to see me, he didn't show it. I looked past the wooden balcony railing covered in ivy and felt the illumination of the string lights above me. Gordon gestured to a closed restaurant with the same hand that held his cigarette.

"Sure," I said. I could make out the faintest blue light coming from within. It gently kissed the glass that made up the store front.

"Oli and Ash are in there," he said.

"Why aren't you?" I asked. I figured it was a question representative of all the questions I had.

"I think we'd sorta been ignoring the fact we're not that young anymore," he said slowly. He took a drag of the cigarette. "We're not in that 'whole life in front of us,' stage anymore. It made us angry. Angry at you, at each other, at the world."

"It's a foul world," I said. Gordon looked at me. He wasn't as jovial as usual.

"I've found myself wanting to go back in time half to do it all differently, and half to just do it all again." I nodded as he paused. "I don't blame you anymore for so desperately wanting to make something out of our music this evening. 'Cause if we give up on that, who even are we?'"

I sat with Gordon and let his words and his smoke linger. It felt nice to sit with an old friend late into that warm night. "I'm sorry," I said. I felt bad for lashing out at the group when they pulled me from the depths of my desperation. I knew that I needed to see them not as my vehicle for success or an inhibitor of my success, but merely as friends. Maybe if I'd done that all along, I wouldn't have been so unhappy.

"You should go to Oli and Ashley, Reza," said Gordon. "That's where you go next." He looked around and I looked with him. I saw a young man with an angular face and a pointed chin, and another with red swooshing hair and a mole on his left cheek. They were milling around the bar. Their eyes were dead, yet efficient in their gaze. I recognized them not for their individuality but for their collective association with Vitality Media. "And you should probably go now."

"What about you?" I asked.

"I'm finding that some of these things we go through together and others we go at alone," he said solemnly. I figured I knew what he meant.

Whether the guards were looking for me or not or even guards at all, I did not want to be found, so I slipped out of the bar to an exit on the other side. This time I took the stairs down.

When I reached the hallway that spilled out into the lobby, I saw three Vitality Media goons talking with the concierge. The small man pointed down towards the elevator and then up to imply that someone went up the elevator. Then he started making sexual thrusting motions to imply something else entirely; something I was unsure of.

Luckily, I saw them before they saw me, and I turned the other way, back into the room with all the elevators. There was a door in the hallway with an exit sign above it. I quickly pushed my way through it and braced myself for an alarm that never came. Just like that, I was back on the streets of the strange town, safe once more. I looked up to the roof to try and make out Gordon, but I couldn't see him. So instead, I made a beeline to the closed restaurant to see if I could find Ashley and Oli. Maybe in them, I could find something, anything, to reverse the waves of despair within me.

I got closer to the building and could more clearly see the flashing blue light sneaking through its windows. I could hear the wail of a guitar coming from inside. I looked at the menu outside the front door— burgers, chicken sandwiches, and wings. I was disappointed, but I wasn't really sure why.

I looked around for Vitality Media goons but didn't see any. Then I tried the restaurant door to see what would happen, and to my surprise, it opened.

Once I was inside, I felt the misery of a closed establishment. I was out of place, and the accompanying discomfort washed over me. There was a security guard on the other side of the room, but he was asleep. Next to him was a door that led to a staircase— the source of the flashing lights and trance-like music. It was beckoning me. I walked over to the doorway and looked at the sleeping guard. Next to him was a sign that read *To enter, you must give up something you love*. Then in smaller print it said *Something you like is also fine*. I was about to just go down the stairs to whatever destiny lay before me, but at the last second, I removed my tie dye bandana that sat loosely around my neck and placed it on the floor beside the guard. I liked that bandana.

I descended the stairs towards a hell that I desperately craved. The music rang louder in my ears, and once I got to the bottom, it was suffocatingly loud. What I found down there was a dive bar with a live band playing punk music. The front man was slamming on his guitar and yelling words I could not understand or remember in a melody I could not forget. There were hundreds of people worshiping his every movement. They were loopy from the journey into the late night and rode the wave around them. At that moment, the world did not exist outside of the basement. I eased my way into the crowd and stared at the lead singer.

I was jealous of him. More jealous than I'd been of any musician I'd seen all day. Because his spot on stage, a God to these people, seemed attainable. And still, he was there, and I was here. I danced to the rhythm and conceptualized each note as it came. I was willing to give up anything to bottle up that exact moment, but I wanted more. I wanted this scene to not just be a fleeting moment, but a life.

When they say there's more to life, this is what they mean. I didn't even notice the crowd around me. I felt like the music was speaking directly to me. "Reza," it said. "Reza," it said again. Not even metaphorically. "Reza!" I heard once more, this time more emphatically. Then I felt a hand on my shoulder, and I spun around. It was Ashley and Oli calling out to me. I looked at them, and tried to decipher their temperament towards me. They smiled, and I gave them a big hug.

4

"How did you find us?" Ashley shouted over the wailing music.

"You found me," I said. I then collected myself to understand what she meant. "But Gordon told me where you were. He told me to go to you. He's just alone at a bar across the way."

"Gordon is in a contemplative mood," said Ashley. Oli nodded. "He keeps saying that he's going to change some things in his life, and if he changes some things, then he can keep the things he cherishes rolling forever. Whatever that means."

"After we left you, things have started to feel hopeless," said Oli. "I guess we sort of got angry and then we just became lost. Lost in regret or something. I don't really know, it's kinda hard to follow."

"I think we're just looking for ways to take back control," I said. Oli nodded emphatically. "We're looking for something that is *us*. Something to hold onto, to have an identity within." I became flush with knowledge or even purpose. I looked at the stage and the crowd. Everyone there wanted to be there and had a reason to be there. They had traded in their sleep for that moment. "I think we've found it," I said. I smiled a genuine smile.

"I know!" said Ashley. "And isn't this place amazing?"

"Yes," I said looking around at the pure authenticity of the punk dive bar. "How did you find it?"

"It called to us," said Oli.

"Well it called to me," said Ashley. "But Oli tagged along." Oli nodded. I laughed.

"What I would give to be a part of this," I said, looking around. "They're in their own world and happier for it. Kings of their own domain."

"Maybe it's not living a famous successful life in the real world that you need to aspire to in the first place," said Oli. "Maybe it's trading in that big depressing real world for a small utopia, a scene that we can live out our dreams in." I looked at him and felt overjoyed by his epiphany. "Maybe we could do this forever."

"Maybe," said Ashley with excitement bubbling within her. I could see her staring at all the bohemian art on the walls. There were characters all around us, each one authentic to themselves, and most importantly, authentic to their dreams. These were the people that didn't give up on their dreams; they just gave up everything that wasn't their dreams. I stared at the front man of the band with pure admiration.

"This is our last song," he said into the microphone. It was perhaps the first words I could actually understand from him. "And I need you to get fucking rowdy!"

He played the first note, and the people around me went absolutely nuts. People were getting trampled and loving every minute of it. I felt my feet come off the floor, and I let the flow of the crowd take me. My body could take any damage the crowd saw fit, because I no longer lived within it. I lived inside the music. The lead singer, or rather the leader screamer, belted out the lyrics.

I went to the market.

At least I think that's how it started.

I gave the man my soul and when I came out, I had charted.
Once, I was good-hearted. At least that's what I wanted.
But I gave it all away.
Man, I must just be —uh, developmentally disabled."

Then he and the crowd just yelled "developmentally disabled" over and over with different inflections. I guess it was
a valiant attempt to censor his language, but it came off just
as bad. Still, the vibes of the room and the energy of the song
kept my enthusiasm intact. I might have even chanted "developmentally disabled" with the crowd once or twice, but I'll just
chalk that up to it being around 4AM. When the song ended,
the front man jumped into the crowd and crowd surfed. Ashley, Oli, and I helped move him past us as we acted with the
crowd as one unit. He was a God to these people, and I was
one of these people.

I'd just caught the end of the concert, but I was so glad I did.
It felt so raw and real. I was delirious yet had the most clarity
I'd had all night. The crowd dispersed, and we saw the band
standing in the corner with a small group gathered around
them. We went and joined them. The band was laughing and
thanking the fans, and we just waited patiently to talk to the
lead singer. I wanted to ask how he came to be the local legend he seemed to be. And also where he got his electric guitar.
Just musician talk. Finally, he glanced at us.

"Man, that was awesome," said Oli on the first chance we
got. The lead singer gave us an appreciative yet dismissive nod
and turned to a different member of the crowd.

"What're you guys called?" Oli said again. He seemed to
have waited for me to chime in, but I forgot everything I was

meaning to ask. The lead singer turned back to us with a pleasant but annoyed look.

"The band is called The Hanging of Traitor Joe," he said. "And my name's Barton, like, uh, like the movie Barton Fink."

"Like Bart Simpson!" I said.

"Nah, his name is Bartholomew, dipshit," he said. He turned away in disgust. But then he did a double take and looked at Ashley. "Hol' up, what's that tattoo?" he asked. There was an arm tattoo peeking just past her sleeve, and she pulled back her shirt to reveal the whole thing. It was of a cartoon duck, and it had the words "See why quack checkers say this is false" written around it.

"This ol' thing?" asked Ashley, excited at the attention. "This is my pride and joy."

"My word, I got the same one," said Barton. He did in fact, in quack, have the same one. He pulled up his sleeve to prove it. He walked over to us and shook Ashley's hand.

"I'm Ash," she said. "These are my friends." Barton shook our hands with a much more attentive demeanor.

"I'm Oli," said Oli. "But some people call me Ollie."

"What's the difference?" asked Barton.

"One has two 'L's' and ends with an 'I.E.'"

"Which one?"

"Either one," said Oli.

Barton very much enjoyed that eccentricity. He also liked that my name was Reza because he had a really close friend named Reza. It turned out that the other Reza was an infant, which was weird, but still cool.

Barton was biracial with curly brown hair. He wore converse and black skinny jeans with a brown leather suede jacket.

He had multiple face tattoos, the most prominent being the word "Give" above his left eyebrow and the word "Receive" below his right eye. He also had a slanted beamed sixteenth note on the right side of his forehead below where his hairline started. He had a slacker coolness to him that made him much larger than his roughly 5'9" stature.

"We're having the after-show symposium in the field out back if you want to join," he said after determining that he liked us. We wanted nothing more than to join. He pointed to an exit next to the stage and implied that it was a backway that led outside.

Barton walked over to the door and a couple of the hangers-on walked alongside us as we followed him. Barton stopped the guy next to me as we walked outside. "Woah woah woah, where are you going?" he said to him.

"I'm just going to the after show thing, man," said the guy in defense of his actions.

"What are you willing to give up for it?" asked Barton. "This isn't just some party. This is where we become who we want to be at the expense of who the world wants us to be. Gimme your shirt."

"What, no," said the guy. He pointed at me. "What have they given up?"

"These guys?" said Barton. "For these guys, it's what they're willing to give up to be here. You can see it in their eyes. Reza, if I asked you to give up your shirt to be here, would you?"

"Yeah," I said.

"See?" said Barton. "Now get the hell outta here, shirt man." Shirt man walked off in disgrace. We all looked at him as he left. We all hated shirt man.

Barton ushered us outside, and we were met by a gorgeous field that spread for acres on end and housed a small barn way in the distance. There was a smattering of people who basked in the night's glow, and they all looked to Barton for guidance. I could see it in their faces. The most noticeable aspect of the whole scene, though, was the stars. There were hundreds upon hundreds of stars in the sky, something that hadn't been there when I entered the dive bar just a while earlier. The sky was beautiful, almost extraterrestrial, and the stars seemed to speak to me. I didn't know where they had come from, but I was more interested in where they were going.

Barton pointed up towards the sky, and the whole group looked up to them. I lay down on the short grass and took in the vastness above me. The stars began to form patterns in my mind. Patterns that changed every time I blinked. They told a story.

The patterns first showed all the nights I wasted staring at the TV or playing silly games. As I grew up, I knew I wanted to be someone special, and I tried as hard as I could. Or so I thought. But I could have been hungrier. All that the stars wanted me to see was that I didn't do enough. I watched as I spent my nights in college drinking when I could have been playing gigs and making a name for myself. I did get to see that time when I hooked up with Rowan Sinclair at Tanner Johannsson's Halloween party Junior year, so that was actually a dope change of pace. She was dressed as a slutty Rutherford B. Hayes.

But what the stars really gave me was regret. Regret that I didn't do more. That I didn't put myself where opportunity meets practice at the juncture of confidence off the road of intuition or whatever it is. There was a kid in a music elective class that I'd taken on top of my statistics degree. He was pretty talented, but more importantly, he was exceptionally driven. When we were driving to the festival, one of his band's songs came on the indie radio station we were listening to. The fact that he made it at least that far made my dream seem more attainable. Which in turn made my failure to actualize my dream seem more painful. All of this was made abundantly clear by the stars.

The stars asked me, in a vague way, if I would give up my positive family life, my safe statistics degree and steady job, my college experience of making friends and binge drinking away the weekends for one more chance to truly make it. I hesitated briefly to give my answer, and then all I saw in the stars was stars. I think I might've seen the Lil' Dipper, but not the rapper.

I closed my eyes and felt soft tears stream down my face. Who was I? Who was I, if my life story was just a series of events that could apply to just about anyone? I opened my eyes to see, in the stars, my arrival at the music festival. I saw that couple who we met when we arrived who had set their tent up by ours. I'd forgotten their names. I saw Ross Kluber's stone face outside the port-a-potty as he stared into my soul. I then saw him younger, grieving at his daughter's funeral. His face was softer, and his demeanor was more approachable. But I watched as he hardened at the hands of his suffering. He let himself become my antagonist.

I watched him build his army. I saw Denny utilize her talents. I saw myself again, wind blowing my hair as I stood in front of a pile of dirt. Angus and I looked at each other. And then I saw Lacey Lexington lying dead on the marble floor. I was an accomplice to her death. It all flashed past me in the sky. And then I saw the cave.

The cave stood alone with smoke arising from the top of it as the dawn of man occurred by its side. There, I saw early humans gather around its mysterious aura. Their jaded movements were told to me by the sky. They all trembled in fear except for one of them who entered the cave without hesitation. He returned a modern man. And he fought wars around the cave. He weathered storms and natural disasters around the cave. The smoke kept its steady presence as man evolved around it. I watched as time sped up within the stars. Groups of people prayed to their Gods by the cave. Civilization grew around the cave, infected with its viral diseases, but the cave stayed pure. And then slowly an army built around the cave. Never did I see what was inside, but my belief that it would forever change me if I did grew ever fortified.

And then the stars went dull again. I saw nothing of note in them. I began to hear murmurs around me as people got up from their own introspective stargazing. I began to exist in the present again when Barton came and sat next to me. He smiled and looked into my eyes with a wicked intensity. "Look," he said, pointing to the sky. Again, there was a young boy in the stars. "That's me."

The boy was a studious lad and an heir to a great fortune. He was loved by his teachers and classmates. He had a charm and a focus that was intoxicating. He was too driven and destined to even inspire jealousy. Even his rivals rooted for him. He was a respected physicist as a grad student at Princeton. And then he disappeared. I saw a star go supernova in the image. He stopped attending research labs or classes. He got into terrifying fights with his parents. He burned down a dorm room. He covered his face in tattoos and took to the streets. He traded in his success in academia for success in bohemia. He became a legend in his small world and a ghost to the big one. I turned to him, the real one, and saw his massive grin. "Inspirational," he said. He wasn't asking if that was how I felt, he was telling me.

And I couldn't help but agree.

Barton called over Ashley and Oli and brought us close. Then he spoke in a whisper. "You three are new here," he said. "But you fit right in. There's a beautiful choice in desperation. You can give up, or you can give up everything. Enjoy the night, please. But don't forget to let the night enjoy you." Then he called over to a woman across the field. "Helena!" he shouted out. "Bring the caldron."

I saw Helena walk over to us with a massive glass growler filled with steaming gray liquid. But while that was what caught my eye, it wasn't what held my attention. Past Helena was a moody girl in black clothes with long, jet-black hair. She was the only one there that didn't hold, on her face, complete admiration for the moment. She noticed my long stare, and I quickly turned away. She had a silver nose ring in her right nostril and wore a black and white striped long sleeve under a black graphic tee depicting a promotional poster for the movie *Sunset Boulevard*. She had numerous black bracelets on her left wrist. I studied every inch of her, in part because of how out of place she was among Barton's entourage and in part because I felt an immediate deep attraction to her.

Barton handed me a glass of the hot gray liquid, and I turned away from the girl. It did not taste good. "We must punish ourselves with the Gray, lest we find ourselves having too much fun," he said. "Don't worry about taking too much, it never can get empty." I looked at the smoking caldron with a mix of confusion and late-night delirium. It fascinated me, just as everything did in that gorgeous valley. We were somewhere tucked far away from the real world, and I felt most at home.

5

Barton sat in a circle with Oli, Ashley, and me. There was also a fifth member of the circle named Journeyman Joseph. We talked briefly about our lives. There were six total lives to discuss, as Journeyman Joseph claimed to have lived two. Barton told us that he first got his facial tattoos to force his own hand. He wanted to make himself unhirable to any professional company so that his only avenue in life would be to find success in the arts, in the seedy punk rock landscape of whatever town this was. I looked around and noticed that all the people had grouped themselves into circles like this, and each one seemed to have their own conversations. The secluded valley belonged uniquely to us at that moment. I knew, through Barton's confidence and the intrinsic knowledge within me, that Vitality Media goons finding us was an impossibility.

Barton asked Oli and Ashley about themselves, and they didn't say anything that I didn't already know a million times over. Maybe I liked it that way. Or maybe that was a symptom of the stagnation my life seemed to have hit.

"The sun doesn't come up for a few hours," said Barton. "We have plenty of time to give ourselves back to the Gods." I didn't know much about what he meant, but I gave little resistance to anything he said. Because like Denny, he manifested hope, but unlike Denny, he actually lived that hope. He showed that you get what you put in. Where Denny filled the gap between reality and dreams with delusion, Barton filled it with pragmatism. There was something real in his charisma and success for me to grab ahold of. He became increasingly interested in me despite me having become increasingly less interesting. "Have you ever heard anyone say that if they could do it all over again, they wouldn't change a thing?" he asked.

"I have," I said.

"That's bullshit," he said.

"You don't think I've ever heard that?" I asked.

"No, I mean the phrase itself is bullshit," he said. The words left his lips with such confidence. Journeyman Joseph watched him intently, as did I.

"There are many things I would change if I had the chance. There's so much I could have done to not be who I am today," I said.

"It's only natural to want to have done those things. It's naive not to. When you die and go to heaven, as some believe, are you even going to like the person who is ascending? Why does that version of you get to experience paradise while all other versions suffer on Earth?"

We sat in silence, mulling over what he had said. I don't think Barton had put much thought into it, but still his words lingered in the air. He represented something I wanted to be. He played music for a living, was revered and seemed to be building a legacy in his community. He was what I could be if I ever fully committed. But my cowardice was my enemy.

I watched Ashley play with the grass that reflected sparks of light back up into the sky. Nature at night had such a special look to it. It was like I was looking into a secret that I wasn't supposed to know.

"I have a time machine," said Barton abruptly. The three of us perked up, and Journeyman Joseph perked down somehow.

"What do you mean?" asked Oli in awe-inspired bewilderment.

"Come, my friend," said Barton as he lifted himself from the ground. "Come all." The five of us weaved our way through the groups of people who had found themselves lost in their own little conversations. Barton led us towards the shed. As we walked there, again I made eye contact with the black-haired girl, and again, I looked away quickly at the sight of her gaze. She seemed to suck in the energy around her. She felt familiar. She felt as though she was someone that my future self knew.

We got to the shed at the other end of the field, and we all entered. It was completely empty except for a computer with a glaring screen in the corner. I shielded my eyes from the brightness.

"Ignore the computer," said Barton. "It will surely come into play later, but I have my time machine right here." He pulled out a red pocketknife and unfolded it. It sparkled from the computer's light and Barton wielded it in a flashy manner. "Do you want to see how it works? Oh, if only I could go back and fix the mistakes I made."

"Yes, absolutely," said Ashley. Journeyman Joseph also gave an affirmative reaction. Barton sliced down the middle of his hand, drawing blood immediately. I winced, and Ashley jumped back in horror.

"There," said Barton. "My future self just went back in time and punished me. He cut me. Now every time I am about to choose the lazy way out, to not strive for my dreams, I'll look to my scar and remember that my future self went back in time to prevent me. You may not be able to punish he who got you to this point, but you can be punished for not getting yourself further in the future. And just like that, I've gone back in time and fixed a bad decision."

He turned the knife to me, and I looked at it and his bleeding hand. I very much liked the sentiment, but perhaps not the blood. I could see in his eyes that he held resentment towards my hesitation to take it from him.

Then Journeyman Joe grabbed it from him and sliced deep into his own hand. I could see the concern wash over Oli and Ashley's faces, and the approval on Barton's. Journeyman Joseph was about to offer me the knife when there was a howl from outside the barn. "Ah it's begun," said Barton as he took his knife back. "The rest of you can go back in time after the ceremony." We nodded along and followed him out of the shed.

There was the most adorable dog running around amongst the other night owls looking to find meaning where they should be finding sleep. He scampered around, and everyone was petting him and rubbing him. His face beamed with excitement from all the attention. I refer to him as a he without any confirmation because my brain had been wired by the patriarchy, but I was too tired to do anything about it. I rubbed the dog, and his little paws grasped playfully at my leg. A middle-aged woman, covered in tattoos and weighed down by the punishing hand of time and drugs, turned to Barton.

"It's time for a sacrifice, Admiral Barton," said the woman. Barton looked at the sky and then back at the group.

"Yes, it is," he said.

"No," said Ashley softly.

"Not the dog," said Barton. We all gave a collective sigh of relief, and Barton got the whole group to circle around him. He put his hands out in front of him with his palms facing the sky. A woman behind him played a soft, haunting melody on a flute. Barton put a big tunic over his clothes that he'd been handed by another member of the group. And then he began to project his voice.

"In the beginning, there was only a dark beach. The waves hit the sand, and the Gods spent their eternal lives staring out into the horizon. Until one moment, there was change. It is unknown what caused it, perhaps the moon hitting off a wave just right, but Castaedes, an eternal being, rose and turned to Zahir, the first of his kind. 'I would like to live,' he said." Barton paused, and the whole group chanted "I would like to live" in unison. Only Ashley, Oli and I, the newcomers, didn't join in. And Journeyman Joseph, who had passed out from the blood loss. He lay motionless on the grass with ghoulish pale skin, but no one seemed to pay it much attention.

"'In life, there is suffering,'" said Barton. "This is what Zahir said onto Castaedes."

Oli turned to me as Barton spoke.

"This is kinda just made-up BS," he said in a whisper. I nodded.

"It's kinda cool though," I said.

"It is pretty cool," said Oli. We turned back to Barton.

"Castaedes nodded but responded that doing nothing but staring into the ocean was its own form of suffering. He had grown restless. Zahir pondered the situation. 'If I were to grant you life,' he said, 'to make you into a billion fragments of consciousness, you will still grow restless again. And you will want more. I can create the laws of the world, but I cannot stop inertia. If I grant you this, it will ruin the universe.' And so Castaedes acquiesced. But the thought was in his head. It wasn't long before he asked again. And this time he mused that surely there was something he could give to Zahir in exchange. Zahir offered that if he gave Castaedes a beginning, then he must be allowed an end. So Castaedes traded death for the opportunity for life."

"I would like to live," chanted the crowd. Barton soaked in their enthusiasm. It was cool that he just sort of made up vaguely Greek sounding names for his mythological tale and everyone was so into it. I enjoyed the sentiment thoroughly. I wondered if whatever force there was out there that Zahir embodied in that tale could be reasoned with. I knew there was more that I could give, because there was so much more that I wanted to get. Barton, in all his logic and realism, allowed me to still feel the presence of my dreams while also being grounded in reality. I knew if I stuck with him, I could pinpoint what it was I needed to give away to receive a life I wanted.

"Today," said Barton triumphantly, "a piece of Castaedes concludes another deal with Zahir. And we may joyously bear witness." The crowd pushed a thirty-something year old man with a strong build into the middle of the circle. "Billington Gray, tell us your story." I recognized Billington's name, and I slightly recognized his face as well. But I couldn't tell from where.

"Hello everyone," said Billington. The everyone that he referenced hooted and hollered. "Today is a special day for me, for all of us." Billington spoke with much less confidence than Barton. He had personal confidence, but he did not have conviction in what he was saying quite like Barton did. His eyes darted around, and his oration was stilted and nervous.

"Since I was a little kid, all I ever saw myself doing was playing professional baseball." When he paused after saying this, I realized immediately where I recognized him from. He was a pitcher for the Minnesota Twins who had just won the World Series the October prior. I couldn't fathom what he was doing here. We seemed so far away from the realm of professional sports.

"Well," said Barton. "How did that dream go?"

"For those of you that don't know, uh, it went well for a while," said Billington to the crowd. "I was drafted in the second round of the draft and was in triple A by the time I was twenty-three. But then I had my first major arm injury. I missed two full seasons. When I came back, I didn't throw nearly as hard, and I was released by Tampa Bay." He paused. His face was strained, and he winced at each memory flooded back into his thoughts. "I signed on with Colorado and played three years in Albuquerque as a minor league middle reliever. I slept on floors and skipped meals just to chase a dream that my arm no longer wanted. On July 13th, they called me up to make my major league debut at twenty-nine years old. But on my very first pitch, I got hurt again. I had my second Tommy John surgery, and I was released by the Rockies. That winter, I met Barton here." Barton patted him on the back and nodded quickly to the crowd. He had a distinct pride in his expression like he was presenting a piece of art to an adoring crowd. He returned his hands to their resting position clasped behind his back.

"He helped me make a deal with the Gods," continued Billington. "Let me recover from my second major arm surgery and get just one more chance at the big leagues."

"Ladies and gentlemen, our sacrifices can come to fruition," said Barton.

"After missing another season, the Twins signed me to their minor league team because they had just signed my old Albuquerque manager to a minor league job, and he put in a good word for me. In early June, the Twins had a rash of injuries to lefty relievers, and I was the one lefty relief pitcher that was doing well in their minor league system. So, at thirty-one, I made a second major league appearance. I was mostly just known as the guy who got hurt on his only major league pitch. I was just a footnote in a book of weird baseball stats. But this time, I was good, or at least decent, and I kept my job. And the Twins started winning. In a blink of an eye, I went from out of the league to pitching in the World series. In game five of the World Series, I was inserted into the game in the seventh inning with men on first and second and one out and I got an inning ending double play." His voice started to break a bit.

"Two days later, in game six, we won the World Series, and I celebrated the dream of any kid who's ever thrown a baseball." The crowd cheered and consoled him as Billington broke down in tears in front of us.

"And now," said Barton. "We give back to the Gods, we complete the trade. In exchange for having one more chance, you shall never throw a ball again." The older lady, who seemed to be Barton's assistant, put on safety goggles and walked over with heavy-duty wire cutters. The flute continued to play in the background. "Give me your left hand," said Barton as he gently caressed Billington Gray's hand. The woman put the wire cutters around Billington's pointer and middle fingers.

"We'll have to leave your ring finger, of course," said Barton. Billington laughed sweetly through his tears. Then there was the most awful snapping noise followed by a howling of pain. I cannot give much detail on what it looked like, because I could not dare to look, but my hands grabbed each other tightly and I felt Ashley tense up next to me.

"The deal is complete!" said Barton triumphantly, and the whole crowd cheered except for five people. Oli, Ashley, and I were stunned by our own squeamishness. Journeyman Joseph was still passed out from blood loss. And the raven-haired girl I couldn't stop noticing scoffed at the whole affair.

It was barbaric in nature, but I wondered if Barton was right. Billington had achieved his goal. He did what millions failed to achieve, and he will go down in history as a World Series winner.

I couldn't help but think that I would have done the same. I turned to Oli. "Would you have done that?" I asked. I needed to get my ponderings out of my own head.

"I guess the difference between those who are successful and those still enshrined in anonymity is their willingness to fully commit," he said, more insightful than usual. It was like he was working it out on his own with each word. "I've never been so profoundly affected by any display of such commitment." Oli generally went with the flow, but I could tell that he was perhaps finding romanticism in effort for the first time ever.

"If we half ass our life, our life will be half assed," I said in agreement.

"We need full ass."

"A one hundred percent ass life."

"What are you two talking about?" asked Ashley.

"How we envy Barton and his subjects," I said.

"It's like how we felt about Denny…" mused Ashley. "But it feels right this time." Sure, we'd run into pitfalls in the past, but this time, we all agreed, our philosophical leader was finally righteous. He didn't just talk about actualizing a promising reality, he lived it. And he continued to show empirical proof of his ideology working. I was willing to believe he had our best interest at heart, just like he did with Billington. If the game was rigged, we just had to play harder. How could that possibly be a bad lesson?

I walked up to Barton to let him know how much I loved what he was doing. The moody girl was standing next to him. Oli and Ashley followed me.

"Barton, man, that was amazing," I said. "We… we want that for us." Barton chuckled.

"I bet you do," he said. "Maybe we can work something out." His posture was somehow impeccable and slouched to convey coolness. He squinted at me to read me, and he chuckled.

I turned to the girl standing next to him.

"I'm Reza, by the way," I said with a smile.

"Okay," she said, without a smile. Her skin was pale, bordering on translucent. Her collarbone protruded sharply through her shirt.

Barton spun me away from her.

"Come with me," he said, leading me away from the crowd. "Let's discuss what you want and what you're willing to give. He sat me down about equidistant from the murmuring crowd surrounding the groaning former baseball player and the barn on the other side of the field. He called his assistant over, and I saw her walk towards us from the crowd. Oli and Ashley were still mingling amongst the rest of the group, as was the angry-looking girl, in her own sort of way. Barton's assistant brought two acoustic guitars and placed them by us before turning around and rejoining the crowd without saying a word.

"You play?" asked Barton.

"I do," I said. We both picked up a guitar and sat criss cross applesauce facing each other. Barton played a few chords and noodled a bit. I copied his key and tried to add to what he was playing. It felt natural.

"So, you were at that festival tonight?" asked Barton softly. His voice seemed intimate but not romantic.

"I was, yeah," I said looking at the guitar strings. "It was pretty good."

"It was a Vitality Media festival?" he asked. His eyes picked up the moonlight and delivered it to mine.

"You're aware of them?" I asked. We played an identical melody, as if something were guiding us symmetrically. It was a somber yet hopeful melody in a minor key.

"Quite," he said. "I've been to one myself. It was a long time ago." He pointed to his tattoos. "Before these, and before my success as a musician. It was around the time when that leader, um…" He snapped his fingers, as if he was egging on his own memory.

"Ross Kluber."

"Right! Ross," he said. "His daughter committed suicide. It made its way across the music scene. Very sad stuff."

"Yeah," I said. I played a sad minor chord.

"But they prey on your ambitious spirit, this Vitality Media."

"Yes, that was my experience."

"And then you find yourself scorned by the whole affair. You feel so much anger towards them," he said. It's like he was speaking into my mind. In a way I guess he kind of was. That's just sort of how speaking works.

"Yes, I blamed them for my perceived failure."

"I've felt that same anger before, but then I met a man who showed me the way of Zahir. He taught me that in life, you get what you put in. Pain is a currency. I never looked back after meeting him, and I've become something."

"I want to become something as well," I said.

"Have you seen the cave at the Vitality Media festival?" asked Barton. It seemed like the climactic question of his interrogation.

"I have," I said. Barton's eyes grew wide, and he perked up.

"Inside?" he asked.

"No, just the outside," I said. All the tension in his body left him, and he smiled.

"I knew one woman who saw the inside," he said. "When I saw her after, she had changed. She seemed to understand something greater than I could grasp. She had this sense of satisfaction about her that I envied. It seemed like it wasn't about what she'd seen, but what had seen her. To be truly known, seen, understood—it's a great envy of humanity, and I'd never met anyone who seemed to have experienced it until I saw her. They have something there that is special. They say there's a great twist that pulls everything together. It may be life-changing, even. Yet another wonder withheld from people like us, Reza."

"A twist?" I asked. I'd heard that before.

"A twist ending," he said. "Or perhaps a twist beginning."

I mulled over his words with amazement. It strained me to mull, but I considered myself one of the great mullers of my generation, so I powered through. I felt like all the conflicting ideas I'd been presented through the night had left so much unanswered in my mind. I knew it would mean everything to see the inside of that cave if there was, in fact, something that tied it all together. I decided to let myself be hopeful, at least to the power of the cave.

"I've experienced many anxieties tonight," I said. "Many introspective questions about who I am and where I am to go, but for whatever reason, I feel unequivocally that the answers lie in that cave."

"Perhaps we'll never know."

I improvised a melody that I liked, so I played it again. Barton nodded his head to it and on the third repeat, he sang softly with it.

"I thought I was dead," he sang.

"All I felt was dread," I sang. Then we sang together: "But it was only in my head."

"You grew up around here?" asked Barton, returning to his natural speaking voice. I couldn't remember if I'd told him that already.

"Yeah, about an hour north. Went to school around here too. And then I moved to Sacramento recently."

"What do your parents do?" he asked. He seemed genuinely curious.

"My dad's in city planning and my mom works in real estate." Barton nodded along and thought for a second before subconsciously messing with the guitar for a bit.

"Do you ever wish they'd pushed you more?" he asked. "You know, like one of those famous parents like with the Williams sisters or Michael Jackson. It's sort of like they traded in their childhood for a life worth living."

I thought about it for a second. It was a question worth pondering. So much of what is wrong with parents who push their child is that the child doesn't consent to being brought up in such a harsh environment. But if as an adult, I could choose that I wanted my parents to have been hard on me to turn me into a prodigy, then I think it would have been something worth considering. I told Barton a variation of this, and he smiled. I could tell that he was enjoying the cracks that were forming and leading to my radicalization.

"You want to become a star, don't you?" he said. "Maybe not in the mainstream world, as that is impossible, but you want to be a central part of some scene. You want to be, even semi-anonymously, a contemporary of a Kerouac or a Van Gogh or an Abbie Kaufman. A revolutionary. Or a Barton even."

"Precisely," I said. I strummed a little on the guitar. He knew exactly how I felt. I wanted to be a part of something. I wanted to lead the life of a figure in a documentary, even a minor figure. There's life that imitates art and art that imitates life, but my life was neither. It had no relationship with art. I sat patiently in the waiting room in the lobby of death and passed the time by doing small things that made me happy. And when I thought about it, I mean the few times where I really reached deep and thought about it, that wasn't enough for me. Barton helped me truly think about it. He taught me to trade the things that made me happy for things that make me remarkable.

"You need to get fired from your job," said Barton. I saw a darker side of him emerge in his expression. "It's too safe. It's impossible to chase any dream when doing so causes you to leave money and luxury and comfort."

He placed his guitar on the ground and stood up, turning to the group a ways away. "We're going to the shed," he said quietly to me. Then he whistled loudly, and the crowd turned to him. "Helena," he shouted. "Come now." Helena was his assistant, and she got Ashley and Oli to come with her towards us. She had a large bag by her side, and she struggled to walk under its weight. The dark-haired girl followed them, seemingly out of boredom, and Billington Gray came too, carrying the corpse of Journeyman Joseph.

We, as a collective, reached the barn. I looked at the twins, who looked at me. There was a whole lot of looking going around. "It's time to indoctrinate our new members into a connection with their inner Castaedes," said Barton. There was a daunting, villainous look in his eyes, and I found it ever intoxicating.

"Full ass," I mouthed to Oli.

6

Billington Gray laid Journeyman Joseph's body on the floor of the shed, and we all analyzed our surroundings. I hadn't noticed before, but the walls were covered in large, surreal murals. There were faces in clouds that dripped down to the ground and a massive hourglass that sat in a desert surrounded by clocks. It had an unintended creepiness to it. Helena placed her bag on the ground and opened it. The contents included a tattoo gun and a plethora of other tools that were likely needed for the process. I looked at Billington's wound, which was wrapped in a blood-soaked cloth. The constant purr of the computer in the corner mitigated our silence.

"Reza!" exclaimed Barton. "Do you see this computer here?"

"I do."

"This is our pride and joy," he said with a sinister smile. "This computer serves one purpose. And it's been used by every member of our group. It is special to us." I nodded along. I looked at it in awe and ran my fingers over the keyboard. It was a model from sometime in the nineties. I realized for the first time that it was the only source of light in the shed. Perhaps I'd gotten used to everything being dark as I wandered through the night. I stared into the computer, and Barton got very close to me as I did. Everyone else was focused on Helena's tattoo kit.

"Why didn't you save that dying little kid, Reza? Young Maxwell?" asked Barton quietly and with anger. I turned around quickly. His irises, usually a hazel that leaned more green, were almost entirely dark brown. The skin on his face under his tattoos was more rugged than it looked in the moonlight.

"What? How do you know about that?" I asked.

"Hmm?" he asked. His face lightened up.

"You just said—"

He cut me off.

"I didn't say anything," he said quickly. I turned away with unease. We stared at the computer for a long time. The blank white screen spoke to me, but it had nothing to say. It kind of just went like "Uhhhh… uhhhhh." Then a voice broke through. It was a nice voice.

"Are you showing him the computer, Barton?" asked the dark-haired girl. I spun around to look at her. She had just a couple freckles on the bridge of her nose, and they perfectly tied her symmetrical face together. She was exceptionally pretty to me, and the fact that she seemed to hate me with every fiber of her being just amplified my attraction. It was an unwelcome feeling, yet one I felt all the same.

"I am," said Barton. "See, Reza, this computer's one purpose is to send a hate-filled letter to your boss. That's all it does. It burns bridges because only complacency exists across the way. Try it." I looked at them both in confusion.

"Yeah, actually try it," said the girl. "It's so dramatic and stupid, but the tech is actually pretty cool."

"What do you mean try it?" I said.

"Press a button," said Barton. "Type anything you want." I turned to the computer and pressed the enter key on the key-board in front of it. Immediately an email draft opened up. In the "From" section it had my work email. In the "To" section it had Andrew Frost, my boss.

"How?" I muttered softly.

"Never mind how," said Barton. "Just try to write a message." I typed the word "Hello," but on the screen, it said "Hey, Fucko." I stared at it with a mix of horror and amazement. I wrote "Just checking in to see if there was anything needed on the Miller account. Nothing that can't wait until Monday, but I was just thinking about it." and when I looked up, the words on the computer said, "Just wanted to let you know how I really feel. I was thinking about the Miller account and how I can't wait to deliver my findings to a bald-headed dipshit who can't tell his dick from his ass. Nothing that can't wait till I finish getting topped off by your whore wife, though. Cheers, Reza."

It made me uncomfortable just looking at the message before it had even been sent. Maybe uncomfortable was what I needed. Maybe this was the only way to force me to not take the easy way out like I always do and actually make something of my life. Barton could see into my soul. "That discomfort you're feeling is natural," he said. "Embrace it."

The girl gave a disapproving laugh.

"Is something funny?" asked Barton.

"Yeah," she said, with her face returning to the bored, annoyed expression that had been its default all night. She did not elaborate.

"I don't know if I'm ready," I said. Barton smiled both warmly and disappointedly.

"It's a leap of faith," he said. "If you know you're ready, you waited too long." He was only a few years older than me, but he presented himself as such an authority on the ways of the world. In a way, he was. You daydream all the time about crazy things you can do and fantastical futures you could have, and there he was, the madman who actually went and did it. I couldn't help but feel that he deserved my respect. But his ideas still received my fear.

"Perhaps one of you would be inclined to go first," he said, turning to Ashley and Oli. They winced. I could tell that they, too, liked his ideas in theory but were terrified of them in practice. "Ash, in this computer is a means to blackmail that girl who got the job at the gallery over you. What's her name? Karolina? Oli, there is a way to cut off your parents who force their antiquated ideals onto you, holding you back from finding passion."

"I'd get a tattoo," said Ashley meekly. I knew she was friends with that girl who went for the same job as her, and she wasn't willing to sacrifice her morals. Not just yet at least.

"On the face?" asked Barton.

"On the ankle," she said, trailing off. She made a face, as if she was bracing herself for disappointment. Barton scoffed.

"You know, if you don't make a sacrifice, you can always be the sacrifice," said Barton. He did not smile as he said this.

"I'll get a face tattoo," I said quickly. I couldn't tell if it was Barton's threat or the threat of eternal complacency that drove my decision, but regardless I was willing to dive in headfirst. "And I'll go back in time to right my wrongs like you showed me, and I'll send that email. I'm ready to trade my life in for a new one."

I felt all the eyes in the room on me. Never had I been so determined in my life. There was a tension caused by Ashley and Oli's mix of admiration and worry and Barton's elated gasp. They did not hold me back like they had when Denny asked me to eat the mound of dirt. But the tension broke when the black-haired girl burst out laughing.

"I'm gonna bleh and then I'm gonna blah," she said mockingly. "Can't you see it's already dead? You cannot bring it back to life. No matter what bullshit Barton has you do." Barton shot her a dirty look.

Her words pulled at my mind like a small, militant uprising of ideas, but I kept my philosophy steadfast in alignment with Barton's. Barton seemed to be somebody, and she seemed to be nobody, as fascinating as she was.

"Why are you even here?" asked Barton. She just shrugged and sat on the floor against the wall. He turned his attention back to me. "So, what kind of tattoo do you want on your face? Something that conveys how authentic and committed you are." I looked at the needle Helena was preparing and winced but did well to shake off the fear.

"Well, Ashley's the artist," I said. She nodded and approached me. We sat on the ground next to each other. "Maybe you could help me out." There was an "I can't believe we're doing this" excitement between us. I felt like it was the only time I'd ever had my life in my own hands.

It was an ironic thought to have, considering I was deferring to someone else for this big decision, but the principle of it held up, nonetheless.

"My father, bless his boring heart, always told me what you did matters most to you in your youth, but who you are matters most to you as you age. But I always thought they were the same. I always figured he just said that because he never really did much outside of, like, family things," said

Ashley. "Maybe you need to focus on the what? Like Barton's musical note on his forehead, what is it that you are going to lean into?"

"Music, guitar," I said.

"Maybe just a little guitar under the eye?" said Ashley with a laugh.

Barton's attention was no longer on my tattoo.

"What would you get, Ms. Ashley?" he asked. "Can I call you Ms. Ashley?"

"I don't know why you would," said Ashley. "But I also don't know why you couldn't." Barton turned to the door.

"Billington," he said. He was probably talking to Billington, but you can never be too sure of one's true intentions. "Go check if I'm legally allowed to call this girl Ms. Ashley."

Billington, using all eight of his fingers, opened the door to the barn and hustled outside. We sat in silence for a minute or two as the computer purred. I would be lying to say it wasn't awkward. Billington finally returned, completely out of breath.

"Yeah, it's perfectly legal," he said with his hands on his knees. Well, one hand on one knee, and then some of a hand on the other knee. Barton nodded and turned to Ashley.

"So, what would you get, Ashley?" he asked. I swear to Zahir he didn't even say Ms. Ashley. She thought about it for a second.

"Well, I like art," she started, her attention primarily in her thoughts. "And I guess it stems from my past, but I want it to be my future. I first got into it when I was a little girl, and my family went on a vacation in Amsterdam. Which feels kind of silly to say out loud. Here I am complaining about my life and a lack of fulfillment when I was vacationing in Amsterdam as a child. But you can't experience the world, truly, from any other upbringing but your own, so I try to teach myself to not invalidate my feelings through comparisons with others. Anyway, I was in the Netherlands, and I just felt this extreme passion for the culture of being an artist and biking to a little bakery and drawing by the river. There were artists that would have showcases and residencies where they'd unveil their work to packed crowds. I saw a Van Gogh exhibit there, and even through the miserable life he lived, there was romanticism there. That was what I truly fell in love with. I became a crazy romantic but not towards relationships, you know? Towards the life of a creative." She stopped for a second.

"I associate Van Gogh so heavily with my awakening, with my romanticism. But I don't feel that romanticism tending bar. I thought it would be more about the Bohemian lifestyle, but it's just drunk guys in sports jerseys hitting on me. So, I guess all that is to say, I'd get a night sky modeled after Van Gogh's *Starry Night* curling around my right eye like Mike Tyson's tattoo. It would have the swirling sky all the way down to just the top of the little town below."

Barton smiled.

"How dramatic that would be," he said.

"But it's Reza's time," said Ashley with a laugh. "Reza goes first with all this." I could tell that she was both excited and nervous about what she was saying. I figured if I took this leap of faith, she would too, and so would Oli. It was a lot of responsibility that fell on my shoulders.

"Alright," I said. "I'll get a little acoustic guitar below my left eye." I thought about the one that hangs in my childhood bedroom. The thought of it brought peace to my tense body. But perhaps it was just my childhood bedroom that brought peace.

"Excellent," said Barton. "Then we can get that email off to the old boss and get you started on the correct path of sacrifice and reward." I heard a buzz as the tattoo gun revved up and I closed my eyes to envision the life ahead of me.

My boss called my phone. He was angry and panicked and wanted me to confirm that I'd been hacked. But instead I doubled down. I had to move back towards college, and my parents didn't understand what happened. I got a small apartment in the city neighboring my hometown, and I worked as a bartender at a dive bar. All the while, all I did in my free time was write music. I developed some buzz as the kid who told his boss to fuck off. There's nothing more punk rock than that. I ditched all those Gordons and formed a new band of like minded, committed members of the underground scene. We started to perform at seedy nightclubs, and we were damn good at it. All the grimy, punk girls threw themselves at me. Worm Man was there too, for some reason. You remember Worm Man?

After a while, we cut an album that was a cult classic. We became local legends and national unknowns. A new underground club opened called Reza's, and you weren't allowed to go in the bathroom without doing coke. All the young kids pissed their parents off by trying to be like me.

Then I sat down one evening to reflect.

All ties to my previous life had been severed. My parents died having no respect for me. I knew nothing of the world of steady employment. I didn't start much of a family besides a few mystery kids who might have been floating around out there. But there was a whole new crop of kids who worshiped me. My songs provided a backdrop to all sorts of debauchery. My name lived on in the tales of my glory. I wasn't who I once was, but I was somebody, and it was all worth it.

I found it difficult to acclimate back into reality, but not that difficult. Once you open your eyes, reality is kind of hard to miss. And the reality of the situation was that Helena was moments away from giving me a permanent facial tattoo. She raised the gun into the air.

"Alright, we're all set," she said. "Ready?"

"As ready as I'll ever be," I answered. Who knows if that was true. I heard buzzing as the gun got close to me. It represented the sealing of my fate. Mostly because of what Barton said next.

"Alright, I'm going to go ahead and send this email for you, man," he said. I was about to journey into a new life by giving away the old one as a sacrifice. Then everything froze to the sound of a loud scoff.

"Are you kidding me?" said the fair-skinned, black-haired girl in the corner. There was a lingering anger intoxicating every decibel she let out. "Seriously? You get tattoos for self-expression. You quit your job for the betterment of your own life. Not to follow some philosophy you thought was profound from some false prophet at 5AM. I really don't care if you get a big face tattoo, but doing so for some weird motive that doesn't even represent your own self is so stupid. Who cares if you're not some worshiped rock God? Or not some pretentious art dealer? It all sucks anyway. Every life anyone lives is just unhappiness and sorrow. So, what, you're sacrificing things that make you happy for a chance to just be unhappy in a new different way? That's this grand philosophy? If you're not a face tattoo guy, don't get a face tattoo. If you're not unhappy with your employment, don't call your boss a fucko. Stop trying to be somebody you're not when there's nobody worth being anyway." She got up and stormed out of the barn.

There was a hush that fell over the entire barn. Billington Gray cleared his throat and said, "Umm, awkward!" in a sing-song voice, but it just made things worse.

Barton was silently fuming. Only the purr of the outdated, single use computer and the whizzing sound of the tattoo gun performed the soundtrack to our thoughts.

"Check, please!" said Billington. Then there was another long pause. "Yeah, I WON'T have what she's having," said Billington. Then he said, "That'll leave a mark" and "She's right behind me, isn't she?" in rapid succession.

"Shut up," said Barton, finally. "Petulant girl," he then muttered under his breath. He tried his best to whip the excitement back up for my big moment. The tattoo gun was raised to my cheek, and it hurt as it pierced my first layer of skin. I jerked my face away, not from the pain, but from something else. The action was a result of some war that waged silently within me. The twins looked at me in shock. I pushed everyone away from me and ran out of the barn. The fresh air felt good on my skin, but even better on my mind. It was like a fog had been lifted. I felt how one does when they finally relax after a long bout of extreme concentration. A trance had ended.

The girl was pacing around on the opposite side of the field from the barn by the restaurant above where the concert was. I squinted to see her through the darkness. There were no stars in the sky. I didn't really understand much of anything at that moment. Perhaps that was why I ran to her.

"You left," she said. I couldn't tell if she was asking a question or not.

"I did," I said. I looked nervously back at the barn.

"Don't worry," she said. "He won't chase you. He can't anyway."

"How do you mean?"

"Barton is confined to this area. That stage and this field. He's stuck here. He never got past it, so now this is his only domain forever. It's a sad existence, but it's sadder for those who follow him." I looked at her in amazement. I could see, in her eyes and in the way she pursed her lips, that behind the front of annoyance, she had a long relationship with sadness. Above all else, she pitied Barton.

"Ashley and Oli," I said quietly.

The girl smiled, maybe for the first time.

"You have little faith in your friends. They're smart enough to reject his idiocy," she said. "I mean, if you are, they definitely are." We both laughed. She had a wonderfully bright laugh. Her warmth was so guarded and rare that it felt special as it lay upon me.

"What if he sends that horrible email to my boss as revenge for my leaving?" I asked.

She brushed off my worry.

"Ah, it doesn't work like that. That machine is designed in the philosophy of its creator. It can only serve its purpose if the sender is fully bought in on the sacrifice. That email is long lost in the void, a remnant of a forgotten feeling." She grabbed my hand after she said this. "Come now. I know a place where we can watch the sunrise." She pulled me gently away from the field. For a small moment, watching the sunrise with her was all I ever wanted.

PART 4

I

The streets outside the restaurant rolled onward through the epicenter of suburbia. The township had done all it could to manufacture a community in the form of a small downtown area with shops and eateries. I saw a retail clothing store and a bakery next to it that had delicate pastries on display by the front window. It all served only as a sad attempt to capture the bustling nature of a city that it would never have. This town would never be anything and would soon be forgotten, overshadowed by the brilliant metropolises that stand in immortal glory. Was it worth it for this town to have ever existed? Perhaps, but only as a backdrop for a moment in my life in which I may hold this mysterious girl's hand.

She led me into the middle of the road and pointed out the tallest building in the whole area. It was maybe nine stories tall, and it stood at the very edge of downtown.

"There," she said. "Atop the roof there, you can see just how small the people and their lives are. It's breathtaking."

We walked towards it, but I began to feel incredibly tired. With every step I took, the building stood unchanged on the horizon. But I felt the toll on my tired body exponentially. It was like I'd made a great realization about my own exhaustion, and then it became all I could think about. The girl could hear my breath grow heavier.

"Have you ever heard of the hedonistic treadmill?" she asked.

"Yes," I said. I technically wasn't lying, but it wasn't a concept I'd gone in depth on.

"I don't really believe in it," she said. "I don't think it's wrong, but I don't think it captures the whole picture."

"What do you mean?" I asked, through many pauses to catch my breath. I felt like I was on something of a treadmill myself. The sidewalk was antagonistic in my plight to reach the building before us.

"Well, the idea is that people's happiness levels adjust to their circumstances over time. A person in jail who's been in jail for a while might rate their happiness similarly to a rich person who flew to Venice for dinner that evening. Maybe so, but I feel like the theory vastly overrates how much our day-to-day happiness levels contribute to our lives."

"Yeah, sure, I guess being a content nobody who does nothing of importance never really appealed to me," I said.

"Exactly, and the saddest part of it all is when it finally does," she said. "But being cognizant of your trivial place in the world makes even the happy parts sad. I just can't seem to care about anything when I know that everything I do amounts to nothing."

"And all we ever get to compare ourselves to are those who amount to something," I said. I watched in real time as my ideas aligned with hers. It would be a beautiful, bordering on romantic, moment if it weren't all so sad.

"Or those too dumb to give up, which was almost you there for a while," she said. I laughed. "At a certain point, though, there are lives you realize you cannot live," said the girl. "And lives you realize you can. So, what is there to do when the entire array of lives that you can live reek of unhappiness? It's why Barton annoys me so much. There's nothing you could have done and nothing you can do to live this fantasy life we all dream of. If there was a God, I'd say our suffering is God ordained. But in the end, it's just the result of an ambivalent world that looks different from what we once thought it was as a child. Love doesn't feel as serene as we thought it would. Our small successes aren't as satisfying as we'd envisioned. Every day we live with the thought that life is not as good as we thought it would be or that it's not as good as it could be. That's the cruelty we endure." I looked at her. There were no tears in her eyes. Her gaze was avoidant and distracted. Her posture was slightly slouched, and it accompanied a sigh. She was not coming to these revelations, just repeating them. She had long disconnected herself from the throes of hope.

"So why were you there?" I asked. "At the field, at Barton's concert?"

"Because there's nowhere else to be this late at night or this early in the morning."

I realized that I'd been looking at her the whole time she spoke. When I looked up, we were right at the base of the tall building. It reminded me of my mother's office. It was beige and drab. The worst part was how well it fit into the scenery around it.

I asked the girl if she knew how to get in. She led me around back and picked up a large rock with an emergency key under it. She gave a wry smile and unlocked the front door.

"Do you ever wonder if being exposed early on to the idea that there are lives worth living has ruined us?" she asked as she casually trespassed.

"No," I said. It was a bleak thought, even for a girl who looked and dressed like one big bleak thought.

"When life began, the young were prepared for battle against the harsh world, and by passing on their lineage and continuing the species, they'd won their battle and were embraced by the sweet release of death. But with consciousness, we crave more than just to pass on our genes, and we crave more than just an empty death. But as we are lowered into the ground, that's all we get," she said as we entered a lobby full of elevators.

"I felt anger towards those feelings earlier tonight," I said. "Something about the festival made me livid about the unfairness of life."

She laughed, almost mockingly.

"Anger? That's so much effort. There's this implication of hope with anger. You're upset because you know things should be better, and by God you're gonna do something about it. That was you, wasn't it? Hatching plans, plotting revenge." She gave a cackling laugh. "Oh, the futility!" She pressed the up button, and I stood next to her, quietly embarrassed with myself.

She was right. The whole night, I'd acted rashly and foolishly, and at each step of the way, the culprit was hope. This girl seemed to embody a freeing release of hope, and I was drawn to her like I'd never been drawn to anyone before. She was easy to spend time with. At that moment, I craved something easy.

We stepped into the elevator when it came.

The girl pressed the button that corresponded to roof access, and we stood next to one another looking at each other through the mirror on the ceiling of the elevator. We both looked tired. There was something in each of our faces that resembled peace, but only in a somber, broken way. The girl's bottom lip protruded in a pout.

"It's good to see you've come to your senses about this whole dreadful affair," she said softly. Then the elevator started dropping quickly.

"Why is it—"

She cut me off.

"We'll get where we're going," she said. Her voice was cold, and I started to feel as if there was nothing in the elevator that wasn't metal. But when it opened, though we seemed to have dropped many floors, we were on the roof, just as we'd intended.

The early morning air hit our faces in greeting, and we sat down near the edge facing east as the very slightest glimmer of the new day's sun peeked over the horizon.

"It's a beautiful view," I said, allowing the sky above and trees below to shake off any uneasiness I was feeling. She grunted neither affirmatively nor negatively and shuffled closer to me as we peered off the roof. "So, what's your name, anyway?" I asked.

She did not answer for a long while.

"I don't use it," she said eventually.

"You don't use your name?"

"Well, first, I'm just not fond of the name," she started. I could see something in her eyes that craved more identity than she had. "And second, if I'm to be no one remarkable in life, what's a name matter? It's foolish to be so obsessed with the identity of nothing."

"I guess," I said. The trees in front of us flowed with a slow wind. I could see the faint outlines of the festival in the distance. It felt like I was looking into a memory. The outlines reminded me of my unhappiness. "I guess the only point of a name is to leave a legacy," I said. I internalized her point of view.

"All the millions of people who were born, died, and promptly forgotten by time. What was the point of them even having a name?" said the girl.

I had no answer for her. I, too, felt nameless and anonymous. Soon there'd be no proof that I'd ever even existed. But as the sun crept up and the world illuminated in front of us, I lost myself in the breathtaking view. If it wasn't exhaustion that took my breath; it was beauty. I could see the smoke from the cave and the massive structures that had been erected to put on a music festival. I imagined all the guards running around by the command of their manipulative leaders preparing for another day. It made me sad that I was no better than them. We were all just passing the time until we were forgotten.

"It sure is beautiful," I said. "Maybe beautiful enough to make life worth living, yet."

"Maybe," she said with a snide chuckle. I could tell she didn't agree with me. And perhaps she was right not to. Obsessing over fleeting moments to cope with the calamitous nature of our existence was a pathetic way to live. But it was all I had to cling to.

"You can see Woodhill Park from here," I said. "Have you ever been?" She smiled, as if she too were looking at a memory. She had a quaint habit of never matching her eyes to the expression of her mouth. No happiness was ever full, and no sadness was ever strong enough to consume her. All there was in the end was numbness. She had lived her whole life in the sad thoughts I was only just beginning to conceptualize, and it had broken her.

"Once or twice," she said. She said that the festival had pure intentions but that it failed to truly understand its audience. I wondered if we were even talking about the same place. I couldn't tell if she was referring to Vitality Media or the Woodhill Park festivals of the past. I found that most of all, though, I just liked listening to her talk. She exacerbated my delirium brought on by lack of sleep. She made me feel tired in the most pleasant and comfortable way. If it weren't for the frenzy of thoughts that still ran through my head, I could have fallen asleep next to her while staring out over the vast morning view.

"You can see the main stage from here," she said abruptly, pulling me out of my own head.

"Ah yes," I said. "The great divide."

"It's what separates the living from the lifeless," she said. "The viewee exists because the viewers do not."

"Oh, to be on that stage," I said somberly. In a past life, just maybe an hour ago, I might've said, "What I would give to be on that stage," but I'd grown since then to understand not to partake in silly delusions. She had taught me to find comfort in unhappiness at the expense of any motivation at all.

"You can," she said. "We can go stand on it right now and see what we're missing." I looked over the horizon at the stage. I told her that it was too dangerous, that the guards were after me. But she looked me in the eyes with her knowing, confident, dark brown eyes and told me not to worry. I couldn't bear the thought of blindly trusting someone into the pit of danger, but at that moment I also couldn't bear not to.

"The cave is over there too, the climax of my journey," I said softly. The girl looked forward.

"Ah yes, the cave," she said. She grabbed my hand and pulled me to my feet. "You know what? I want you to see the uncaring world with me! I want you to journey with me into the darkness of our sad existence. Together we can see how small and alone and pointless we are!" She was smiling a genuine smile from ear to ear.

"Sure. Let us journey back into the darkness of Vitality Media," I said. I had much to learn from the girl who had it all figured out. And I felt a stunning apathy to the danger of what I was about to embark on.

2

It felt like I was on an Odyssey, but there was no longer any discernible goal. There was no sweet revenge or better life in front of me. In fact, my actions weren't important at all save surviving the wrath of brainwashed soldiers. The world afforded me nothing but a night of insanity soaked deeply with aimless walking. What was it all for? I put my hope for answers in the cave on the festival grounds but had little in terms of plans for entry. It seemed the aimlessness of my movements, that I was yet again headed towards Woodhill Park to embark on some odd adventure, was paralleled by what I truly learned. Life is not filled with profound revelations that give us meaning. Whatever divinity there might be that writes our stories doesn't care much about mine.

The girl I was with asked me a question as we made our way down from the roof we'd trespassed onto. She asked me if I'd noticed how many tropes and stories include a nobody who, through grand adventure, learns that they are a part of a great lineage. I found that I could think of a few immediately. She theorized that we do not have nearly as much interest in finding our own greatness as we do in being chosen for greatness. In the end, why lead the revolution when you can be the son of the king?

I thought about how small my life was, and it made me sad. I wanted to be somebody, but everybody I could be was taken. At least it briefly felt good, in the early morning, to just be nobody. I'd spent the whole night fighting it, but in peeling back all the emotions but sadness, I felt a cruel liberty.

"Well, we didn't see much sunrise on the roof," I said to the girl.

"Complacency is neither of our fortes," she said as we walked through the streets of the small town.

"What's the name of this town, anyway?"

"Oh, I have no idea," she said.

"What? I thought you lived here," I said.

"Nope."

"So where are you from? Why are you here?"

"Ah, all over," she said. A fitting answer for a girl who wouldn't even tell me her name.

"Why are you here?" I asked again. I didn't mean to interrogate, but she seemed to know more about me than I did her.

"I suppose I'm with my family," she said. "But you know family."

I did know family. I thought about my mother and father. I imagined that they were asleep in their nice, quiet bed. I wondered if they thought about the pointlessness of their existence or became saddened by the lives they could have lived. Their lives were slow, but they never took the time to think. Perhaps it was better for them. And perhaps I didn't really know that much about them at all.

I thought about the Gordons. I wondered if Gordon was still up on that roof coming to whatever epiphany he found so important. I wondered if Ashley and Oli had gotten face tattoos and committed to becoming someone new. Or maybe they gave up on the whole charade and went to sleep. Maybe they were snorting Benadryl with Worm Man. Maybe they were as lost as I was, and I should have been there for them.

They played a massive part in my past, and maybe I wanted to push them away because I didn't want my past to be indicative of my future.

When I looked up from the thoughts that I'd traced in the cracks of the pavement below me, I found that I was in a familiar neighborhood. "I was here earlier," I said brightly.

"Okay," said the girl darkly. She was not a fan of trivial speech. She spoke only in philosophy. But she smiled at me when she realized that her coldness was not enjoyed quite as she might have intended. I looked just past her smiling face, and I saw the lawn that I'd ripped up hours before. Elise, the mother who'd taken me in, was out on her front lawn, but she was not looking at us.

She dug a shovel into the grass, further defacing its appearance. She went at it rhythmically and aggressively. There was a distraught look on her face. One of anguish and hopelessness. I noticed that she had dug quite a large hole. She was trapped in her own head in the wee hours of the morning, performing exhausting labor under the rising sun, and she paid no mind to me, who she'd earlier kicked out of her house.

I stopped walking and watched her as she went back into her house. The girl I was with paced in front of me. She was uninterested in Elise. I stared and waited as Elise stayed inside. Then I watched her come back out holding her young son. She did not look at me or even seem to notice me.

A bit of rain began to fall, but only over her house. I stayed dry, at least for the moment. The rain ran down Elise's face as she held her child and looked at the ground. Then she jolted her head up and looked me in the eyes. She had more wrinkles on her face than I remembered. A jovial spark in her eye that once glimmered with every glance now seemed dull and uninterested. I felt a horrific connection as we stared at each other across the way. Her in the rain on her lawn and me on the cold concrete under the watch of pure ambivalence.

"Into the grave you go," said Elise as she tossed her son into the hole she'd dug. She did not break eye contact with me. Tears streamed down her face, and I could not look away until the black-haired girl next to me pulled my arm. I wanted to go up to Elise, but I had nothing to say. I could not be sympathetic. I did not share her pain. I felt great shame for feeling so despondent in a world where true pain and sorrow does exist. But I could do nothing to help it, so I trudged on.

"Come now," she said. "Let others live their own sadness." She pulled me onwards, towards Woodhill Park, and I watched in my peripheral as Elise filled the hole back up until she could no longer see a trace of her son.

I didn't speak much to the girl as we kept walking. I thought about Ashley and Oli and Gordon experiencing their own sadness. I thought about just how much sadness there was all around at all times. It seemed unnecessary, as though life could have existed without it.

We passed a church, and the girl said, "Look at this church."

I said, "This church?" pointing at the church.

And she said, "No, this church," and pointed at the same church, and I looked at it. It was half charred and rundown. It had a wooden cross at the top that had been pecked away by birds. Half of the roof was missing on the right side, and the ornate door on the front taunted passersby with the haunting reminder of what once was and what horrors remained. A raven sat atop the building, daring me to succumb to its macabre whims. But when I looked into its eyes, it turned away from me, as if the dark symbolism of my own being was too dark for even it.

"What say you of this church?" I asked.

"Who talks like that?" she asked.

"I don't know," I said. "It just sorta came out that way." She answered my question regardless. She said that apparently an old pastor used to run that church for twenty-five years. He and his God were a centerpiece in a thriving community until it burned down one night in an electrical fire. He tried his damnedest to blame agents of satanism for arson, but all evidence from an extensive investigation pointed to an unlucky electrical fire. The old pastor tried to raise funds to build it back up, but the community had more or less moved on. He spent his days reading the bible to people on the streets and died unceremoniously in an alleyway a year later. The church marked his grave. His entire life's work was rotted wood that further fell apart each day.

"What if he's wrong?" I asked after hearing the dark story. "About the heaven and the God he dedicated everything to? Even if it feels impossible in his mind that he's wrong, what if? Then he will have dedicated his life to nothing, and he'll end up in the same place as the rest of us."

"Yeah," said the girl. "The God who he'd given everything to did nothing but burn his livelihood to the ground. In a way, he's all of us. That which we give everything to has a habit of giving nothing back, no matter what Barton would have you believe. It's a crazy thing, how much there is to give and how little there is to get. Makes you wonder if it's worth giving anything at all."

"Do you wonder that often?" I asked, looking into her dark eyes. Was she a person with a negative take on the world, or a reflection of a negative world?

"I do," she said. When I turned back, I found that we were right at the forest that connected the edge of the town to the edge of the Woodhill Park festival. I took a deep breath as I looked at the vastness of the forest I was about to enter and the danger that stood before me.

"Don't worry," said the girl, placing her hand on my shoulder. "Nothing lies before you that doesn't lie behind you."

3

I watched the faint sunlight hit the trees of the forest. It was the light from the past that had just now made its way to my eyes. Perhaps it was light from a happier time. The world dawned on me. I saw how faint and colorless my place in it was.

The girl stood in front of me and stared into the sun. "How often do you see the sunrise?" she asked, taking her first step into the forest.

"Almost never," I said. I realized again how tired I was. The sunrise felt like something I wasn't meant to see. My body prayed that my mind would rest, but that was not its intention.

"There's supposed to be a joy or excitement at the dawn of a new day," said the girl. "But I see only futility. It's cyclically torturous. How can you have a new life when the old one happens over and over, unending?"

"Maybe it's not that bad," I whispered, if only in self-persuasion.

"Maybe," she said. "I think you'll find at these festival grounds a microcosm of what I mean. To see this all again in a new light might make you laugh or cry, but the hope is that you at least feel something."

"How about tired?" I asked with a tongue in cheek nature to my tone.

"Oh, we're all tired," she said with a smile. I was only a few paces into the forest, and I found that the trees had grown to form two distinct paths. The girl stopped before them. The sunlight peeked through the one on the left, and I saw the branches around it sway gently in the breeze. The trees joined together high in the air to create a shelter over the enchanted walkway. If a cartoon bird had flown out to enlist me on a heroic mission, I wouldn't have even been surprised. The path on the right was pitch black. I knew without looking which way the girl's feet were pointed.

"This way," said the girl, walking into the dark path in the forest. I followed her, and my legs struggled to keep me up. I wondered what would have happened had I gone the other way without her, but I didn't dare leave her side. There was some mixture of admiration and friendship and attraction that kept me near her. But in large part, I stayed by her out of laziness and fear of loneliness. Her cynicism was heavy and exhausting yet so comfortable.

Again, we reached a path that branched two ways, and again we chose the darkest path. Together we heeded the advice of a demonic Robert Frost, and I felt increasingly claustrophobic from it.

Eventually, we reached the end, and I was attacked by the festival lights. I shielded my eyes, but only for a second. When I looked again, at the entire scene of the sleeping festival, I saw that my vision was entirely in black and white. And I felt cold. I was colder than I'd ever been, but I did not need a jacket. "Wh—" I began, with no direction to a sentence's end. The girl understood, still.

"The world looks different to a mind devoid of hope," she said. "Behind you, you've left delusion, vengeance, desperation. All pitfalls riddled with hope. You're free now. This is what freedom looks like." I shuddered as I looked at the once vibrant campsite that was now the remnants of a battlefield in an old 40's war movie. The wind through the tents and the trees made an aggressive roar that oscillated between a whistle and a crumple. I focused on a tire track in front of me. The tread had cut the dirt in a way that felt painful. The power and urgency of the vehicle had long since left behind any serenity once written onto the terrain by nature.

"I'm not free from the guards," I whispered. "I'm a wanted man." The girl laughed. Just as she did, I saw a guard in the distance, heading towards us. His eyes widened as he saw us. I turned in panic to the fence we'd just hopped and prepared to flee back into the forest. But the girl grabbed my arm.

"Ma'am," said the guard. "I didn't expect you." He had a mole on his left cheek, an angular face with a pointed chin and red, swooshing hair. His skin tasted salty. Probably. Maybe. He was familiar in the same way that Woodhill Park as a whole was familiar.

"We're going to the main stage in a bit. Can you make sure it's clean?" asked the girl.

"Surely," said the guard as he quickly redirected himself towards the main festival grounds. He never even looked at me. I stood in shock. Who was this girl, that she could have such command over the guards?

The girl turned to me as he left.

"See, we'll be just fine," she said with a chuckle. I didn't even bother to ask for clarification. I was along for the ride, and she never answered any of my questions anyway.

The girl walked me through the northern campsite, and we looked at all the tents. Each guard who stood firmly at his post nodded in deference as we passed. The world felt upside down, and I thought that I might fall off of it without the girl to cling to.

As we paced through those northern campgrounds, and I looked at each zipped-up tent with a hint of longing. There was beauty in the black and white scenery, but it was overshadowed by an uneasy sadness.

"Who are you anyway?" I asked, again prying with futility at the locked door. I had been stewing on the question long enough to just let it out again.

"Who am I?" she asked. "Who are you?"

"I'm just, like, some guy," I said. It was the exact, honest truth. The truth that haunts me the most.

"Well then I'm just, like, some girl," she said.

"Yeah, but the guards don't stop what they're doing to call me, sir," I said. She just laughed.

"No, they do not," she said, emphasizing how pathetic I was. At least that's how I took it.

I couldn't tell if I really even cared about all the little mysteries of my night. Everything I'd learned so far was just that there was nothing out there worth doing or learning at all. I was in the abyss, but it wasn't that I'd just fallen; rather I'd just been made aware of where I'd always been.

I passed over rows and rows of tents, all filled with someone uncomfortable yet happy. It was hard for me to put into perspective that the Woodhill Park Festival was just another weekend in all these people's lives. It was a time to get a glimpse of the wonders of the world as a break from its realities. It made me sad to think that we'd been conditioned to need to savor and relish the beautiful moments in our life. Somewhere along the line, life itself stopped being beautiful. I felt as though the girl was speaking through my thoughts, but I was too tired to stop her.

Up ahead, before the entrance, there was yet another row of tents, but these were all black. Next to each of these tents was a hearse. By nature of the early morning, this image before me was quiet and still. I felt as though I were in the face of the simmering low tide of death.

"What is this for?" I asked. "I didn't see this before."

The girl merely nodded and kept walking. I dodged the rough terrain that had been softened by the morning's ejaculate. I promise I didn't want to phrase it that way, but my mind was being tugged on by knavish forces.

In front of my step was a small white splatter. "Aw man," I said while looking at it. The girl stopped and looked at it too. "A man took a bird shit right here."

"What do you mean?" asked the girl.

"A man took a bird shit here," I said again. "How vile."

"Like a man pooped here, and it resembles that of a bird's?"

"No, it is a bird's," I said. I was entirely convinced of what I was saying. The girl looked to the sky.

"Well, birds shit all the time," she said.

"This was no bird though," I said. I wasn't really getting frustrated. "A man did this."

"That doesn't make any sense."

"It was a man who took this shit," I said, raising my voice, but without exasperation or anger. My tone was almost triumphant except with a neutral connotation. "He took that which was not his to take. Because it was a bird's. It was a man who took this bird shit!"

We both looked at it for a beat more and then no longer.

"Let's move on," said the girl.

We did precisely that. We got to the northern gate and walked in without struggle. The morning guards looked at us in awe. It was the most emotion I'd seen conveyed by them yet. It felt uneasy.

The wind got a hold of me as we walked. Its harshness tried to wake me further, but my body fought against it. I really had no say in the fight. We entered the festival through the northern gate, and I could again see the dramatic castle before me and above me. It was beautiful in black and white. Although the day was beginning, it felt like I was at the end of something. Everything around me was different, sadder, and more indifferent to my presence than it was when I was there before. The girl led me through the Zen forest, where I had experienced my first delusions of grandeur. I froze, because next to a tree in the corner of the garden sat Denny. She did not look at me, and I prayed that she'd keep it like that.

"She has no interest in you," said the girl, sensing my fear.

I approached Denny slowly as we walked by her. She was ghost white and sat with her arms crossed. Her tight blonde ponytail had loosened off her scalp and singular, wiry hairs frizzed out of her hair tie. Her eyes were paranoid yet focused, and red lines erupted like lightning from her irises. She shivered in the wind and muttered slowly. I couldn't help but lean in to hear what she said as I passed.

"In death," she said to herself. "There's life. In desire. There's suffering. In admiration. There's envy. In life. There's greed. There's lust. In death. There's grief. There's mourning. In the morning. There's nothing. In nothing. There's you."

She was a shell of herself, but who was I to say that? So was I. The night seemed to have been equally cruel to her as it was to me. The night had protruded her pale cheekbones to ghoulish proportions and twisted her limbs around as she squatted against an old tree. Her condition represented how the whole area had lost its luster.

"What happened here?" I asked the girl. The garden had once mesmerized me, but now only saddened me.

"This is a music festival at six AM," said the girl. "When the thoughts and ideas and hopes and dreams and feelings all melt away in the face of the harsh morning chill. Real life retakes control at six AM and with it comes…" She gestured around her. "This."

We soldiered on through the garden. I looked at the stump of the tree I'd cut down those many hours ago. Through the clearing my labor had left behind was the smoke arising from the cave. It was maybe the only constant in the world.

When we got outside of the Zen forest, the girl grabbed my arm. "There," she said, pointing to the stage. "Where Gods do their work." The stage was almost glowing, perhaps more in my mind than in actuality. Looking at it, in its majesty and emptiness, was like looking at paradise through a reinforced glass window. The grass is always greener, they say, but I felt assured that the grass was objectively greener on the stage than it was in the trampled valley that once housed the audience. Kendall Paulson never looked from his view on the stage and yearned to be in the crowd. My only wonder was whether yearning at all was even worth it.

There was a small patch of flowers between us and the stage. We barely noticed them while we marveled at the great wonder in our view, but we turned our attention to them eventually. They were white lilies, a fact I didn't know off hand. Well, I knew they were white. Each petal flowed outward from the center writing its own melody, a piece of a greater whole. There were small dots, a color I could not make out of course, maybe purple, in the middle of each flower and they were clumped together in perfect chaos; they were both the benefactor and the beneficiary of nature's embrace.

The girl picked one of them up. It wilted in her hand immediately. It almost made me laugh, but instead I watched silently. The girl made no expression, and she dropped the flower to the ground. "You should get on the stage," she said.

"Is that not trespassing?" I asked. I was mostly joking.

"I feel as though I've been where I'm not supposed to be my whole life." I thought about this as she said it. I wondered if it applied to me as well. I think, behind the front of apathy, the girl secretly wanted me to agree with and believe the things she said.

I made my way around the flowers and approached the steps leading to the large stage. This was where I'd seen those dramatic shows what felt like lifetimes ago. This was where I'd witnessed such outward beauty and yet felt such inward pain. I was ignorant; I could not appreciate talent for something that was beautiful without seeing it as merely something I could not attain. I felt a great deal closer to myself than when I'd last seen the stage and yet a lot further from the world. It was worse; it was a worse place to be.

I took my first steps up to the stage and looked back to see the girl squinting up at me. There was no real glare, but she squinted into it nonetheless. She had a bit of prideful anticipation on her face, as though she was watching someone do something she'd done many times over to life-changing effect.

My feet felt lighter on the stage. I could almost float, and I knew exactly where to float to. The pain of indecision lifted off me like a great weight. I found my mark on the center of the stage and looked out over the festival, over the audience that was not there. Not only was the world in color again, but it was in more vibrant color than it had ever been before.

I felt a roar around me, an excitement buzzing. A crowd began to populate, all focused on me, and they made their admiration audibly known. It was as if I were experiencing surround sound, but in real life, which I now realize is how it always is, but it was somehow better in that moment. I was no longer tired. I fed—feasted, even—on the energy around me. I twirled around taking in every feeling I could. I looked back at the crowd and saw a sea of people. They sang along to my thoughts like they were hit songs. It became an objective fact that the things that I thought mattered more than the things the commoner thought. It should have been snooty and narcissistic, but instead it was just awesome. In the crowd, I saw my parents with beaming faces. Their adjacency to stardom had made their lives tangibly better. I had made their lives better, something I never could feel through my years of extreme normalcy.

"Woodhill Park..." I yelled out. There was an incredible echo, reverb and slight autotune caressing my voice. The crowd cheered. I singled, or zeroed in, anything below doubled, on a member of the crowd. They had a whole life with feelings and tasks and relationships and a foot fetish that was getting so extreme that their roommates had to have an intervention.

They had thoughts and aspirations. There was so much to just one person, and yet it was the highlight of their month just to be within one hundred yards of me on that stage.

"… I am a king!" I bellowed out.

"I love you, Reza!" yelled a girl from the crowd. I could barely hear her. I looked in her direction and saw her. She was pretty, with no discernable facial features. She was a million girls. She threw a pair of panties at me. I watched as they danced in the air against the vibrant colors of the sunrise and landed at my feet. It was cliche and dumb, but I loved every second of it. I then heard a much deeper voice.

"I love you, Reza!" it screamed. I turned to see a very large bald man who was giddy to see me. I smiled at him until I noticed he was holding a balled-up diaper like a shot-put ball. That thing had some serious heft to it, and he was stanced up like he was about to absolutely launch it.

"Woah!" I said in reaction. "Let's maybe keep our clothes to ourselves." The crowd went absolutely nuts. I noticed a girl holding a sign that read *Play Let's Maybe Keep Our Clothes to Ourselves* going so crazy that she almost fainted.

It was difficult to conceptualize how much I meant to these people. Everything I'd assumed about the profundity of fame was correct and then some. To be famous was to live the human experience on such a grander scale that it didn't even feel like the same reality as my previous life of anonymity.

It felt so real, and I wanted it to never end. There's no reason one cannot live entirely in a single moment. This was my dream, a culmination of everything I'd aspired to have. So, I began to sing. I sang my favorite song from my band, which I suppose is called Fury and the Gordon Three. As I sang the intro, music rendered in behind me, and the crowd sang along with every word. These were words and melodies that I'd spent weeks toiling over and trying to perfect to little end, and here this audience of peers hung on every second of my performance—no, they were not peers. They were fans. As a collective, they meant everything to me, they were the catalyst of my success and the proof of my worth. But as individuals, they meant nothing. I was on the stage, and they were on the ground. It didn't matter if we were where we deserved to be; we were there regardless.

As I performed my song for the adoring crowd, it felt good to no longer be who I was to myself, who was just a guy, a regular guy looking for purpose, and instead be who I was to them: a genius and an idol. This was what life was about: Admiration, success, just being on the stage. How could it be anything else?

I finished my song and just looked out over the sea of people in the audience. I took it all in. And then in my peripheral vision, I saw the girl up on the stage with me. Her black clothes and black hair pushed back against the vibrant colors all around. The crowd booed her. They were angry about her presence. They wanted her to go away and let the show rage on, but she just kept approaching me. "Reza," she said as she grabbed my arm. "It's time to come off the stage."

"No," I said. That stage was all I had. I was living in that moment. To leave it would be to kill me.

You have to," she said. "You've seen it. You've seen it all."

The crowd became angry.

"No!" someone shouted. And then another. The girl tried to look at me warmly as she pleaded with me to leave, but I could only see coldness in her. The coldness of a corpse.

"Kill her!" said someone in the crowd.

I looked at them—they all had pitch black eyes. It was scary. A bottle whizzed past the girl. "She's trying to derail your happiness!" shouted a shrill voice from the crowd. It came from a woman with an intense voice, she began to melt into the other angry crowd members around her.

"She doesn't belong up there, but you do!" shouted another woman. She was right.

"Rip her head off," said a man with a visceral anger behind every syllable.

Another lady in the crowd then said, "Rip off her kneecaps and wear 'em like a bra like *The Little Mermaid*."

"Oh I'm actually in on the kneecap thing, can I change my vote?" asked the first guy. Then the two of them started polling the crowd, member by member, and the kneecap bra thing seemed to have a significant advantage.

I just watched them, frozen in place in the face of their empty pleas, as the girl dragged me down off the stage.

And just like that, the crowd disappeared. The world was back to black and white, and I was nobody again. I sat on the grass, and the girl sat beside me. We did not speak.

4

Sometimes I think I'd rather have a nightmare than a good dream. Because waking up from a good dream only to realize that the perfect life you were living was fake all along brings a unique pain. A pain that outweighs any terrors a nightmare can conjure up. It's better to be relieved by your reality than to be saddened by the life you lead. Although honestly, I don't always feel as though I lead my life at all. I tend to follow.

Stepping off that stage, back to reality, was like waking up from a tremendous dream. It only made my life sadder by comparison. I picked up one of the white lilies in front of me and it died in my hands. It was not funny at all this time around.

I looked at the empty field that once housed an adoring audience. Where there was once so much life, there was now nothing at all. There wasn't even death. This world didn't even have the decency for that. A plastic bag thrashed in the morning winds and made an aimless, ambivalent journey across the field. It was like a dystopian tumbleweed delivering the message of my life's emptiness.

"I thought I told them to clean this place up," muttered the girl. She was staring at the ground, but still took notice of the calmly moving debris.

"Ariel's bra in *The Little Mermaid* isn't human kneecaps, right?" I asked slowly, looking at the ground. "It's like clams or something, right?"

"What?" said the girl. I just sat there in silence.

"So, that's what it's really like?" I asked, again cruelly laying my thoughts onto her. "Up on that stage? That... that feeling exists?"

"Not for us," she said. She wasn't angry, and neither was I. We were just tired. It felt like everything was too heavy. "There are so many things to do and feel and experience, and it seems we occupy our whole day, every day, doing none of them."

I shrugged, not because I didn't believe it, but because I wanted to not care. I was happy before I sat down and thought of all the reasons not to be.

Off in the distance, there was a guard approaching us. He held a rifle to his chest and walked quickly but devoid of direction. He wasn't so much eager to get where he was going as he was bored of where he was, and with that came hustle. I wasn't afraid of him because I seemed to have a bizarro forcefield at my side in the form of this sad girl. So, I just looked at him. Even if his intentions were more nefarious than I'd calculated, I thought to myself, I didn't have the energy to stop him anyway. He was going to do to me what he was going to do to me, just like everything else in the world. He got up close to us and stood completely straight.

"Is there anything I can do for you, ma'am?" he asked with manufactured warmth. He ignored me.

"No," said the girl. "No there is not." She released a frustrated chuckle with her response. She was in a place where there was nothing anyone could do for her, and she was slowly dragging me there as well.

She turned to me. "You know, it'd be fun to show you all these realizations if it wasn't so disheartening."

"Yeah, it's always a pleasure spending time with you, until it's not," I said. The guard was still there, standing perfectly straight, and he kind of nodded along to this personal conversation I was having with the girl. "In other circumstances, I think I'd be interested in spending a lot of time with you." I looked her in the eyes. Her cheeks did something in the same classification of a blush and the corners of her mouth did everything they could to turn up against the tyranny of her brain. And then returned to her resting cold stillness.

"In other circumstances," she said coolly.

"Yeah," said the guard.

"Dismissed, Marcus," she said with an annoyed tone. The guard leisurely walked away without saying a word. "His name's not Marcus," she then said to me.

"Oh," I said. I didn't know if she was telling the truth, and I didn't really care. She looked over my head and into the sky and then back into my eyes. Parts of her graphic tee had become untucked on her left hip as she sat on the ground. Her hair on the right side of her head had been tucked behind her right ear. Our time together had all kinds of small effects on her appearance.

"Well," she started, as if she'd exhausted every option and all that remained was an ever-existing thought deep within her mind.

She looked intense, like she was bracing herself for my reaction to what she was about to say. "I guess it's time you see the cave."

My eyes widened. I did not know how to feel about this, and I had no one to turn to for advice. I was in it alone. Was I really prepared for these promised truths? She said it so casually that a weird shiver went down my spine. All night, I'd been given a messy tangle of loose threads and ideas to see the world through, and now here I was, poised to enter the one place where it supposedly all got pulled together. All because of the whims of some strange girl. I guess I wouldn't have it any other way.

"I'm…" I rose to a standing position. "I'm ready."

"Yeah, they all say that," she said with a smile. She took my hand and led me across the field. Marcus, the guard, or whatever his name was, watched us from a distance.

We stomped the grass covering the field on our way towards the cave, and I felt the weight of my despair fade with every step. I surgically killed each blade of grass that dared show me my reality. Everything behind me was still shrouded in black and white with long shadows and harsh angles. It was a world that would be filled with horror if it weren't so boring. But in front of me, faint colors began to reappear.

All the sadness was in the past, and only excitement remained in the future. I looked at the line of smoke in the air and followed it to the promised land. I was a fool to trust the world's promises, but I couldn't afford not to. There was just as little to a life of doubting as there was to a life of deception.

"This way," said the girl as she tugged me along.

"I know!" I said. "We're literally walking towards the giant black smoke in the air."

"Oh yeah," she said. "A constant reminder." She had a connection to the Woodhill Park Festival in the weirdest way. There was a knowingness to her, and the remnants of a love/hate relationship that no longer existed because she no longer had the capacity to muster up either emotion. I wondered if it was whatever she'd learned here that broke her or saved her in her own twisted way.

I took exalted steps through the main road and watched as all the frivolity melted away. Food stands and picture booths fell against their backdrops like liquid down a wall. Shops selling overpriced T-shirts and a guy in a T-shirt selling under-priced shops faded away in my vision. A stand to get tempo-rary tattoos and permanent regret because of the weird things the guy says to you while drawing on you went away as well.

I was on a journey, and all the details that did not matter showed reverence to the great truths that did. Everything I'd done and seen was all for something, and I walked the path to that something with my head held high. It was like I was in a memory where only the important remained; a memory I'd hold for the rest of my life.

In all the lies I'd been fed from Denny and Angus and Bar-ton and even this sad girl, there was one truth that linked them all together: I would find myself in the cave. I'd passed all the tests, or at least failed them correctly, and now I was ready. It was all in my head, exacerbated by delirium, but it fell onto me so heavily that it brought tears to my eyes.

Through my blurry, tear-soaked vision, I could only see darkness in my peripheral vision and colors ahead as I walked perfectly straight on a golden path to the now rainbow-colored smoke. What was once a girl next to me became a dark mass, and it pulled color into it with every step. I no longer thought in thought; I thought only in colors.

Then I snapped back to reality in the face of a hundred armed guards who froze in their busy and well-regulated tracks to stare at me. All of them looked identical. They had red swooshing hair, an angular face with a pointed chin, and a mole on their left cheek. One of them had a mole on his right cheek instead, but the guard next to him picked it off and placed it onto the left one before filing back into position. Between myself and their gaze was paradise in the form of revelation.

"Oi, what do we have here?" said the lead guard. He was the only one to deviate from the uniform physical appearance. He had a shaggy black beard guarding a resting sneer. He stood in the middle with the others in a V shape like a flock of birds or Superman in the Justice League. He spoke with a rugged British accent. "Little birdies strayed too far from the campgrounds." He turned to the cave and then back to us. "In fact, you mighta seen too much to be allowed back." I saw the confidence in his eyes as he clutched his gun and prepared it. Unlike the other guards, there was life in his eyes. He was a worthy adversary that stood between me and my climactic finale. He was a soldier of Vitality Media that retained his humanity. I readied myself for the final obstacle and dug my feet into the dirt. Then a second, more lifeless, guard approached him and whispered in his ear.

"Oh my God," he said, no longer holding that rugged accent. In fact, he wasn't even British anymore. "I'm so sorry, I didn't know who you were." The girl just yawned.

"We're going in the cave," she said, and all the other guards remained tense.

"Do you want us to kill him?" asked one of those dead-eyed idiots around us, gesturing to his once confident colleague.

"Eh, no," said the girl after some deliberation.

"We can't get in, ma'am, but we can fetch—" said the guard who'd taken de facto leadership after the previous cave guard was removed for his transgressions.

The girl cut him off.

"No!" she said sternly. "Fetch...fetch Orion. He can get us in."

"Right away," said the guard. Three of them sprinted off like machinery receiving its latest input. The girl sat down in front of the cave, and I looked up and marveled at the massive ongoing trail of smoke.

"None of these guards have ever been in here?" I asked her without looking at her.

"Of course not," she said. "You can tell who has or hasn't seen the inside by how they act."

"You've been in," I said. It was perhaps a bit of a question.

"I have," she said. It didn't seem to have "fixed" her, whatever that meant, but maybe she wasn't someone who could be fixed. "There are two types of people who have ever interacted with this cave: Those who've seen inside, and those who want to see inside. That's the magic of it."

"Can you be both?" I asked. The girl laughed.

"No," she said using her most mysterious voice.

I sat down next to her.

"Who's Orion?"

"He's coming over here. Why be told when you can just be shown?" she said. "He's just a guy anyway. You're making me go through a lot of trouble to show you all this."

"Why are you?" I asked. It was an obvious question, but I'd never bothered to ask it. "Showing me all this?"

"Misery loves company," she said. It wasn't an answer I found myself all that fond of. I heard a loud bit of hubbub off in the distance. I tried to peek through all the trees to put images to the noises. It was hard to be interested in anything but the cave, but the struggle through the trees was a fine enough appetizer to wet the palate of my growing impatience. Finally, the source of the noise came to view.

There was a thin, lanky man with wiry black hair and wire-frame glasses being dragged over by three guards who pulled him aggressively towards us.

"Unhand me!" he shouted. They did not obey, and just pulled him roughly until he was right next to me and the girl. "Okay that's enough," said the man to the guards in a much calmer tone.

They let him go, and he stood up perfectly straight. He jittered a bit as he stood. There was art to him, the way his thin body moved and the way his presence fully conquered the scene around him. He moved and looked like an artistic animated character, and an artist's signature one at that.

"Oh darling, it's always good to see you," he said to the black-haired girl next to me. "Even if…" He trailed off.

The girl nodded, and I did not, for I had no idea who he was or what the hell he was talking about. He then looked directly at me. I could almost see his opinion of me waver dramatically as he did. I was either someone who wanted to know the great truth of the world or deserved to know the great truth of the world. "So, you're the lad who wants in the cave?"

"I am," I said. I couldn't have been characterized any better at that moment.

"They have the meaning of life in there, at the source of that smoke," he said. "Once you see it, you seen it. Can't unlearn that. Well, I guess you could get a good bonk on the head and then lose it. I betcha I could make a killing in the bonk industry, just getting people to forget all kinds of stuff. Imagine you read a good book, but it don't have good reread value, so I bonk ya and then you can read it for the first time again. Imagine that. Imagine there's no heaven. It's easy if you try. I guess you won't have to do much more imagining after you see in there. Doesn't leave much to the imagination, unless you leave before you see anything or close your eyes or something. You really learn why everyone does what they do when you see in there. You ready for that? Huh?" He spoke extremely fast, and it was almost as if the only way he stopped was by pursing his lips together to prevent the flow of words.

"I think I'm ready for that," I said. "It's a scary feeling, like I'm becoming who I'll always be, and everything I've learned tonight about myself and about the world has led me here."

"Tonight?" said Orion. "I'm Orion, by the way. Tonight? It's morning, lad. It's mourning time, mourning he who you wanted to be. He died a slow, painful death. At your hand. The cave at least tells you more about the world you live in and the world he doesn't live in. It won't bring him back."

"Well, I made it this far," I said.

"Hazzah!" said Orion, for some reason. "You know I used to change this girl's diapers?" He motioned to the girl.

"Yeah, I had a bad bout with food poisoning last year," she said.

"Oh, okay," I said. I touched the tips of my fingers together, and they felt numb. While my mind urgently fixated on the cave, the rest of me was content to fade away into sleep or obscurity or both.

Orion pulled a small key out of his back pocket and walked us to the entrance of the cave. There was an old black door guarding the inside. "Look away, all!" said Orion to the guards. They all faced the opposite way and watched the empty clearings in front of them for trespassers. "I wouldn't dare go in again," he said more quietly to us. I stared at the cave door and felt my breathing increase. Orion inserted the key and wiggled it a bit. "Aw, they must have changed the locks," he said. He just shrugged and removed the key and began to walk away. I felt a bubbling rage within me. I knew it was silly to care about anything, but I knew, in the exact same way, that the cave was the only thing worth caring about. I would not be denied so callously.

"No, I'm just kidding," said Orion as he reinserted the key and opened the door. "Get in there, kiddo!" he said. "Answers await." I looked into the cave in awe, but all I saw was a dark tunnel. I closed my eyes and took a deep breath before walking in.

The girl scooted in behind me, and Orion closed the door, swallowing me in darkness. It was then that I took my first step towards the center. It was one small step towards large revelations. I knew I was on a journey, in an odyssey, and this was the climax.

5

When I was a kid, my parents took me and the Gordons on a hike to a beautiful national park in the northwest. It was just the six of us. It was refreshing to go on a trip with my friends instead of my extended family, because in those days, it seemed like whenever we did anything, we'd have to have extended family around. I loved my extended family, but they also got old fast. Especially Uncle Lloyd, who had wrinkles and gray hair by age twenty-six. I'm sure Ashley and Oli's mom was glad to have the twins off her hands for the week as well. We all explored the wonders of nature together, without a thought given to anything outside of the dramatic landscapes. I was old enough to see the beauty in those moments, and still young enough to not worry about the stressors we were escaping. I was simply experiencing tranquility with my friends and family. It was a moment that meant a lot because I was naïve to how little it meant.

I did nothing there to leave my mark; it was actually discouraged by the park rangers, yet the memory always left a mark on me. This memory came to mind as I wandered through Woodhill Park, because during our exploration on that vacation, we came across a cave. I remember every detail of the cave, the ridges and edges, and also every detail of my excitement. I was excited to explore, to look into the unknown. There was no feeling that ever matched the idea that I was out here and in there was something cool. "Can we go in, can we go in?" I shouted out. A part of me knew the answer. I knew the danger and the risk. What I'd always seen as excitement in the unknown, my parents had seen as danger. It was a product of their vast experience with the world compared to mine.

But my father said, "Sure, buddy, let's see what's inside." I remember jumping for joy. Gordon sprinted to the mouth of the cave yelling nonsense. The moment stood in a vacuum in my mind, and thus it was untouched by my future unhappiness. I did, however, feel a somber nostalgia.

Not for my childhood, but for a time where the past and future weighed so lightly on me. Also, I was better at geometry back then. I hadn't done geometry in so long that the little kid version in the memory was probably better than me as an adult. That was also pretty sad.

We walked through the cave and my little brain, which had the formula for the volume of a cylinder memorized, was buzzing with interest at everything I saw. Ashley yelled, "Ew look!" and "Woah, look!" with equal fervor at the things she saw in the cave. We turned our flashlights on as the light from the entrance got further and further away, and we saw the damp walls and jutting rock that engulfed us. It was an area of the world that very few people had ever seen. That was impactful to me back then. Deeper in the cave, we saw a small beam of light come from a crack in the ceiling providing a spotlight for a gorgeous lake in the middle of the cavern. It was angelic. It rewrote all the ideas of what the world was capable of in my little area of a rhombus knowing mind.

I'll never forget looking at that lake. I had thoughts that I couldn't put into words, but not because of my limited vocabulary. It was perhaps the first time I was truly floored by existence. The shadows from the beam had minds of their own and they reached across the floor on their own personal journeys. My eyes followed them to a corner that my father was staring into.

"Woah, what is that?" he said, with great interest in his voice. "Buddy, look at this thing." I walked over and stood in front of him. I looked intently into the corner, trying to make out what he was looking at. "It's like a—it's like a monster. Oh, it's moving!" I looked harder, trying to find it, and fear boiled up within me. Then I felt something on my ankle, and I screamed and ran towards the lake.

When I realized it was my dad who'd grabbed at my ankle to scare me, I laughed and laughed. Gordon and Oli were tripping over each other and rolling on the ground laughing. My dad picked me up and swung me around the cave as my mom laughed too. It was a moment we brought up frequently in my house, and it was funny every time. But I did not laugh in the cave at Woodhill Park. I ran my hand along the wall of rock and realized how similar it felt to the cave I was reminiscing about, but I paid it little mind. I had walked about halfway in, and I saw the glow of a fire around the corner of the upcoming wall. This was it; this was the promised land, the source of the big smoke.

The girl with me grabbed my hand. "Clammy," she said softly, and she let go. I was about to see the most profound revelation of my life, so I was a little nervous, what did she expect? Whatever.

I got to the corner and took a deep breath before rounding it. I felt like a fool for remembering that moment of my childhood at such an important time. That vacation to the national park was just something for my parents to do as an alternative to the nothing of every other day. It was something kind of cool to look at to pass the time until death turns its attention to them. They were victims of an apathetic world, and they either didn't know it or didn't care. Having that frivolous memory be a core memory was an indictment of how pointless my life had been. I was ready to begin anew when I left this cave. I was ready to do that Matrix thing where the guy ate that candy.

When I turned the corner, I saw a guy. He was five ten with brown hair and tan, white skin and about 30 thirty years old. He looked at me with slight surprise in his eyes and stopped what he was doing immediately. Then he saw the girl round the corner behind me.

"Uh… hey," he said to her. He then looked at me again, darting his eyes to the girl a few times before focusing on my face. "Uh, okay. Uh, welcome to the climax of your journey, the…the meaning of life. I'm Dave." He was tossing newspapers from a giant stack onto the fire to keep it going, and the smoke from it emerged from a large hole in the ceiling.

"What is this?" I asked. I was so confused that I almost felt scared. I felt like I was standing on a cliff.

"This is it," said the girl. "The meaning of life."

"It's just some guy burning newspapers!" I exclaimed.

"I'm Dave," said Dave. "It's the smoke in the sky that we make here. The mystery, the setup, the driving force. It's something that's always there, letting you know that you're working towards something."

"But inside, there isn't anything," said the girl.

"Well, there's Dave," said Dave.

"Life is all set up and exposition with little payoff," said the girl.

"Why would you bring me here?" I asked. I felt tears begin to fall. I saw my legs tremble. They were legs that had fought exhaustion to push me through the night and ultimately to the cave. And this was their reward. I was overcome by an involuntary shiver. The moment felt like ice.

"This is the most important place of all to truly understand. This is the visitation room to see the body of hope as it lays in its casket," said the girl. Dave burned an entertainment section of a local newspaper. I watched as a positive review of some young woman's directorial debut withered away into smoke.

"I was told I would find the meaning of life here," I yelled. "I was deceived!"

"That deception is the meaning of life," said the girl.

"Yeah, man, you're supposed to see the smoke in the sky and know there's more to all the meaningless, pointless things you do. You aren't really supposed to see all this," said Dave.

"You aren't supposed to see Dave," said the girl.

"Then why bring me?" I asked. I felt like the last bit of hope that I had pretended to not carry had finally been ripped from me. It was what the girl wanted. Why did she want that of me?

"Because you are like me," she said. "Is it better to know the saddening truth or live your life in blissful falsehoods?"

"Blissful falsehoods!" I said. I exclaimed this like it was obvious, and to me it was. I began to hate the girl, but even that emotion meant nothing to me. Nothing meant anything at all.

"Yeah, I gotta agree with the kid on that one," said Dave. He continued adding paper to the fire like a robot. The rising smoke stayed steady.

"You just couldn't bear to have this knowledge alone, could you?" I asked the girl. My eyes were stern and scornful.

"Your hopes, dreams, and ambitions are dead," she said. "The smoke is just a delusion of lingering possibilities, an unhealthy coping mechanism. I freed you from that."

"And how do I cope now?" I asked. "Knowing that the one place I might find meaning and gain something from this twisted, godforsaken night is a fraud?"

"Perhaps you just don't," she said somberly. We all stood in silence. The tears rested gently on my cheeks.

"I'm sorry, man," said Dave.

"Why do you do it, Dave?" I asked. I wanted to know why there were so many happy cogs in this twisted machine.

"You cannot enjoy the morning lest you make it through the entire night," said Dave.

What the actual fuck does that mean, Dave? That's what I wanted to say, but I was too tired and angry and sad and let down to say anything at all. I sat down against the cave wall and just watched Dave feed the fire of deception one paper at a time. The girl sat next to me, and I tried to scoot away, but to little ends. The anger dissipated, and the sadness bubbled up, and in a way, that felt more comfortable. All the sharp pains were replaced by a lingering dull one, and with my growing comfort, I thought to myself that the girl was right: Misery loves company.

I guess other people say that too.

We sat with each other and thought about our predicament. I thought about how the fact that the cave was talked about so frequently made its nothingness pack so much harder of a punch. I was finally devoid of the hope of making something of myself or finding meaning in my life. It would have felt good if it didn't feel so numb. None of my thoughts were straight, as I hadn't slept in over twenty hours, but I got more out of their swirling nature than I would have otherwise. I wanted to get up off the cave floor, but then I realized that there wasn't anything to do.

The world truly was black and white. Everything except the fire. It was bright orange, and it was mocking me.

"Look at you," it said. "You wanted to be a famous musician. Eight billion people, and you thought you were special enough that you deserved millions of others to care about the things you created. What a pathetic narcissist. You think you're better than your parents because you whine about this profound unfairness the world has dealt you while they actually are out there trying to enjoy themselves in this brief, pointless existence. Boo fucking hoo, you aren't a generational talent who is immortalized in history. You're just like everyone else, but you're somehow better because you complain about it?"

The fire was right. I resented it for being right. I hung my head until the girl spoke up again. "Get up; we've got one last place to go," she said softly. Dave did not pay us any mind. He continued to tend to the fire, and he hummed somberly to himself. I used all my might to get myself back on my feet, and the girl slowly led me towards the exit.

As we rounded the corner, Dave yelled out, "You can finish this, yet, Reza!"

I did not look back. We got to the end of the tunnel and the white sunlight hit me, causing me to wince. When my vision finally found its focus, a black interruption of the sunlight cut into my vision. It was the hair on the head of Ross Kluber, the head of Vitality Media. I jumped back when I saw him star-ing directly into my eyes. His stern expression did not waver.

"Hello, Father," said the girl.

"I heard you've been all around my festival grounds this morning, Debra," he said. I could see the similarity in their eyes. It was scary seeing this figure I'd vilified in my mind speak so casually. But I had more pressing questions.

"Oh, your name is Debra?" I asked, softly, looking only at the girl.

"Yeah," she said.

"Oh," I said. "Okay."

"Yeah, that's why I never told you."

"What, you just don't like your name?" I said. "I thought you were just being mysterious or something."

"Yeah, no, that's a hundred percent the reason," she said.

"Are you done?" asked Ross Kluber. He was just watching us interact with a tinge of amusement. He had rugged skin and his head stood high on his neck. His jaw was ever so slightly tilted up. His mouth, with the faintest smile, was kinder than I'd ever recognized it before.

"Yes, sir," I said with unwarranted deference.

"Has my daughter shown you everything you aim to learn?"

"I-I suppose so."

"Remember to think your own thoughts, too," he said. Debra gave him a glare. Ross stood perfectly straight; he was so much larger than his six-foot frame.

I thought briefly about Angus and how he hated Ross. This was a man who ran the machine that chewed up and spit out me and everyone I knew, but I couldn't even muster up enough emotion to hate him. To fight this villain was not my calling because it had become abundantly clear that I was no hero, no protagonist. So instead, I just stood there venerably and watched Debra interact with her father.

"What are you doing here, Dad?" she asked.

"Overseeing the festival," he said. "For it is my job."

"Well, we've been running around all over the place, so you and your stupid little army are doing a shit job," said Debra. She was upset. She seemed to resent her father, as I once had and perhaps still did. He was starting to seem to me as merely a facilitator of a horrid world that would always exist.

"You've always been afforded any freedoms and opportunities you want, daughter," he said calmly. "It upsets me that you never saw that." Debra scoffed. There was a small silence.

"What, uh, what about Lacey Lexington?" I said meekly. I didn't mean to pry, but I was curious as to why I wasn't considered an enemy of the festival after my affiliation with Angus.

He said, "Lacey Lexington died two years ago. It was a horrible tragedy, but I hardly see how that's relevant now." He gave me a look, and that was the end of that. I wondered if Angus's fate was similarly finalized and forgotten.

I started to feel like I just wanted to go to bed. I wondered if the numbness and misery would wear off in the face of some calming delta waves. I doubted it.

"Are you going to the castle again?" Ross asked Debra. There was a deep sadness or dread in his voice. It was the most emotion I'd seen in him yet.

"Yes," said Debra, and with that, she stomped past him.

He hung his head and looked at me.

"You should go with her."

I felt no obligation to obey, and yet I did.

6

"Your father..." I called out to Debra as I lagged behind her furious pace. I was a bit out of breath. "Isn't as scary as I thought he was."

"What?" asked Debra as I caught up.

"Your father isn't as scary as I thought he was," I said. It was the same thing I said the first time, but you already know that.

"No," said Debra, with a blank expression. She slowed her pace so I could walk with her. I couldn't tell if her beeline for the castle was for her or for me. We walked urgently, nonetheless. We could no longer see Ross Kluber, but I still felt his watchful eyes on me. "Nothing's as anything as you think it is." She paused. "He's just a fool. A regretful fool."

"What does he regret?"

"All of it," she said. The magnitude of her words made my image of Ross seem small in my mind. I used to think he was the king, and we were his pawns. But as I saw him as merely a person, a father, with emotion in his face, I realized that he was the pawn. And Debra and I were just specks of dust on the chess board soon to be wiped off by the hand of our God. And our God had the losing position anyway.

I could see the castle towering above the trees, but we were still a good ways away—a good ways is a measurable unit if you use vibes instead of measuring instruments.

In the nighttime, the castle was scary in a traditional way. It loomed large and cut through the moonlight, seeming to act as a beacon for the nefarious and foul. It imposed its macabre nature onto me and used the shadows it created to hide the world around me. It knew that *what might be* struck more fear in me than *what is* so it hid everything behind its sprawling walls of old architecture. And it knew that in my mind, old was synonymous with death. Yes, the castle at night terrified me.

But the castle in the backdrop of the early morning glow embarked on a fear-mongering journey of its own. The stillness around it and the stillness of the morning took a hold. The mystery and danger of the night prior had been replaced with uneasiness and unsettling feelings. At night, the castle was scary because *it* was out of place. In the early morning, the castle was scary because *I* was out of place.

As we walked in silence, I felt a numbness in my mind and heart. It was an emotional pit that I'd never really encountered before. That's not to say I'd never felt sad or felt the urge to do something brash, but, rather, I'd never had those feelings while so clear of mind. Usually, being in a dark place comes with a fogginess in my thoughts, altered by alcohol or trauma or often both. But in that moment, I felt the darkness and emptiness in me coincide with my perceived mental clarity. I finally saw the world with a sound mind, and I saw only darkness. It was eerie. As eerie as the stomach-dropping look on Debra's face as we reached the base of the castle.

She looked so despondent and yet determined. The revelation she held close and that she'd given to me, that everything in her life, and maybe even in the world, was aimless finally gave her aim. It was like looking at the face of a machine that had a process kicked off within and no abort button to accompany it. Something had more or less initiated within her, and there was no stopping it. More, actually, not less at all.

We entered through the front door of the castle and stood in the middle of the large, Draconian room illuminated only by the daylight creeping in from the windows high above us. I felt small, perhaps a common theme. I needed to hit the gym.

It was the same area we'd seen earlier, with all the girls dancing chaotically as a hypnotized entertainment for the elite. They were all asleep now, ready to again dance on command the next day. The floor was characterized by scuff marks that were illuminated by light coming in from above, and candles hung on the walls around the entirety of the room. The gray walls had ornate depictions of people carved into them. The actions of these figures seemed ritualistic, as the artist had rendered a possessed look on the face of each of his subjects. Some of the sculptures reached out towards the room and at me. They were trying to escape the hellish nightmare of being castle wall art.

"It's scary when it's empty," I said.

"It's scary when it's filled too," said Debra quickly. "Come, this way." She had no time for my mundane comments. She led me to a stairwell that spiraled though one of the jutting cylinders in the corner of the castle. Last time I was there, I had taken the elevator as a visitor, as Angus's plus one. I was an intruder, and I took the vague route to the top, fueled by rage and a thirst for knowledge. Though I did not come from Greece. I'd never been.

This time, I took the pointed route up through the stairs. With Debra, I was above the illusions. We knew exactly where we were, and she knew exactly where we were going. My thirst had been quenched, though I'd spit that which quenched it if I could. We walked up each step deliberately and spiraled our way to new heights. We got to the top and found ourselves in a medium-sized bedroom. Think about a tiny bedroom. Now think about a massive bedroom. Yeah, it wasn't like either of those.

It too was candlelit and had a bed off to the left side. The walls were a gray granite, like the outside of the castle, and it had a window that opened up to a small balcony. It was the balcony I'd seen Ross stare pensively from. It looked like Rapunzel's bedroom, with considerably fewer haircare products scattered about.

"Is this your bedroom?" I asked.

"When I close my eyes."

I thought about that for a split second until I saw three figures sitting in the shadowy corner opposite the bed. I jumped back slightly.

"Is that…?" said one of them, a girl's voice. They stepped into the light.

"Reza!" said another voice. It was Ashley, Oli and Gordon. We embraced before I could even say anything.

"Where have you been?" I said finally. I was shocked, and I felt myself smile involuntarily for the first time in a while. But it faded slowly, as it always does.

"I found them," said Gordon. "We've been journeying." He looked less contemplative than before. His face was worn down, but his eyes were kinder than when I saw him at the rooftop bar.

"We've been doing misadventures," said Ashley. Her pig-tails had come undone, and her wavy hair was in high tide down her shoulders.

"Yeah, Gordon and Ash were doing misadventures, and I said I'd be remiss if I missed misadventures," said Oli.

"Wow," I said.

"What have you been up to?" asked Ashley. She had no massive facial tattoo to speak of.

"Nothing good," said Debra, cutting in. I nodded in agreement. We'd just been coming to the conclusion that everything we aspire to is impossible, meaningless and dumb. Nothing major. I couldn't help but feel that I wanted to be happier upon seeing Gordon and the twins than I was. I kind of hated them because they hadn't seen the cave. They were just naïve souls who lived in the false embrace of hope. I pitied and envied them.

"We're never gonna be anything," I said. I just sort of blurted it out. "Anything remarkable. We have one life, and we're just kind of doing nothing with it."

The room fell silent. Ashley, Olivia and Gordon had been on a similar journey to what I'd been on for the most part, and Debra had lived that journey. We were five sad souls wallowing in our insignificance. The castle walls looked like the backdrop of a play, and it was a tragic comedy. Or a comedic tragedy.

Debra grabbed a bottle of whisky from under her bed. It was one of those cartoon bottles with "XXX" on the label.

"I can't drink; I haven't eaten or slept in forever."

"Oh, shut up," said Debra. She walked out onto the balcony.

I looked at Gordon, and he slowly shook his head with a sad smile. Ashley did the same. It didn't indicate that I shouldn't follow her, but rather that they weren't also going to. Oli was watching a butterfly that danced around the room. I walked past the three of them towards the balcony.

I whispered, "It's good to see you," and stepped out into the fresh air again. Debra sat on the balcony with her legs slipped below the railing, straddling a pillar. They dangled in the air as she looked out over the park and used two hands to take a big sip of the whisky. "You come here often?" I asked. I don't know why. I just did.

"Yep," she said. "Every time. Over and over and over again." She took another big sip of the whisky and handed it to me. I sipped it and immediately felt warm and tipsy. I didn't concern myself with the inherent dangers of sharing a drink such as infectious mononucleosis. I took another sip, and the liquid worked its way down my throat and found my tired, depleted body the perfect host for its wicked intentions.

"How do you wake up?" asked Debra.

"Alarm."

"How do you find the motivation to do something so unnecessary and at times painful," she continued. "Sometimes I find that if I'm going to go about my day putting nothing of meaning out into the world, then why even put myself out in the world?" I got what she meant. I felt it deeply.

A lot of days, I'd go to bed and realize that I did basically nothing, and other days I found a pathetic sadness in the accomplished feeling I would have when I'd achieved something completely trivial. And I would sit around and watch TV or play video games or drink with friends. The only moments I was happy were moments where I could successfully distract myself from reality. If that was really true, what was the point of living in reality anyway? I would sit around and wait for the weekends, and when the weekends came, I'd blow through them hedonistically. And then I sat around and waited for a music festival I bought tickets to, the highlight of my year, so I could watch other people be successful. I had the ultimate struggle trying to define what success really was in terms of this whole life thing, but it sure as hell wasn't this. That's what Debra understood so deeply, which is why I hung on every word of her depressing philosophizing.

"The world out there doesn't need us," she said, presumably looking out over the world. "It's indifferent to our existence. We're all like that guy pushing that ball up the hill."

"Sisyphus."

"You're a sissy!" she said angrily. "And how am I fussing anyway? You saw all the same truths I did."

"No, that's the guy's name," I said calmly.

"What guy?"

"The guy pushing the ball—well, it's a rock—up the hill aimlessly," I said.

Her angry face settled.

"Oh. Well, anyway, we're all him. And if we stop, the ball crushes us…"

"Rock."

"And it's like, who cares, really?"

"I suppose, like, our loved ones?" I said meekly. It almost seemed sarcastic, but I didn't know much what my intentions were. She chuckled softly.

"Loved ones," she said, repeating my phrasing. "The people that we suffer with." This part wasn't repeated because I didn't say that. "It's somehow our duty to slightly ease their suffering. It's all frivolous. We can't control anything. It's hard to tell what's broken, human existence or society, but there's a break nonetheless." She seemed to be packing as many thoughts as possible into the disjointed things she was saying. I could tell there was a battlefield within her mind, but the war had been fought and the winner declared ages ago.

The world remained in black and white in front of me. It had been since the cave. I wanted to go to sleep, but I wasn't that excited to wake back up. That's a troubling thought, to say the least. It was kind of funny, in a stupid way, that the realization that I wasn't special or destined for historical greatness had shattered my will to live this heavily. It was unlikely that I'd ever have a Wikipedia page, or that I'd ever be a part of a revolution or romanticized scene. A biography written on my deathbed would be one page and it would read, *You know, like, a normal guy? That.* My daughter would tell her kids, "Your grandfather liked to play guitar." And they would respond "Oh" and that would be the last time I was ever thought of again. The answer to why I wake up each day to do what I do would be because that's what I have to do. The meaning of life is made up and represented by a random, insignificant guy burning newspapers so that people could look up in the sky and know there was some greater reason to keep pushing. People just need a reason to keep pushing because there's no other option. Is there?

Debra looked down at the ground and let out a small sigh. "We don't have control of anything, do we? Born rich, born poor, smart, dumb, happy… sad. It's all genetics and luck. Only 0.00001% of lives appear worth living, so we consume media about people living exciting lives to distract us from our boring ones, and then you come to find out that even the rich and famous aren't happy. So, at some point you come to the conclusion of fuck this. And then once you feel that way, there's still nothing you can do about it. The simulator or that weird angry Old Testament God or Buddha or all those Greek dudes or that made up shit Barton keeps talking about or whoever is in control just sits there and laughs and mocks us. Have you ever been asleep, and half woken up to start doing some weird task until you wake up fully and ask yourself, 'Why am I doing this?' That's what gaining consciousness all those years ago was like. And there is no answer to the question." She finally took a breath. I could see tears developing at the base of her eyes, but she was doing well to hold them back because she thought that any emotion at all was silly and contrived. "The worst thing that ever happened to the world was a sense of self," she said quietly after gathering herself. I felt a shadow fall over me, and I shuddered.

"You think?" I said softly to Debra.

"I do," she said. "I think the root of my unhappiness is that a part of me died. A part of me that never existed. It's not enough for there to be beauty all around me. I needed to be beautiful and special too. I needed to become something that I couldn't become, and it hurts to compare myself to those who did. I can't just be; I have to be exceptional. And it could all be undone of the concept of 'I' never existed to begin with."

"You're just being right now," I said, trying to reassure her and myself.

"And I'm doing a shit job at it." She stared down at the concrete below us. We were about seven stories up, but the world revealed itself further because we were atop a hill. It was odd, but we weren't really in any kind of exact moment in time, yet we were in an important moment. Our feelings and thoughts were so heavy that it kept the rest of the world out. Where was I? I was in a state of intense sadness. When was I? I was at a crucial point in my life. And that was all there was.

"So, we have no grand future, no meaning, no control, no motivation," I said. "So where's the 'why' for our continued existence?" I asked. As you can see, I was real caught up in my who, what, when, where, and whys.

"I grapple with the same dilemma," she said. I thought briefly about my job. It was a perfectly fine job that gave me the means to live the rest of my life. But if there was no substance to the rest of my life, then it was an unfulfilling job to be the focal point of my existence. It's interesting that I'd never pointed my ambition to fulfillment in general. There was never anything appealing to me about being fulfilled without logical reasons to be fulfilled. And the only logical reason to me was living a life of greatness. Perhaps people like Debra and I were incapable of being fulfilled by the little things. We were more alike than I cared to admit, and we were both broken.

I looked over at her, and what I'd always thought was intelligence and authority looked so scared and confused. She was young, as young as I was, and she was worried that the world was different, worse, than she'd wanted it to be, and she just couldn't cope. I wanted to be strong for her, but I couldn't. I was too tired and too despondent in my own right. We thought the same thoughts and they ate at our happiness, at our will to live. I felt a little drunk and a little brazen. I wanted to do something to take control. I could tell she felt the same way. I wanted to kiss her. I wanted it to be us against the world.

"You want to kiss me?" she asked.

"Yes," I said. I kissed her. My already narrow focus tunneled further as I did. All that existed was me, her and the balcony.

"You wanna take control, Reza?" she asked.

"Of what?" I said softly.

"Of everything." She gestured out over the horizon.

"No," I said. "I just want control of me, my life."

Debra chuckled. I thought about the empire her father had built that she rejected so wholeheartedly. Everything I was standing on and looking at was created by her father for power and control, and she felt so small within it. Denny was a subordinate of it, creating an army of delusion that Debra, like myself, had once fallen victim to. We believed that the childish delusions of grandeur were still in touch and thus we were grifted into idiocy. Ross taunted us, mocked us, angered us. I felt the pain that she must have always felt. She would have given anything to escape the perils of her upbringing until she eventually turned to nothing. Nothing filled the massive void created by the cruel truths of reality and she wallowed in it. I experienced, in a night, the life that she lived, and together we stood at the pinnacle of it, atop the castle. I so deeply wondered about her. I wanted to peel back the mystery that sat beside me.

"You had a sister?" I asked. It seemed like my final attempt to understand her, the person. Not just her, the idea; the philosophy.

"No," she said. "I took on the world alone." I looked at her, but she did not look at me. I felt confused, like there was no linearity in my world. There were just puzzle pieces scattered all around me.

"Funny, I'd always heard Ross Kluber had a daughter that killed herself," I said.

"How is that funny?"

"I guess, peculiar," I said.

"Well, he does." She laughed in a horrific, dead manner.

The laugh ended abruptly. I could see the determination, the darkness in her eyes. She stood up beside me. "It happens every time." She pushed herself up onto the railing. I just watched with wide eyes. I was frozen, tired, rigid, paralyzed by shock and numbness. "You and I are the same, Reza. There's only one thing in life we can control, one beautiful thing: the end." She didn't jump, she just sort of leaned off the edge and gave in to gravity. She was Ross Kluber's daughter, she embodied a deep sadness, and she was his greatest sadness. I wanted to yell, to scream out to her. I wanted to fall apart and convey my horror. It was time for my grand performance. But I just softly muttered, "No," and my expression did not change as my eyes followed her until my ears heard the most detestable crunch.

In a way, her movements and the expression on her face as she let the world lay its final blow upon her were so eloquent. Until they weren't. She didn't consider, in her intense climactic act, the horrid, mangled state of her body below. Her limbs twisted every which way on the concrete as blood oozed out of any crease it could find. She twitched a couple of times and fell limp. It was a dreadful scene. The nauseating ugliness was the world's final revenge on her for thinking she could take control for once.

I was still in her embrace. There was still a magnetism between us; I could feel her body pulling mine towards it. It was a pitfall in my divine journey, and the fall was more literal than it had ever been. I was sad and scared, I worried that I could see my fate in her face. Her cold, lifeless face. I looked down at the ground while the girl pulled me towards her, and there just wasn't enough holding me on the balcony. The death of my ambition was the death of me. I could not untether them. I began to cry until I heard a voice.

"Reza," it said from behind me. It was Gordon. He came to embrace me. I fell limp and Ashley grabbed my other arm to hold me up. The pull from down below gently washed off of me in the face of my friends. Oli grabbed me under my arms as my three friends pulled me away from the balcony railing. Tears flowed from my tired eyes, and the world came back to dull color.

PART 5

I

The cave let out, the one from my childhood, into a vast view of rolling plains. The plains took my little mind with them, and it stampeded with the wind. I could not look at everything, and I felt as if I saw nothing at all. It was too big. It was bigger than I was little, and that was the grand fear, that I'd never be big enough. I could see small blemishes and etched-out paths where some people presumably lived and many more had died. I was too young to conceptualize what I was feeling, but the gist was certainly that I understood that nature did not care about me and my life, and it wanted me back.

Those plains in front of me needed to exist. In the grand scheme of things, or even in a scheme of lesser grandness, the beautiful and massive terrain needed to exist. My own existence was arbitrary. I felt smaller than I ever had, and I began to lose focus. Focus of anything.

Then I felt my mother's hand rest gently upon my shoulder. Her fingers pressed the cloth of my shirt onto my skin, and I felt all the prior eeriness dissipate. My father rubbed his hand on my head, messing up my hair, transferring it from one weird little kid hairstyle to the next. The three of us looked out over the view, and I felt normal. I could hear my best friends giggling behind me. I felt happy. I was not nearly as in my own head as I soon became.

I kept coming back to that moment. Perhaps it was just being high up and insecure looking over a world that was entirely apathetic towards me. Or perhaps it was just a joyous memory to ground me from the perils of the present. Either way, the memory had become paralleled with the present like a self-fulfilling prophecy, and I looked over the whole of Woodland Park while my friends gently brought me to the ground, and my uneasiness faded off into the distance. It was there, or maybe it was a good bit later, that I realized that the memory of that cave and that view were not important for how small I felt. I was not the central figure in that scene. It was my parents, who looked out over this gorgeous view with their loving spouse and their incredibly remarkable son and felt bigger and grander than anything in the universe. It was the unit as a whole, friends and family who held onto the moments they had with each other in the face of beauty.

I couldn't bear to look at Debra down below, and I finally staggered back into the bedroom on the top floor of the castle.

"You weren't going to jump, were you, Reza?" asked Oli.

"No, I..." I stopped. "No. I—no."

"I knew you wouldn't," he said. I felt a break in my mind, a release. It was just as I'd felt when I didn't eat the dirt or kill Jenna Jameson or email my boss. These forces held me so tight, but as I was yanked from their embrace, I stood before them, able to recognize their absurdities.

The wooden floorboards in the bedroom took in the warmth of my hands more than my hands did their coolness. I pushed myself to my feet and studied each of my friends. I could feel the steady uproar of tears bubbling up in the bottom of my eyes every time my mind caressed my memories of Debra. But I also could barely remember her or even what she stood for. I was lost in a realm of uncertainty but it beat a previous inclination towards certain despondency. Gordon looked carefully at his watch.

"I really gotta learn how to read a clock."

"That's a digital watch," said Ashley dryly.

"Oh," said Gordon. He looked at it closer. "Oh! It's almost time for the show." His tone turned somber on the last syllables as he remembered the horrible nature of the moment. His words felt mechanical and rehearsed as though a playwright had used Debra's death to give him the most wretched cue. I took a step out onto the balcony and looked out towards the main stage with curiosity in my gaze. I saw above the screens backing the artists' platform a banner with the logo for Vitality Media.

The first time I ever saw that logo was on my laptop at work. It was my 23rd birthday. A coworker had made muffins for the office to celebrate my accomplishment of existing. It was a particularly dull day, and I was feeling the dullness longer than I generally had before, a devilish preview hinting towards its intentions of becoming my eternity. There was a note on my desk that read, in scribbled handwriting, "email record label." For the first time ever, that note, and the sentiment behind it, felt comical. I knew that I would leave it at my desk as I packed up my things and that night it would be thrown away by the office cleaners, never to be seen again. With that thought, I simply looked away.

But as I did, I received an email. It was from Vitality Media, and it said that they were excited to present this year's edition of the Woodhill Park Festival. Attached to the email, floating in digital magic, sat an image of the artist lineup. I remembered that day's dullness shrivel up as I feverishly texted my closest friends the picture of the lineup and found myself swept up in a whirlwind of excitement.

Gordon watched me stare at the Vitality Media logo. He waited for me to finish my memory. Then he said, "Not there."

"Show? What kinda festival has a show at this hour?" I asked into the breeze.

"Yeah, not there," said Gordon, with a wild grin. "It's at The Acorn Diner." I returned his grin, involuntarily until it fell off my face. The Acorn Diner was a 24/7 diner in our hometown. It was a willing backdrop for our high school debauchery. And sometimes, to the dismay of every customer they've ever had, they had live music. The Gordon Three and I were even known to grace the stage.

"The Acorn Diner!" I yelled out to the group. I smiled through my crying eyes. "Well shit, let's go." Ashley giggled and I watched the bags under her eyes dissipate in real time. Immediately, in antithesis to the previous moment and perhaps to the entire night, I took charge of the group. I both needed to get away from the horrible scene and longed for a place of familiarity and comfort. Such was surely to be found at the old Acorn Diner.

I walked down the stairs to the base of the castle and exited into the crisp air. The air was different down there, newer. I didn't peek around the bend to look for Debra's body. I wondered how long she'd been dead for. I mean really dead. I didn't really feel pain about her, or grief. I, rather, felt *her* pain. It was far worse.

Ashley patted me on the back as she followed me. "It's all gonna be okay," she said. For some reason, I believed her.

We walked through the festival grounds, through lingering tensions reflecting that the whole area was soon to awake. But we pressed against it in the opposite direction.

"Are you good to drive, Gordon?" I asked. My mind was focused on emotions, but it still had just enough time for logistics.

"Yeah," he said with his usual brazen confidence. I kept leading the group and looked around as I did. I was disturbed by how normal everything looked. I hadn't been face to face with normalcy in so long that it was the weirdest thing in the world. The open field of inch tall grass lined with closed vender stands did not elicit some dreadful thought or tangled metaphor. The clouds in the sky were ones I'd seen before, and they reminded me of ones I'd seen even a time before that.

Much of the mysticism around the park had dissipated. Very nearly, as I took in my surroundings, did I think, *This is just a park*. This is just grass and around me are just people. I almost saw it for what it was: just a place for fun.

But the nefarious demons of pointlessness scampered around me yet. They whispered that I'd never be the same, and I interpreted that it would be for the worse. I couldn't displace the feeling that I didn't matter, even as the associated sharp emotions dulled. We passed through rows of tents that housed people who also didn't matter. Some of them were awake, but they were in the stark minority. I rubbed my scalp and took pleasure in the feeling. I was too tired to be tired, so I felt energized.

When we got to our campsite, I caught the gaze of my tent, the one housing my pillow. It laughed in my face, and I laughed back. I caught a whiff of the sweet morning dew clinging to the grass around us as it slowly got incinerated by the sun. I didn't get incinerated by the sun. I stood and enjoyed its warmth. I was better than the dew.

"Alright, everyone pile in," I said to the group. I knew that the show was about to start at the Acorn diner, and I wanted desperately to get there on time. I somehow innately knew about the show more than just from Gordon's words. I felt that, in this terrible world that abandoned Debra and abandoned me, at least there was a place I might belong, if just for a moment. So I implored my friends to get us there, and they needed no persuasion.

The further I got from where Debra lay, the more I thought I could distance myself from what she had taught me. I was antsy in the backseat urging Gordon to put more distance between me and the ghoulish scene. In the car, I remembered how alone Debra was in the face of reality. But any discomfort I felt by being crammed in the backseat of the small car was a symptom that I did not have to go it alone. Whether the Gordons, who traveled partially with me through the night, understood everything I felt was academic. They were there with me, and that carried far greater value than any deep understanding could.

We got onto the interstate and listened only to the hum of the car on the road. The tune was unrelenting. We passed an apple orchard that I was quite familiar with. It was the one the kids from my area would go to on a Saturday morning. We'd pick apples and the lady there would make cider and pie. We'd throw apples at each other, at first in good nature and eventually out for blood.

I'd had my first kiss, with Katie Blunderson, there. But then she kissed three other boys that day. So then I kissed Mallory Wright, and I was the only boy she kissed that day, so I consider that my real first kiss. There was a lot of kissing that day. As I saw it again, that wash of fond memories came upon me. Except for that whore Katie Blunderson. She actually grew up to be really cool, and she was in med school. And women shouldn't be slut shamed anyway. But still, four boys at the apple orchard in one day. Whatever, that apple orchard was special to me. Special enough to make me forget all my sadness and become overwhelmed with nostalgia.

I noticed Oli, in the seat in front of me staring out the window. He too, I could only imagine, was internalizing these sights of great familiarity.

"Hey Reza, you wanna see what this town would be like if you were never born?" he said without looking back at me. In my mind he looked older and wiser. If my mind could bend time, then perhaps Oli could speak to me from a place of wisdom.

"Oh, uh…" I didn't know how to respond.

"Nah," he said, with a laugh. "I don't know how to do that. That'd be a rip-off anyway." Oli's face was and had always been just Oli's face. I watched a speck of dirt on the widow dance through the outside environment.

"It'd probably be pretty similar," I said.

"Yeah," he said. I laughed.

The world around me started to get even more familiar as we approached the diner. I laid my head against the window, and my eyes darted across the sprawl of suburbia, settling briefly on reminders of my past before moving to the next. There were places where I'd hung out with friends, where I'd been to dinner with my parents. There were streets where Gordon and I had run from the cops and venues where all the Gordons and I had blessed nine people with dreadful music. It was silly, because all these places in this world, in this terrible world, brought me joy.

Somewhere along the line, I was wrong. Either the naïve kid who couldn't grasp his insignificance was wrong or the delirious, drug-riddled adult who'd journeyed to the center of earth's cruelty and hated what he saw was wrong.

Either way, as stupid as I felt smiling at these reminders of my dumb life playing out in these dumb suburbs, the smile never faded. Ashley, sitting next to me, also smiled. It was a smile that danced to the tune of her own thoughts. Gordon's Subaru pulled into the mostly empty parking lot of the Acorn Diner.

The diner had an all glass front wall with a low ceiling. The top rim of the outside decor was a bright red cylinder set horizontally across the building's frame. Directly in the center of the tubular top sat a cartoon acorn jutting up into the sky.

The concrete on the parking lot was not well maintained, and Gordon's car jostled against it until we came to rest somewhat between fading white lines across from the establishment.

I walked the familiar walkway and opened the door, holding it for my three friends. We were greeted immediately by Alfredo, the head waiter at the diner. He was an older man with white hair that seemed out of a Seurat painting. It was as if he'd covered his bald head in glue and then dumped salt all over it.

"Ashley!" he said with excitement. Then his face dropped to utter disappointment. "Oh and your friends, hey."

"Hi," said Ashley. We sat ourselves down at one of the many empty booths. The table and leather benches were as sticky as ever, and we never knew if that was on purpose or not. Alfredo had been our waiter every time we went to the Acorn Diner, regardless of the time of day. We theorized that he lived there. Oli often claimed that he once saw a pillow in the kitchen. These memories flooded back to me and brought a smile to my face.

I took a quick look past Ashley and Oli on the other side of the table and studied the old diner. On the back wall was a whole array of photos of celebrities obviously photoshopped into pictures shaking hands with Alfredo at the diner. It could have even been a funny bit if we didn't know in our heart of hearts that Alfredo thought they looked real. Next to the wall was a semblance of a stage. It was basically a cleared out section with an amp plugged into the wall. The patrons sitting near it glanced at it in nervous horror.

But when I turned my attention to my immediate vision, it was I who became immersed in horror. Before me sat two twins who were about twelve years old. They resembled Oli and Ashley except in that one extremely key way. "What the fuck?" I said aloud, involuntarily. They simply ignored me and turned to Gordon.

"Guys!" said Gordon, who also looked like a child. "We should start a band!" He spoke in a child's voice. I steadied my breath and felt myself fall slowly into the ocean of a memory. I took one small lunge towards the surface, but then gave in to the current. I leaned in towards the middle of the table and looked at my own tiny hand.

Through all my ambition and suffering, I'd forgotten that it was one arbitrary day at the Acorn Diner that launched our musical journey. "I've been learning guitar," said Gordon.

"That would be fun!" said Ashley. She was so young and hopeful.

"It'd be like the Wiggles," said Oli.

"Well we wouldn't make, like kid's songs," I said. Oli's ridiculous statement launched me into the role of an active participant.

"No but we'd be all playing at the same time and making songs together."

"That's just a band!" I said.

"Dude is your only concept of a band The Wiggles?" asked Gordon. Oli shook his head and leaned back defensively.

"No, I was just making sure you guys knew."

"I've been taking lessons!" I said with an excited smile pasted onto my face. I was totally in the moment. Each of the Gordons began to buzz at the thought of the band's inception. I reached into my mind for my inner drive. I looked for that excitement I must have felt to record songs and then start selling tapes. I searched for a plan to get a record producer to notice us, or to disperse our catchiest songs on social media platforms that were nearer to their infancy. But I could not find any of that.

All that existed in the channels of my brain was the excitement for fun. I was so ready to just pull out a guitar and jam with Gordon, to let Ashley hold down the bassline and Oli bang away at a drum kit. I could only find, searching the ambition section of my mind, the urge to yell and laugh while playing my instrument, to melt away a day in my garage with my friends.

I was jolted away from my confusing thoughts by the ringing of microphone feedback. I looked up and saw Alfredo holding a microphone by the makeshift stage. "We're gonna do a concert," he said. The scattered patrons enjoying their breakfast groaned.

"Here we go," said Gordon. When I looked back at him, I saw an adult with a smirk on his face. I took a deep breath, grasping at whatever intended to present itself as reality in each fleeting moment, and prepared myself for another good old concert at the Acorn Diner.

2

A group of four teenagers came out from the kitchen and Alfredo handed the microphone to the one in front. "Test, test," he said into the microphone, filling the diner with unwanted sound. I recognized the kid from my high school days, from the mirror. "Is this thing on, testing, testing," he continued.

"Dude, it's on!" said fifteen-year-old Gordon while plugging his guitar into the amp. I glanced at the adult versions of my friends sitting at the table. They were grinning ear to ear, looking at the spectacle.

"We're called Kill the Banana Man," the young version of me said into the mic as the rest of the gang set up their instruments. I remembered that being our first band name. Ashley thought it was too violent. I gave a short laugh at the false confidence of the lead singer. "We're gonna rock the goddamn syrup bottles off the table all morning long." A dad sitting near the stage covered his young son's ears and guided him to a table further away from the ruckus. The mom grabbed their plates and followed.

The young me started off with an out of tune A chord, and Gordon struggled through a beginner melody. What it lacked in technical excellence it made up for, or rather exacerbated, with sheer volume. The smiles on our faces did not match the horrible sound waves emerging from the amp. As I leaned in to listen, I thought to myself, "This is not music." But when I looked at the faces on the stage, as young Ashley and I leaned into the same mic to sing a harmony for the chorus, I thought, "This is the most music of anything I've seen all day."

Orangutan daydream, what does he dream about?
Probably banana
Probably orange

The lyrics sometimes merged with the melodies and beats around them but more often clashed with them. I leaned to Gordon and whisper shouted over the music, "I forgot how amazing these shows were!"

"Probably banana," he responded.

"Probably orange," I said.

The kid from the family that had moved away from the nightmare began to cry. It was a fair reaction. I studied the kid singing the songs up on that stage. His light blue jeans fit a little too loose, because he thought trying clothes on in the dressing room at the store was for girls. His floral Hawaiian shirt was a poor imitation of how guys in bands actually dressed.

I once thought, when I entered Woodhill Park with my troubled mind, that the dreams of this young kid were dying out. It was unconscionable that I, at my more advanced age, had let him down. But I saw, on that stage at the Acorn Diner, that he was actualizing his dreams then and there. His dreams were pure and real, and they weren't mine to mess up anyway.

He played that terrible music not for a producer or for fans, but for him. And for Oli and Ashley and Gordon. I teared up watching that simple fool somehow find a chord progression that actually worked and then follow it up with one that absolutely did not. It brought him great joy that this was the worst music he'd ever make for the rest of his life, not that it was the best music he'd ever made. He was wiser than me.

As the fourth or so song came to an anticlimactic conclusion, the young Reza looked directly at me. "Thanks, everyone, you have been great," he said. He paused for a beat that was filled with a metal fork hitting a porcelain plate through a pancake. "We're honored to be the opening act. Now give it up for Fury and the Gordon Three." The Ashley, Oli and Gordon at my table robotically stood up and made their way for the stage. I followed them, swept up in the rush, and assumed my position at the front of the band. Whatever form of fate that had guided me through the night had now placed me in an early morning gig at the Acorn Diner. I wanted to give fate a piece of my mind, and not any of the pieces she'd already taken a wicked hold of herself.

When I plugged my guitar into the amp up there and graced the Acorn Diner stage in front of the scattered crowd of construction workers and dads taking their kids to a weekend little league tournament, the world did not turn into vibrant color. I was no God up there. The girls didn't faint and there were no adoring signs. But the guitar felt comfortable in my hands. It felt nice.

I looked at Oli and mouthed, "Cripple Me Elmo." He nodded.

"C.M.E.," he said for Ashley and Gordon to hear. Then he tapped his sticks against the drum kit and counted us off. Ashley played a familiar bassline and Gordon came in right on cue with the patented riff of Cripple Me Elmo. I held down the rhythm guitar with a simplistic but bright chord progression.

When I sang, the hoarseness thrust upon me from dehydration and sleep deprivation actually worked in the context of the song. Compared to the younger versions of ourselves, or maybe even in some small realm of objectivity, we sounded pretty good. My first thought, as the electricity of the sounds shot through my body from the marble floors of the Acorn Diner, was not, "Let's get this to a record producer immediately," but rather, "Wow, look at us go!" I wasn't entirely ready to not internalize these thoughts as those of a dunce's, but I didn't feel all that ashamed to be a dunce at that moment.

And then I stopped thinking about it that much at all. We rattled off four more songs. A man sitting on a stool by the counter even conceded to offer a quick applause after our third song. I felt heroic being able to win him over in such an impossible setting.

I realized that I would never lose the jealousy or the envy of being Kendall Paulson. That would be an impossible ask. But I figured that I'd never be willing to give up what I had for what he or anyone else has. I thought about all that I'd lose if I were to become someone else. The darkest moments I'd ever felt were not when I felt that my existence was unfavorable compared to someone else's, but rather unfavorable compared to some ideation in my mind of what existence should be. Depression, in my lowest cases, arose from the idea of me vs who I thought I could be, not me vs him or me vs her. But either way, it came from not accepting my life for what it was and the joys it had to offer. The unhappiest people out there are the ones in pursuit of a life that is not theirs.

"Thank you," I said, proudly into the mic. "We have been Fury and the Gordon Three. Uh, enjoy the rest of your breakfast." There were a couple of claps and one cough and the four of us smiled and giggled as we walked back to our booth.

"Alright, let's get out of here," said Gordon. I turned back and could only make out an outline of the stage. Even Alfredo started to kind of fade away, but that's just how he always looked. We had exhausted our time at the Acorn Diner.

I turned and smiled sweetly at Gordon. "Let's."

3

I sat in the backseat of the moving car, a feeling reminiscent of everything I'd gone through since, well, ever. I was the eternal passenger, yet I didn't let that belittle the weight of personal decisions. Just because we ride the rails of life doesn't mean we don't have the power to derail it. I could lean over and push Gordon's steering wheel, maneuvering us into oncoming traffic at any time. But I chose not to, perhaps a symptom of my excellence. Out the window, I envisioned the car ascending up a hill in space surrounded by a vast planetary sky. It wasn't drugs, it was imagination, the purest drug on the market, no less addictive than any other. We drove on this galactic highway, and the views were magnificent and gigantic. It was as though the illuminated scenery was unending, yet at the speed we traveled, it left my vision as quickly as it entered it. It was the mind that journeyed from one place to another, and I took the brunt of that fatigue head-on.

I unfocused my eyes and refocused them to the sight of green signs and unwavering concrete. The few comrades who helped us create a light Saturday morning traffic rode along with us until they exited or we exited. It's an interesting thing, the interstate. It's all about the exit. We sure spend quite a lot of time on a place we so desperately want to exit. I shooed away the thought for fear of turning into a bad observational humorist. I started to think that I'd never turn into much of anything at all.

I could have begun to worry all over again about not becoming this or that, but I was too tired to be anybody but me. It wasn't apathy, though; it was peace. I enjoyed sitting in silence in the morning stillness with my friends as we headed towards Woodhill Park. I thought about how I'd made this same trip all those hours ago with these same people. I was so tightly wound back then. It was a fond memory, but I couldn't let myself be fully present. I didn't know myself; I only knew a fantastical version of what I thought I'd someday be and the hollow, temporary version of him that I felt I was in the moment. I thought gently about how life would be, without the rich and famous me of the future to reach towards, and I was content. I understood that life would go on without him, whoever he might have been, and by God, that was tolerable. My circling, delirious, exhausted thoughts drew a smile on my face as easily as playing music had.

We exited the highway a few miles from Woodhill Park, and I couldn't help but feel a sense of reality that I hadn't felt in quite a while. The world was more how it is than how it should be, or maybe it was the other way around. There might have still been a guy called Worm Man somewhere in one of those tents, but some things just can't be helped.

We entered through the main entrance and traced the roads through the campgrounds. I could feel the energy of the yawns and stretches from the few waking souls around me. They were the types to come to the festival for morning yoga and fresh fruit paired with live music, not for whatever the hell it was I experienced. Reality, in its purest form, was all around me that morning. There was no Debra or Angus sauntering through the world with me. There were no Dennys or Bartons there to fill my head with forbidden ideas. There was no Reza, not in the way I knew him. But in the distance, there was Ross Kluber, and he was approaching.

Gordon parked the car and looked out over me to the right-hand side to make sure he had enough room between the fading painted lines that marked our campsite. I looked across the other way and saw Ross's flowing black hair, along with the rest of him, make haste towards our location. I got out of the car, and my friends did too, and I leaned against it, watching Ross draw near. I wasn't afraid. I even saw him as a sympathetic figure, having met and understood his daughter.

Ross walked up close to us and stopped a couple of arms lengths away. His face was older and less villainous than I remembered. My experiences with him had always been brief and filled with reverence. But now he looked at me as more or less an equal and his aura was that of a debrief. He gave me a knowing nod, and a strand of his slicked back black hair fell onto his face. I wondered if the onus was on me to speak first, but I quickly realized that it was not. "Mr. Donegal," he said, ignoring my friends. In part, they stooped into the background.

"Mr. Kluber," I responded, feeling a faint uneasiness.

"Let not the mind trick you that it not still be on this journey," said Ross. Who the fuck talks like that? But in the end, he was right. Until I slept, the world could do to me as it pleased. I was at the end of a bitter voyage, but I was all the better for it. Even in its dying light and rising sun, the prior night had more to uncover. This vague thought, I saw in Ross's eyes so clearly.

"I know pain and grief," he continued. "I know the pain of losing a daughter, but also the pain that my daughter once felt. I've spent my life to understand it.

"The name Debra is fine, by the way, I don't know why she hated it so much." He looked down to the ground as he continued. "What she never could grasp or get past was that the youthful existentialism that comes with becoming your own person in this world is not terminal. It isn't the end to think the thoughts she did, it's the beginning. It's human. I can only hope that, in some way or another, you realized that over the course of this festival." I nodded slowly. "This festival is dedicated to her, and the memories you make and the conclusions you draw are to get you past the pitfalls that others, with less support, fell victim to. I failed her, and I don't want anyone to be failed again. To be who you are, you have to strive and fail to be someone else. You have to curse the world for your failings and offer everything for another chance. You have to give up and give in, and then all of a sudden, move on. It is human nature, it is a pillar of growing up, it is everything. Grief in every form is an odyssey, and those who quit before the end fall to the cruelty of the night. I don't want you to hate me for what you've been put through, but if that is required to love yourself, then so be it. Coming to terms with the world is a death of sorts, sure, but it needn't be the death of passion or love or drive. Acceptance is learning to be who you are and learning to be happy. And happiness is not the antithesis of failure."

I stood silent for a second. It was a wonderful monologue, but unfortunately, I tuned the whole thing out. No, I'm kidding. He put into words the feeling that I had been trying to reach. I wanted to be someone special, but I was finding that being Reza Donegal was a mighty fine alternative.

"If you'd be so kind," said Ross, looking directly at me. "I'd like you to follow me around the festival ground. One last following for old times' sake."

"Go, Reza," said Oli, from behind me. I turned to him and saw that he was wearing a baby blue nightgown with a soft, baby blue night cap and was holding a candle. It was obvious that he had an alternative path on his mind. The sunlight absorbed each of my friends, and I turned my attention back to Ross.

"Come with me now, Reza," he said. He walked towards the festival entrance, and I followed him. We made our way up the hill towards the collection of main stages that made up the core of the festival. There was a small tingle of rebirth flowing from the grass below me that had been stamped to hell the night before. I could hear a bird sing an intricate but ultimately forgettable melody.

"You ever have lust or- or wrath?" asked Ross.

"Those are like two of the seven things you're totally not supposed to have," I said. "So, I like to think not. Not in any debilitating sense."

"Hmm," said Ross. We kept walking. He was an odd fellow. His strides were longer than his legs. The trees around us were doing a tip top job at being trees. They were tall and brown and green. Ross walked with a high degree of purpose. He walked like he owned the place, because in some sense he did. He walked in that one foot in front of the other way that guys in his generation walked. Every generation, I guess. I was so tired that I couldn't really describe anything in any normal sort of way. He had the kind of hair that would flow in the wind if it was windy out. But it wasn't. As I walked behind him, my steps were the sort of steps that would have kept going down if it weren't for the ground. The sun was doing that thing where if it wasn't there, like it didn't exist anymore, it would be bad.

Finally, and thankfully, Ross arrived to where he was leading me, and my brain was able to sedate itself and turn its focus.

We were in the Zen forest, as I had been some nine hours prior. This time there were a few stragglers reading books or sitting peacefully. The tree I'd cut down had begun to grow back, and it was about halfway there. It didn't really make sense, but, like, whatever.

"This place," said Ross in a whisper, "is the beginning of the journey of self-discovery. It also stands alone as a scene of tranquility." I did feel peace in the secluded forest. It was a blank canvas for introspection and discovery. But more importantly, and more dangerously, it was a deceiving place of vulnerability. That is what Denny used it for. Ross walked slowly towards the vector of trees that spelled the end of the secluded area, and we spilled out into the open field where I had been so desperate to eat dirt the previous night.

"I knew a girl in high school, one you might have met, who was the prettiest girl in the whole school. Her name was Denny." Ross didn't really look at me when he spoke. While meant for me, they were still entirely his words. He put them where he saw fit. And in doing so, he told me a story.

"She had all the spoils in our small kingdom. The athletes would lust after her. The male teachers would soften their grading scale for her. The other girls wanted desperately to be her. But any time I ever talked to her, it seemed that being her was exhausting. She wanted to be an actress and a model. It was clear that it was her entire ambition.

"After high school, I hadn't heard much about her until one day she reached out to me trying to sell healing ointments in an obvious pyramid scheme. I ran into her at the grocery store in my hometown years later. She looked good, but obviously older, and she looked tired. She was in town selling the same scam ointments and mentoring the young girls with the same ambitions as her. She said one of the girls had an audition and had promised to recommend her if she got the part. I could see the delusion in her eyes.

"I searched her up on the internet and there she was. She had no family or hobbies. She was just selling ointments and getting young girls to sell ointments for her, putting them in the same cycle she was in. It was never clear what the ointments were even supposed to do. I thought about buying one out of curiosity, but the situation was too sad. After that, I never heard from her again."

He walked across the field with his head hung, and he lightly tried to fill in various divots in the grass by kicking at the ground. I followed him slowly behind. "I like to think everyone is special," said Ross. "In that life is precious and those who have it have something to contribute. But it's so crucial to know your own limits. Those who have both perseverance and self-understanding are the happiest and most effective at whatever it is we do from birth to death."

"I've seen delusion and denial consume people," I said. "I felt its pull upon me."

"Overcoming that is the first step." He walked more quickly now, and I deduced eventually that we were headed for the castle. When I saw it again for the first time since Debra had leapt from it, it looked less mystic and more ancient. The walls were reminiscent of a bygone architecture but did not elicit a Disney feeling. I could not taste the lingering smoke of fire breathed by a nearby dragon. It was a relic not from a magical time, but from a forgotten time.

"This castle is haunted, but it beckons only those that will invite its haunting. You have surpassed that in your journey. Enter it one last time with me." He opened the door and ushered me inside. I stood on the ornate ground floor and looked up at the ceiling. This was once the epicenter of my unhappiness. It was the personification of what was wrong with both the world and my life. But I could now see it only as an old, empty building. I had come to terms with the horrors inside and none of them even seemed that scary anymore. The fire of who I was raged in my mind and the light of who I will never be flickered out. And the castle called only to the latter.

Ross pressed the button to go up the elevator, and I joined him in the cab when it arrived. We stood silently as it elevated us. It functioned exactly as its name implied it would. That was appreciated in a world shrouded in mystery. People, places, and things all exist with hidden motivation, with hidden purpose. But not the elevator. It elevated.

Actually, sometimes it lowered. About half the time it lowered. A very sturdy portion of its time was spent doing the exact opposite of its titular purpose. I began to hate the elevator. It opened on the second to the top floor, and we walked out into the golden room that had earlier been the venue for a fancy party. It contained just about the only lavatory in the whole area that wasn't portable and filled with visible shit. And music festival shit at that. That's a whole different breed of shit.

"The blood's all cleaned up," I said. I was looking at the ornate floor. It was Italian marble. Maybe. I don't know anything about floors. It would have been rather out of character, in my expert opinion, as the character, for me to just pull the exact floor style of that floor out of my ass. The only thing coming out of my ass was a music festival shit. And that's a whole different breed of shit, or so you may have heard.

"Yes," said Ross. "So to speak." I looked at him with a tinge of confusion. "Lacey Lexington was murdered three years ago, though, Reza. It was in the news."

"Oh," I said. "Really?"

"Yes," he said somberly. "She was killed by a lunatic 'fan.' The event didn't exactly happen tonight, but the anger that killed her still exists. It exists within you. Within us all. You experienced that anger and what it can do. For some, it overwhelms."

"Man, I must be really out of the loop with the Lexingtons," I said.

"Yeah," said Ross. He was a little annoyed that I was more focused on that than his big message on anger. "When you're on the same journey as everyone else, the one journey of self-discovery, time moves less linearly. When you feel what the killer felt, you're there with him, and it is up to you to move past that anger and fear and hatred."

"I just feel like it was probably all over the news," I said.

"Yeah, it was," he said.

"Huh," I said. It's hard to keep track of which celebrities are dead or alive. Even if they release a new album. There's a rapper, Stick 'em up Joseph, who released seven posthumous albums. And I saw on Instagram that he just announced a world tour. Anyway, yeah that thing Ross was saying about anger is crazy.

"The killer, Angus, released a manifesto that became widespread after the murder. It interested me, because in the beginning, in his thesis, he made some good points. But as I read on, I saw how he took his anger and purposefully allowed it to grow. He felt power from it and misplaced it and eventually let it consume him and ruin his life. While his act was horrible, I found the fact that I could read his work and see a regular, relatable person get led to commit such an atrocity the most horrific aspect of it all."

There was a time where Angus made me feel like martyrdom was glorious, but as I examined how many people got hurt by his beliefs and the perceived unfairness of the universe, the more I wanted to distance myself from it. It's all luck, and we only get one draw at it. It's the stupidest thing. But once I let it roll off of me and stopped letting the roll of a single die define my worth, the world came back to me, and I could see straight again. I felt grateful for the absurd journey I'd gone on, for it showed me so much about myself and the world. Ross was no villain or hero; he was just someone who had seen the world. I appreciated him for that.

"All of this, son, is a big knot of time and theories and thoughts that were in your brain, slowly killing you. All that you've experienced is an effort to untie it. Come now, it's not long before you can finally go to sleep." The idea of sleep was starting to feel as unachievable as my past goals, but I drudged on behind Ross in pursuit of it, nonetheless.

We walked through the festival grounds, navigating stages and temporary art structures. We passed closed up vendor tents, a couple of which were buzzing with activity as they prepared for the day. There were little areas marked off for yoga or for tea or for any way to replace the dirt and grime of a four-day outdoor bender with a profound, self-cleansing and grounding illusion. I ran my vision over areas that once contained memories of music and friends, and now contained memories of eccentricity.

There were far fewer militant guards patrolling the area, and the ones I did see seemed faint, as though they were fading away. It felt like I was coming down off of whatever made me see them as they were. They still existed, those brainwashed and zombified by delusion and anger, but they no longer showed their faces as clearly. They did not scare me; they saddened me. What I had to go through to find a way to be content with myself was an everlasting struggle. I felt a renewed sympathy for everyone, but I walked the tightrope bravely, not succumbing to the temptation to be some sort of sociopathic self-proclaimed empath. I just more familiarly knew the face of turmoil. It's an ugly, spiteful face. Also, like, Greek or Turkish for some reason. That might have just been an accent of flavor I added on my own.

Ross and I approached the fence that outlined the festival grounds. "When you're in here," he said, referring to what was behind him, enclosed by the fence, and not what was in front of us. "This fence is the edge of the world. That's what I love about festivals. For four days, nothing else exists, everything is self-contained. Also, molly. Those are the two things I love about festivals. But, to the first point, it's a great place to discover yourself and understand the idea of truly living in the moment. Everything outside of this fence melts away to the dramatic sounds our artists create. Time becomes warped, and our perception is twisted. We live a whole life in those four days, and then we return to the world, changed, but unaffected. There's a beauty to it."

"I've been to a festival," I started, piggybacking on his point, "where I saw a fella writhing on the ground, foaming at the mouth, and I found out later that he was a project lead at Deloitte. It really is a diversion from reality."

"Exactly," said Ross. He looked out over the fence. "But you mustn't give away what you have out there for just an in-kling more of what's in here. This is an escape. This is no life. You're familiar with the town across this forest?" he asked, gesturing to the forest.

"Intimately."

He continued to gesture. That was his thing, gesturing. If Michael Jordan was synonymous with basketball and Ted Kaczynski was synonymous with manifestos, then Ross Kluber was synonymous with gesturing. But not in an Italian way. I looked at the forest and imagined the town beyond it, mostly because he was gesturing at it.

"It's a small town," said Ross. "One of those places where a person can become lost. You know I grew up in New York before I moved out here?"

"No," I said.

"No, I didn't grow up in New York?" he asked.

"No, I didn't know that," I said. Everything was difficult with this guy.

"Oh, good," he said. "Well, I did. I had Swiss parents, too." I didn't care about that. "And I went to a pretty prestigious college in the area. You may have heard of it. I had a classmate who, really in every measure, was exceptional. He was brilliant and charismatic. He had a magnetism that made me feel inspired by him instead of jealous. He was just a powerful figure. Everyone knew with certainty that he was destined for greatness."

"Let me guess," I said. Ross nodded.

"Yep," he said.

"It was Frank Sinatra."

"What? No," said Ross. "How old do you think I am? It was Barton."

"Oh, that makes way more sense," I said. "Well, you and Barton aren't the same age."

He said, "Not the version you met. That was the version you needed to meet. It was Barton at the beginning of his end. Where he was willing to give up everything to become a punk legend in this small town. There's nothing wrong with where he ended up. There are all kinds of lives of happiness to live. But look at all he gave up. He was an exceptional young man who had his head on straight and one day gave away everything to be a big fish in the smallest pond in America. He doesn't have contact with friends or family, he barely even exists."

"When I met him, or imagined meeting him—"

"Little bit of both," said Ross, cutting me off.

"Sure," I said. "He was infectious. He really did inspire me to want to go for it. To make one final push."

"That is the most dangerous pitfall of them all, in my opinion," said Ross. "It is appealing to give up everything in pursuit of a fantasy when everything you have seems ordinary. But realistically chasing your dreams is different from giving away your life in pursuit of a mirage. Too many Bartons don't realize what they had until they lose it. And in every field, you run into someone who gives up more and you compete until there's nothing left to give up and nowhere left to go. It all begins with a choice. A choice not to embrace who you are in favor of some image of who you'll never be."

God, I was really getting that point hammered home. But he was right. All the things I admired Barton for would quickly become exhausting elements of life if I'd embraced his philosophy. He was on an island, and he had burned the bridge to the mainland. I was so goddamn sick of metaphors.

Ross gave one more look across the way from the safety of the Woodhill Park festival grounds and shook his head slowly as he turned around. I could tell he really did care for Barton. I realized then how deeply Ross had been affected by the sadness in his life. His ownership of this festival wasn't a money-making venture, it was a way to give back to the world. He saw all of these young people fighting against the tide of early adulthood and took it as an opportunity to help them work through the pitfalls of growing up. He created this way to help us grieve the death of that idealistic version of ourselves that never existed and move past it to accept the reality of our lives. I looked at him with admiration. If he was a false idol just like the rest of them I'd met over the last twenty-four hours, then I'd gladly be wrong following him instead of anyone else.

"It's almost time to let you sleep," said Ross with a chuckle. "But first we need to examine one final place. One final gut punch from the world needs to be revisited."

He walked away from the fence, and I walked beside him, matching his gait. Also, by the way, I went to the bathroom a few times over the course of the journey, and I've been drinking water the whole time, so you don't need to be all worried about that. I just didn't think it was worth mentioning, is all.

4

I found that every step of the way, every movement I made hurling myself towards adulthood, I was desperate for an antagonist. At first there were naysayers and doubters who told me what the world was like and in doing so contradicted my delusions of grandeur. They were the enemy that needed silencing. But I couldn't find the malice I needed in their hearts and in their points of view. So, I turned to the man. There was this big bad entity that rigged the world against me, and it was what I needed to defeat. That was my purpose.

But I could not take the fight to that vague, all-powerful antagonist. I could find the cruelty I desired, but not the means to combat it. So, I took the fight to the weak. Those who did not do enough to fight for what they wanted were the true villains. There was a version of my past self there who gave up too easily, and I hated him. But how can you fight a memory? So, I soon learned to laugh at the futility of it all and blame the world. It was the universe itself that I did battle upon, and I had no chance of winning, so I sat next to Debra and let myself lose.

And each step of the way, I encountered a slender, raven-haired, black-coated man who looked me in the eye like he knew what I was going through and was happier for it. Ross Kluber, at each point, was the enemy. I thought he was the enemy of each version of me trapped in each dreadful state of mind. But I couldn't find the antagonist truly, because the antagonist was me. Not me from the past and not me from the future. It was me, right then, right there, thinking of all the ways my life was ruined by some imperceptible force or another. It was my journey to defeat myself and beat the bad chemicals in my brain that caused my previous despondency. And Ross, the whole time, was my ally.

I looked up from thought, because thought is low, and found that I'd followed him to his destination. Our destination. It was the cave, where I'd learned once and for all that my life had no meaning. "This here is everything," said Ross.

"That's what Debra thought too," I said somberly.

"No," said Ross. "She took too much stock in what's inside."

"That's not what you're referring to?" I asked. "What's inside?"

"No. Debra was a complicated kid. She had a lot of thoughts and a lot of opinions. She was cerebral, and that was a celebrated aspect of her. She really was exceptional, and not just in a dead kid way, like how every parent of a dead kid says their kid was the most amazing kid ever. I guess it would be a lot easier on us as parents if we could just say, 'Well, that was kind of a bad kid anyway' after they die. We could move on a lot easier." It was a dark thing to say, but I gave him the benefit of the doubt in using irreverence to talk about the greatest tragedy of his life.

"But Debra had a lot of ideas about how small and insignificant she was, and she dealt with overwhelming depression from that," he continued. "Her mom and I saw signs, but we never knew enough, and we never did enough. She would assign great meaning to small things, and that was her trick for getting through the days. It was like a religion. But when she found out that everything she chose to assign meaning to was, metaphorically speaking, just some guy burning papers over and over and over again, it was too much to bear. She snapped, and I never saw her again."

"So why show me the same message that pushed her over the edge?" I asked. I didn't mean literally, and it felt like a faux pas, but Ross ignored it.

"Because it isn't what's in the cave that gives you meaning and purpose, Reza, it's the cave itself. The cave is unique to you. In this journey of self-acceptance, everyone's cave is something different."

The meaning that I was desperately chasing was within me all along. It was represented by a moment in my childhood where my family and friends gathered together on vacation and explored a cave and took in a breathtaking view. It embodied a time when I lived a life that was truly worth living. The little things, a hug from Mom, throwing rocks at Oli, giving rocks to Gordon to throw at Oli, they suddenly didn't seem so little.

"Don't let anyone tell you what is and isn't important, Reza," said Ross.

"Is this cave important?" I asked.

"Yes."

5

I woke up at 2:00 PM as the sun cut into my tent and got it-self trapped on the way out, creating a sauna. I groaned and rolled around in agony as a sunburn I'd developed in my sleep rubbed against a film of dirt I'd tracked in earlier. Camping at music festivals is fun.

I felt, after a quick spell of grogginess, oddly refreshed. I ripped open my tent, with the aid of its zipper, because it's imperative to treat your things with respect, and felt a slight breeze. It was a pleasant breeze. It was a pleasant day. I yawned and clumsily pushed myself towards our large canopy area. It was the hippie drug-fueled bender version of waking up in bed and heading to the living room. Gordon, Oli, and Ashley sat in a loose triangle, and their faces lit up when they saw me. In the lines on their faces lay the same temperament and expression as the morning prior. But in their eyes was a hint of knowingness. The day was anew.

"Well, well, well, speaking of what the Devil dragged in," said Oli.

"There's no way you think that's the real phrase," I said with a laugh.

"It's a malaphor," said Ashley.

"A malaphor for what?" said Oli.

"More of a simile, I think," said Gordon. I had just woken up, and I was already exhausted. I couldn't tell if my friends were doing a bit or were just idiots, but I also knew it was always a perfect mix of both.

"Last night was a movie," said Gordon.

"Yeah, the most incoherent art flick yet," I said.

"I feel like it was more of a music video," said Ashley. She was right.

"Okay so who are we seeing tonight?" asked Oli. The question elated me. I had forgotten that I had an entire two days of concerts in front of me. I reached for that uneasiness within me that seemed to accompany excitement, but I couldn't find it. I felt free. All I could think about was enjoying the music and the presence of my friends and finding myself as I lose myself under the thick blanket of pounding bass. I was in the present and the part of me that lived only in the future finally piped down for once in his goddamn life. I was as light as five pounds of feathers and as five pounds of bricks, which is heavier but still light.

"The Goober Natorial is on at 5:00 PM," said Gordon. He was a techno infused reggae act, and sometimes he juggled on stage. It was awful, and I was so looking forward to it.

"Okay, let's get in for that and then switch stages for Jan Van Clammy and the Two Man Band," I said. I was borderline giddy. The upcoming schedule of events I had long been looking forward to all culminating at once under that day's uniquely pleasant sun tickled the part of the brain that made one jump with whimsy. Dopamine or whatever, I'm no neuroscientist.

"Duuude," said Ashley, "I forgot she was here. Did you know the Two Man Band is just one girl?" We all groaned. Of course we knew the Two Man Band was just one girl. It wasn't like any of us were gonna be focused on her anyway if Jan Van Clammy was wearing one of her patented clamfits, which I would have bet my bottom dollar on. And that's saying something, because my wallet is filled with ones, but at the bottom, there's a twenty.

"Alright, sweet," said Gordon, looking at a pamphlet he'd picked up the day before that had the lineup on it. "So, Goober Natorial, Jan Van Clammy, and then we ride the night out with Mortician's Daughter into the Crinkle headliner set and then a three-hour jam sesh from The Soggy Trio." We all murmured positively at what was the plan for a perfect night. I took a look around, brought in a deep breath, and smiled.

"Well, I guess we have a couple of hours," said Ashley. She was walking towards Gordon's car while talking. Then she reached in. "We might as well do something." She came out of the car with an acoustic guitar and a ukulele. Oli grabbed a beer out of our cooler.

"Oh, shit, gimme dat," I said to Ashley, and she handed me the guitar. Oli began tapping the now closed cooler with his drumsticks. Ashley played a chord on the ukulele, and I felt a rush fall over me as I placed the guitar in a familiar position resting on my thigh.

I played a few chords to start off, trying to keep up and harmonize with Ashley. Then I deviated with a riff and brought it back. We laughed as we fell off beat but then brought it right back on. Oli helped us with the rhythm. Gordon started goofing off with some vocals and we had a whole four piece going. As I tried to hold down the guitar, I made a mistake. And then another. But I didn't care. I wasn't playing to be the best or to try and show off, I was just having a good time with my friends. There was a looseness I hadn't felt between myself and my guitar in a long time. I looked around and examined the smiling faces and took in the silly sounds we created. I felt the most amazing feeling. I felt nostalgic for the present. You should try it sometime. I knew, wholeheartedly, that I was in the middle of a cherished memory.

Amber, our campsite neighbor, lifted up our tapestry and revealed to us the wonder written across her face. "Oh my God, you guys are amazing!" she said. We all smiled and laughed and thanked her. I felt the sun hit my neck. It was the warmest, most divine feeling.

I noodled a bit on the guitar, but it took a backseat to conversing with our neighbor. "Who are you most excited to see tonight?" I asked.

"Probably Jan Van Clammy and the Two Man Band," she said. She had this infectious excitement in her voice. It was as though she was entirely tethered to the happiness of the moment and the invitation to live vicariously through her was open and welcoming. Her warmth fit into our campsite like a puzzle piece adding to the most beautiful picture you can imagine. That's assuming you can imagine beauty. If not, Google it.

"I heard she's gonna be wearing one of her clamfits," said Gordon.

"God, I wish I could pull off a clamfit," said Amber.

"I know," said Ashley, drawing out the last word in agreement.

"You totally could, babe," said Clayton, Amber's boyfriend, emerging from the other side of the tapestry. He placed his hand on her thigh. He was wearing a scarf-print button up shirt with the top three buttons unbuttoned and two necklaces each with a pendant depicting an almost hieroglyphic version of the sun and moon respectively. He wore a bandana as a headband to keep his hair off his face. There we sat, the six of us, as members of a flowing community. The fading spray paint that marked off each car's territory were but easily crossed dotted lines on the face of one giant community. Except for Jason, our creepy other neighbor. He wasn't a part of it. Or Worm Man. Actually, thinking about all the zany characters I'd met the night before, I was starting to feel a bit more exclusionary. But with Clayton and Amber joining in with us, I felt the true joys of meeting new like-minded people and living the shared human experience with open arms.

"I bought these special underwear from Jan Van Clammy's official merch website that have an apparatus that helps conceal your boner at her concerts when she's wearing her clam-fit," said Oli.

"Nice," said Clayton.

"Nice," said Amber. We mentioned Goober Natorial, and the couple hadn't heard of him, so the lot of us got extremely excited to put our new friends onto new music. If sharing music constituted a love language, that would be mine. The concept of love languages interests me. Liking when your partner touches you seems pretty basic to me, but insufferable people will try to turn that into a gatekept personality trait. But I digress. I guess I could have saved you a lot of time if I digressed about two hundred pages earlier. People don't digress like they used to.

The conversation went on like it had for a while. A good bit of it was less dumb than what I detailed here. Some of it was dumber. Once it hit 4:40, we made arrangements to head in to catch The Goober Natorial and start our second day at the festival. Amber and Clayton tagged along.

We took the small passageway from our campsite to the main road and joined in with the flow of foot traffic ascending up the hill to the main stages. I looked at all the lonely people. And I was one of them. We weren't alone in the present or even in our lives. We weren't alone in our struggle to find meaning. But at the end of the day, when it was time to truly rationalize our lives and our purpose, we were all alone. There was a distinct loneliness in being just part of the crowd, but it was one I was learning to live with. I was learning to accept that just being a face in the crowd was okay. We were all headed to the same place to experience the same joy of watching a woman sing a song while wearing a clamfit, and by God, that was okay with me.

6

That night, after the headlining set, I watched as the crowd dispersed, filled with drugs and endorphins, and headed off to whatever adventure lay next. A very small proportion of those adventures was sleep. Ashley, Oli, Gordon and I bid adieu to Clayton and Amber for the night and went to sit on the outskirts of the Soggy Trio jam session. We let the moonlight come to us and fill us with introspection.

I started sifting through my bag.

"What're you looking for?" asked Ashley, noticing me.

"My apple," I said. I was craving some fresh fruit.

"Are you sure you brought it in?" she asked.

"Yeah, I distinctly remember the security guy making a comment about it in line."

"Oh yeah," said Ashley. "He said, 'you can't bring that in.'"

"Oh, that's right," I said. I didn't get to eat my apple.

While we were sitting, letting the melodies drip off us, I noticed a patch of flowers make what looked like a trail. They were white with a black or maybe deep purple center, and they arranged themselves in a pointed direction.

"I'm going to go to the bathroom," I told the group. I stood up and walked along the flowers as far as I could to see where they came from or were going. I weaved my way around the vendors to a more secluded area in the park and found that they came to a small flower-filled clearing engulfed by a grouping of trees just barely within the festival grounds.

Swarmed by the flowers were two old granite markers, turned slightly green. They were, as I recognized them, gravestones. One of them was behind a mound that bumped slightly above the ground. It read *Reza Donegal, a talent like no other, never to be forgotten, even by the harsh eraser of time.*

The other was unfilled. It sat in front of a hole, about six feet deep and seven feet long. It read *Reza Donegal* at the top, but the rest of it was blank. I stared at the absence of words. I kicked a small amount of dirt into the hole with my right foot. The marker did not taunt me; it did not scare me. I simply lent it my gaze for a moment longer and headed back to the group. We went to bed shortly after.

I dreamt that night that I was running through a train. People don't ever really care about your dreams, but I couldn't seem to get this one out of my head. I could feel death inside me, rotting away the edges of a bygone me. I didn't know where the train was going, but I felt an inherent excitement to get there. A slew of young people brushed past me, racing down the aisle towards the back of the train. I watched them run through my car to the next, and I turned my attention back towards the front of the train once they were all out of sight. I thought perhaps I might like to get to the origin of the train, but no more than to get to the destination. I looked out the window and watched as the terrain passed by, as life passed by. I let out a pleasant sigh, leaned back, and eased myself awake.

EPILOGUE

30 years later

Warlock's Office was on the TV, performing *My Night in Cairo*. Parts of the show were presented in hologram form in front of the TV, a primitive form of media compared to my neighbor's super hologram plus TV. Every wrinkle in Kendall Paulson's face reminded me not only of his advancing age, but also of my own. He was receiving a lifetime achievement award for his role in the musical zeitgeist. The song had been released over 32 years prior, but it still sparkled as it did all those years ago off of his voice and guitar and to the backdrop of the complex drum loop.

I folded laundry while I watched the performance. I took note of little things that went on during the show and ceremony. Symbols, nods to other parts of his career, other famous people that attended. I needed fodder for my conversation with

Willy R. at work the next day. Willy R. and I always had a competitive spirit when it came to who knew more about cool things. This stood out in direct contrast to Willy L. who could barely carry a conversation about a baseball game.

The laundry got folded, passively. Warlock's Office got watched, semi-actively. And my evening advanced on. I stretched out my back and took pleasure in the dull pain. The intervals of sharp pain prevented it from being a fully pleasurable activity. That was the mantra of my 50's so far, it seemed.

"Olivia's leaving," shouted a woman's voice from another room. I watched as Kendall Paulson played the final notes of his famed song. "Reza!"

"Coming, darling!" I said. I walked to the living room and saw my daughter weighed down by an over-packed backpack, holding the handle of a rollie suitcase in her right hand.

"Alright, you gonna be safe?" I asked her.

"Yes, dad," she said, half earnestly, half in annoyance.

"Text us when you get to the train station and when you get off," said my wife, trying unsuccessfully to mask the unwarranted worry in her words.

"Mom...," said Olivia.

"Yeah, come on, Mom!" I said. "But do be safe, sweetheart." Olivia chuckled.

"My Uber's almost here," she said, shuffling towards the door.

"Don't let that driver get fresh with you," I said.

"Dad," said Olivia. "I got an Uber Auto. I haven't had a driver in like three years." I felt old. We hugged her and said our goodbyes. It was nice to have her in the house from college, even for a night. There's less arguing and more hanging out once your kids get to college. It's refreshing, I tell you.

A car pulled up with no driver, however the hell that works. Olivia struggled slightly to get her luggage off the front step, but after that, she was on her way. "Oh, and Olivia," I called out as she neared the car. She turned to me. "Beware of temptations each step of the way. I'll see you on the other side." Her face changed with a hint of confusion, and she nodded slowly. Then she turned again and got in the car.

"These music festivals are no good," said Riley, my wife. I know what you're thinking, Riley is no name for a middle-aged woman. But all those young Riley's are going to grow up someday and here we are.

"Ah," I said. "I got into all sorts of trouble at them when I was a lad and look how I turned out."

"Exactly." I shook my head and laughed and walked into my study. I ran my fingers through my extensive CD selection resting on a shelf in the corner. CDs were super in, they were cool retro, not defunct retro. I had all kinds of CDs. It was a top-notch selection, all my friends said. Even Olivia's punk little friends thought it was cool.

I pulled out a CD from Dreadful Art By Dying Artists, the mysterious band that performed before Warlock's Office at the Woodhill Park Festival. The cover of the jewel case displayed the five members posed on stage with their instruments. I could see them clearly, perhaps for the first time ever. On the far left was Denny with her blonde hair pulled tightly into a ponytail. Next to her was Angus, banging the drums with reckless abandon. In the middle was Barton, serenading the crowd on his guitar. His face tattoos shined off his caramel skin. Then there was Debra on bass. I placed my finger somberly on her image. Then, on the far right, was me. I smiled back at myself from my comfortable position in that photo.

In the reflection of the jewel case, I caught a glimpse of my old face. I smiled softly at the sight of it. Just below my right eye was a black dot. It was a mole I'd developed in my twenties, or maybe the beginning of an unfinished tattoo, the remnants of a bygone philosophy. I stared at the CD case for a second longer and placed it back in its spot.

I walked into my living room and sat next to Riley on the couch with a sigh and a creak. I placed my hand on her leg and smiled at her. I could have thought about all the opportunities I'd seized and all the ones I'd missed. All the relationships I'd had and all the ones that faded away. All the thoughts and feelings and desires that led me to where I was that day. But I didn't. I didn't think about much at all.

"Well, I guess back to work tomorrow," said Riley.

"Ah, tomorrow's a Friday," I said. I went into the kitchen and came back with a bottle of wine, an opener and two glasses. Riley's eyes lit up.

"Fair enough," she said. I poured us each a glass, mine first, which was a longstanding bit I'd always done with her.

"To us," I said, raising my glass.

"To us," she said, clinking it. "And to Olivia's safety at that no-good hippie festival."

"And to Olivia's safety at that no-good hippie festival."

I looked out the window and saw a faint outline of those two graves I'd seen all those years ago. Every now and then, I'd wonder what that second one would say at the end of it all. But every time I wondered, the thought slowly faded away,

and my attention would turn back to what was in front of me.
My wife, my child, my house, my life.

End